Praise for Les Hi
The Bootle Boy: an

CW01336726

'A delightful autobiograph,
and a beautifully written page turner'
William Shawcross

'Brilliant . . . a remarkable book'
The Australian

'A terrific memoir by one of the all-time great newspapermen'
Piers Morgan

'An epic story . . . and a penetrating insight into the mind of
Rupert Murdoch'
Daily Mail

'A great romp of a journalistic memoir'
The Sunday Times

'Pacy and engrossing . . . overflowing with the names of the rich
and famous, from Yoko Ono, John Rotten, Graham Greene . . .
to Bill Clinton, Princess Diana, and Gordon Brown'
British Journalism Review

'Vividly captures the rise and fall of newspapers over 60 years'
The i Paper

'Fascinating . . . a must-read for anyone
with even a fleeting interest in the media.'
Western Mail

DYING DAYS

Les Hinton

First published in 2025 by
KLH Editions LLC, in partnership with Whitefox Publishing Ltd

www.wearewhitefox.com

EU GPSR Authorised Representative
LOGOS EUROPE, 9 rue Nicolas Poussin, 17000, LA ROCHELLE, France
E-mail: Contact@logoseurope.eu

ISBN 978-1-917523-51-6
eBook ISBN 978-1-917523-53-0
Audio ISBN 978-1-917523-54-7

Epigraph from Dylan Thomas: The Collected Letters, Volume 1:
1931-1939 edited by Paul Ferris © Dylan Thomas, 2017,
published by Weidenfeld & Nicolson, reproduced
with kind permission by David Higham Associates.

Designed and typeset by seagulls.net
Cover design by Dan Mogford
Project management by Whitefox Publishing
Printed and bound by CPI Group (UK) Ltd, Croydon CR0 4YY

For all my family.
The lot of you.
With all my love.

I hold a beast, an angel, and a madman in me.

Dylan Thomas

PART ONE

He opened the bedroom window, sat on the bed, and closed his eyes to the chill wind. 'It's a beautiful morning, my darling,' he said. 'The sun is reaching the top of the hill and the sky is a hundred shades of red and there's not a cloud to be seen. Some stars are still out and there's a blue heron on the lake, fishing. Can you hear the owl?'

He stood at the sound of a yelping dog. Four wild turkeys chased a young border collie down the long driveway. The man gave a low laugh.

'You should see Spike, my dear,' he said. 'He's making the same stupid mistake. He'll never learn those turkeys fight back.'

He reached for a pair of spectacles and picked up the brief, hand-written note. It was on his bedside table, where he'd first found it. He had read it every morning for seventy-two days. He couldn't imagine how its author had managed to produce such beautiful script in the circumstances it was written.

'Drink your coffee now, darling, before it goes cold,' he said, picking up two mobile phones. 'It will begin this evening. I'll tell you all about what happens later, but we're following your advice. We're following it every step of the way. We will make them pay, my love. We will punish them for their wickedness and cruelty. Whatsoever a man soweth, that shall he also reap. One by one, they will reap our pain.'

He mounted the exercise bicycle by a window overlooking the deep valley and began to pedal. He pedalled until the sweat was pouring from him, drenching his T-shirt and stinging his eyes; until he could barely see; until there was hardly a breath left in him – as if he were fleeing all the sorrows and guilt of his famous life.

Chapter One

Chatstone House, Gloucestershire, England

Dan Brasher stood on the terrace by an open French window, with a drink and a cigarette. Rose bushes patched the fresh-cut lawn that swept down towards a serpentine lake fringed with reeds and overhanging willows. Beyond the lake stretched a quilt of fields hemmed with hedgerows, their moods and shades of green shifting with the light. Towering cypress trees stood in orderly lines each side of a driveway that coiled beyond the lake and through the fields towards the road and the real world.

Dan flicked his cigarette into a bed of lavender and marigolds. 'God,' he muttered, 'I fucking hate the English countryside.'

There was a crack of thunder and quick black clouds hid the evening sun. The rain was sudden and heavy, and guests ran from the garden balancing drinks above their heads, nudging each other politely as they crowded through the French windows into Chatstone House. Their arrival scattered the ballroom floor with drops of rain that sparkled like sequins in the light of the grand chandelier.

Dan hadn't been invited to the party, not strictly, but he'd turned up anyway. The invitation had arrived in the mail two days after he resigned, knowing he was about to be sacked for assaulting the deputy editor. He'd planned an evening in his local, feeling miserable, but a few large gin and tonics had put him in a better frame of mind and he'd called an Uber for the eighty-mile journey from London. He stood out among the sleek suits and dresses – uncombed, and wearing trainers and black jeans and the worn-out Gieves & Hawkes suit jacket he put on whenever he wanted to look his best.

There was no evening of the year when the circuitry of power buzzed more feverishly than the night of the Chatstone family's summer party. Politicians, CEOs, celebrities, diplomats and editors stalked the room searching for people worthy of their company.

Dan had been here before, seen all the privilege and vanity squeezed together. If power were a place, it was a place like this, and these people were its villagers.

The tradition of this party had begun in the days of Albert Porter, a poor boy from London's East End who'd founded the Chatstone dynasty. It happened every year to mark the summer solstice. The host this evening was the Honourable Cressida Chatstone, Albert's great-granddaughter and most recent heir.

Cressida Chatstone was a few feet away when she saw Dan. She looked quirky, as usual. Her blonde hair was half pinned up, half falling down her back, and chaotic in a way that must have required some consideration. Her dress was patterned with giant, wildly coloured sunflowers. She wore yellow Converse high-tops with pulled-up socks – one sock red, the other blue – and spectacles with thick green frames. Red leather gloves reached almost to her elbows. Two Irish setters sat close by; they followed her everywhere.

The way she dressed and the low sound of reggae throbbing through the great Elizabethan manor house were Cressida's well-known protests at the serious life thrust upon her following the death of her brother, when the family had appointed her chair and chief executive of one of the world's largest media companies. Dan couldn't see which of her boyfriends was here.

He raised his glass to her. 'Good evening, your highness,' he called. He often addressed his ultimate boss this way and usually she seemed to enjoy it. This time she turned away without a smile. Dan guessed he was in disgrace.

She was talking to the chancellor of the exchequer, or at least listening to him. The chancellor was animated, waving the air like the conductor of a hectic symphony. Dan was sure he could make out the words 'He's really struggling in the job – just doesn't get it', which meant the chancellor was most likely putting the knife into his old rival, the new prime minister.

As the chancellor spoke, a short, plump man stepped between him and Cressida. He was wearing sweeping white and a red-checked headscarf. Behind him, two younger men were dressed the same. The short man's smile and his large, ingratiating eyes might have compensated for the fact he ignored his host's extended hand.

'Will Leila be joining us tonight?' he asked.

'Not tonight,' Cressida answered, with a sharpness indicating she did not intend any further explanation. Leila was Cressida's fatherless only child.

'We brought a gift for her,' the man said, bowing very slightly and holding up an orange bag bearing the Hermès logo. 'Would you be so kind as to pass it on?'

Cressida looked irritated, but took the offering before handing it to the next passing waiter. The white-robed trio retreated, huddling together for a moment before heading for the exit.

The chancellor, still talking, shifted position to put himself once more face to face with Cressida. She wasn't paying attention, just gazing absently around the room.

Dan blocked the path of a waiter and switched his empty drink for a martini glass filled with something pink. It was sweet but tasted satisfactorily strong.

Jim Slight was working the room, touching the women too often and leaning in too closely as he made his way towards Cressida. He had been in the editor's chair for more than a quarter of a century, which was a hell of a run at the helm of a national newspaper. He was brilliant at it, too. Last year, he had helped bring down a US president, and that was only the most recent in a long run of triumphs. His high rate of success was part of the explanation for his long tenure; but Slight was honest enough with himself to acknowledge the other part of the explanation – perhaps the greater part – was his enduring popularity with the family who controlled Chatstone Corporation. He had achieved the difficult – perhaps miraculous – trick of balancing the task of maintaining his newspaper's integrity with an instinct for how far it was safe to go when challenging the beliefs and prejudices of his employers. These days, ChatCorp had more lucrative interests in other media, but its proudest possession was still *The Daily Courant*, whose first edition in 1865 had published an account of Abraham Lincoln's assassination.

Slight was heading straight for Cressida when he saw Dan. He worked hard – a little too hard – staying close to The Family.

'What the hell are you doing here?' he demanded, and Dan spilled a little from his glass tugging out the thick, gold-rimmed invitation to wave it in his editor's face. A pink line of the martini clung to Dan's unshaven top lip.

'Hail to you, maestro,' Dan said. 'It's wonderful to see you too. I'm here by invitation, of course, along with all these other fine people.'

'For Christ's sake, son, what's wrong with you?' Slight said. 'You know you can't be here.'

'Really?' said Dan, leaning against the wood-panelled wall. 'You mean this isn't my surprise party? It's not your little farewell for me after all those years trekking round the world for your fine newspaper?'

'Come on, Danny,' Slight said, a firm grip on Dan's arm. 'This won't do you any good, you know.'

'Do me any good?' Dan shook himself free, spilling more of his drink. 'Aren't things about as bad as they can get for me?'

Slight moved a step closer to look up at his protégé, speaking in a low voice. 'Please, Danny – you're simply not allowed to flatten the deputy editor in the middle of the newsroom. It's against the rules. You've become fucking impossible, and you know very well you're the author of your own disasters. You could have been my number two. You could have done anything.'

'Anything?' Dan said, planting his feet further apart for added stability. 'You mean spending my days like you, kissing the arses of the Chatstones? A bunch of billionaires sitting on fortunes they did fuck all to earn? Pandering to their half-witted prejudices? Thanks, pal, but no thanks. I'm heading back to New York.'

Slight was a short, square man with tiny black eyes that didn't look at someone when he was angry so much as take aim. He terrified most of his staff, but that didn't include Dan. Dan stood up to his tirades, retaliating with tirades of his own.

'Jeez, Dan, you must've practised so hard all your life to turn yourself into such a perfect piece of shit.'

The two men were standing eye to eye, trying not to blink, when Fiona Chester interrupted.

'Daniel!' she said, looking hard at him, hands on her hips. Dan liked Chester and hoped it was a look of affectionate disapproval, though he couldn't be sure. She was ChatCorp's communications director, and Cressida Chatstone's best friend.

'No one expected *you* tonight, that's for certain,' she said.

In one sweeping motion, Dan plucked a fresh drink from a passing tray and returned his empty glass.

'Dear Danny,' Chester said, tilting back her head to make eye contact as she cupped his face in her hands. 'Just look at you. Sometimes you can be your own worst enemy – you really can.' She turned from him and seized Jim Slight by the hand. 'The PM's leaving and he's in a rush. He wants another quick chat before he goes.'

They disappeared towards a group where the prime minister and Cressida Chatstone were talking. Years ago, politicians and CEOs would ignore Cressida, but that was when she was the family disappointment – a flighty twenty-something whose name was forever in the gossip columns of rival newspapers. When she was given the top job, for those same people Cressida turned miraculously into a witty beauty whose every thought was profound and every small joke hilarious.

Chester's voice rose sharply as she led Slight towards the prime minister, and whatever she said caused the group to open up instantly. Upon seeing Slight, the prime minister turned on his famous jagged smile. The two of them headed towards the exit, the PM running one hand through his tangled hair, with his other arm around Slight's shoulders as he leaned in to talk into the shorter man's ear. They'd met when the PM was a backbencher and Slight *The Courant*'s political editor.

The bonhomie, though, was a charade. *The Courant* had been the new PM's harsh critic long before he reached Number Ten; but not even a prime minister would risk snubbing a Chatstone invitation.

As they departed, Cressida broke away from the group and went alone to a quiet corner of the ballroom, where she took a phone from a pocket in her dress. It was a trick she employed on occasion to give her a moment of solitude without walking out of a room. This time, though, she was talking into the phone with a hand on her other ear, looking anxious. The normal, laughing Cressie hadn't turned up tonight. She was either unwell or had a lot on her mind.

By now it was gone nine o'clock and Chat House was packed and excited. A great actress arrived, one of the world's most famous and beautiful, and all eyes followed as she weaved through the ballroom. It was like a time-lapse video of flowers turning to the sun. Dan smiled. It took someone like her to turn heads in a crowd so self-absorbed as this.

Many cabinet ministers and their opposition counterparts were present, and most of the proprietors and editors of other newspapers. Their rivals feared and envied the Chatstone family's power, but tonight they wouldn't let it show. The director-general of the BBC was present, as well as representatives of the global digital businesses that had ended the years of comfortable profit newspapers had once enjoyed.

A dozen or so members of the extended Chatstone family wandered the room. Most didn't care much about the business, not so long as their dividends kept growing, though Jim Slight spent too much time fending off protests about *The Courant*'s rough treatment of their rich and famous friends, and companies they had put their money into.

Dan's old friend Peregrine Ainsworth was talking angrily to the foreign secretary, whose face was frozen in an unhappy smile. The Metropolitan police commissioner was with them, looking uneasy. Her head was wrapped in a blue hijab.

Perry was *The Courant*'s most-read columnist, and notorious for insulting politicians. He was once so rude to the education secretary that she pushed him into a flower bed and poured her cranberry juice over him. The incident would have made headlines, but it happened at a Chatstone party, where different rules prevailed.

By the time Dan appeared, the foreign secretary was staging a retreat. 'Please don't leave us,' Perry called after the fleeing minister. 'There's so much you have to learn about this complicated planet we inhabit, and so much we can teach you.' But the foreign secretary kept walking as he mouthed something over his shoulder. Dan could see it was *fuck you*.

Perry ambled towards Dan, still smiling at his little onslaught. 'God knows how long that man will last at the Foreign Office,' he said. 'I swear to you, I had lunch with him when he was in charge of levelling up, and he kept referring to Afghanistan as Abyssinia.'

Dan gave an unsurprised smile.

'I'm astonished to see you here, old boy,' Perry said.

Perry was a good man but also an outrageous phoney – a miner's son, born Ernest Scruggs, who'd reinvented himself with a new name and a new accent. He was always overdressed in impeccably outdated outfits. Tonight, pinstripes with a matching double-breasted waistcoat; a blue-and-white striped shirt, white collar connected with a gold pin behind the knot of a lavishly green tie. The rainstorm had flattened his mane of snowy hair, and the felt-collared camel-hair coat over his shoulders was dripping dangerously close to a Gainsborough landscape. A blackthorn shillelagh was tucked under his arm, as usual. He'd carried one for years without ever displaying evidence he needed a walking aid. He liked to claim it was for self-defence.

'Have you actually gate-crashed this event?' Perry asked Dan. 'Pretty well.'

'Attaboy,' he said, tapping his martini against Dan's. 'Our Mr Slight is very upset with you. Not so much for your drunken violence – more because of you blowing up your marriage. He's exceptionally distressed about that. Always a risk breaking up with the boss's goddaughter.'

'Laura is the closest he has to a daughter,' Dan replied. 'He's blaming me for everything. It's too late now. I'm done with him. I think I'm off back to New York.'

'New York again? You'll never make up your mind where you like best.'

Dan first moved to New York as a teenager when his father had relocated his business.

'Where's Laura now?' Perry asked.

'Santa Monica. She took both the girls with her. And the dog . . . and her new man.'

'So sorry, old boy.'

Dan shrugged. 'What's with Cressie?' he said. 'She doesn't seem to be quite with us tonight.'

'Fiona thinks she had some row with Leila.'

'Why isn't Leila here?' Dan asked.

'Gone to Venice, apparently, to see a pal who lives there.'

'Venice? These days she's usually off to Gaza or Pakistan.'

Leila was Cressida's one true love and her mother's biggest worry in the world – twenty-five years old, and the Chatstone family's rebel and lost soul. Lately, Leila had taken to denouncing in public the policies of *The Daily Courant* and its tabloid sister, *Worldly News,* which were reliably right-of-centre. *The Sun,* owned by ChatCorp's hostile rival, had accused her of being a Hamas sympathiser and implied she was secretly funding the movement. The Chatstones had launched a libel action, but dropped the case when Leila refused to cooperate with the company lawyers.

Perry put a hand on Dan's shoulder and swept his arm across the room. 'Look at this lot,' he said. 'This new crop of ChatCorp executives. Where the hell have all these geeks come from?'

'They're our digital future, mate,' Dan said. 'The life of news is in their hands. We're living in the silicon-coated new age of information.'

Perry emptied his martini glass with a single swallow. 'These parties aren't nearly so much fun, Danny.'

Dan smiled. Perry was more than seventy and an unreconstructed survivor of old Fleet Street, forever rewinding heyday tales of unchecked expenses, eternal lunch hours, and the sound of Remingtons rattling through smoky newsrooms.

'You should be used to it by now, old-timer,' Dan said. 'The days are gone making millions smearing ink on crushed trees. ChatCorp will never buy another printing press.'

Across the crowded ballroom, Chester walked with Cressida towards Slight and detached him from his head-to-head encounter with the foreign secretary. The three of them talked briefly and nodded among themselves before Cressie, the two Irish setters trailing her, led them towards the stage.

'Here we go,' said Perry.

Cressida stepped up on the stage and Slight followed.

Dan turned his back. 'I don't think I can bear listening to the piss-poor jokes and guff Fiona Chester will have written for Cressie. Come outside. I need a smoke.'

They walked through one of the French windows. The lingering sun glowed through a break in the clouds and the breeze sent golden wrinkles across the lake.

Slight's amplified voice hushed the room.

'Hey, listen, it's Jim,' said Dan. 'He's got a promotion. Cressie's given him the job of welcoming everyone.' He walked back to the window. 'You don't often see her standing in the background.'

Slight was by the podium with Cressida behind him next to a grand piano. He stepped back and took Cressida by the arm to get her to stand by him. She took two steps forward, then freed her arm and went back to the wall behind the piano. Slight fastened the buttons of his beige summer jacket, and leaned his small hands on the podium.

'Ladies and gentlemen, welcome again to ChatCorp's annual summer celebration,' he said, then waved his audience towards him. 'Please come closer – the acoustics are dreadful in this place.' The guests moved forward, crowding the edge of the stage beneath the podium.

'Thank you,' he said. 'This is the day the sun shines longest and keeps the night at bay.' He paused for a little laugh. 'Well, I suppose the sun this evening hasn't been entirely obliging . . .'

Then came the explosion.

Chapter Two

For a moment there wasn't a single human sound, only glass breaking and the shrill throbbing of an alarm. Dan was face down, flat on the stone terrace, covered in debris and strips of wood and pulverised flowers and leaves. A hot gust had blown over him with the blast, and there was a harsh, chemical stink he couldn't identify. The Chat House lights blinked through the thick yellow mist. Then voices rose from inside the ballroom. Screams and sobs and groans. The pained yelping of a dog. A woman shouting with urgent authority, 'Get out, everyone get out!' A man's voice, weak and old, crying over and over, 'Help me, please help me.'

The side of Dan's face was wet and sharp, embedded with pieces of glass. He struggled to sit upright and felt a surge of pain all over. The thick air stuck in his mouth and throat. Next to him, against a wall, a body was half buried beneath glass and broken timber. He reached to remove the soil and red rose petals covering the face. It was Perry Ainsworth.

Perry let out a long groan. 'Oh, fuck,' he said, and began coughing and breathing heavily.

'Stay still, old man,' Dan said, crouching beside him. 'Let me get this crap off you. Jesus, for a second I thought you were done for.'

'What was that? . . . God almighty!'

'It's got to be a bomb.'

Dan leaned Perry against the wall.

'You're a mess,' Dan told him.

'I'll be okay,' Perry said, pulling a mobile from his jacket pocket. 'Not sure I can get up yet. Let me tell the news desk. You better go find out what the hell happened.'

'You're a true hard-arse, Ainsworth,' Dan said as he stood to walk through the wreckage into the ballroom, his feet crunching on the carpet of glass. People pushed each other aside as they fled past him into the gardens.

Inside, the big chandelier was swinging crazily, raining sharp chunks of crystal. The long black hair of a woman in a blue sequined dress was tangled in wreckage. Two men lay beside each other; one appeared to be without his head. Dan helped a struggling woman trapped beneath them. When he freed her, she rested her head against one of the men, sobbing. A white jacketed man was against the wall in a sitting position, unconscious or dead, with an empty silver tray on his lap. The chancellor of the exchequer sat dazed on the rug by a tall fireplace, still trying to compute what was happening, his face and hair so caked with dust he looked like a statue.

On the stage, the twisted armour of a medieval knight had landed among the ruins of the grand piano. A green-framed pair of spectacles, the lenses smeared with blood, lay near tufts of red that resembled the remains of a fur coat.

Cressida Chatstone's face was shaped in a soundless cry of pain as three people moved the pieces of wreckage trapping her. Fiona Chester sat nearby, staring at her own blood-covered legs.

The editor of *The Daily Telegraph* held a handkerchief to his bleeding head, talking breathlessly into his phone. 'I've no idea for sure what's happened, except it's really terrible,' he was saying. 'It looks very much like a bomb. The prime minister had only just left. It could've been an assassination attempt. You need to get people here quickly. Give me someone now and I'll dictate what I know.'

A security man turned to Dan: 'Are you a doctor?' Dan said he wasn't and the man pressed him in the chest. 'Get the fuck out of here, sir, right away. Get out of the house. It might have been a bomb. There could be another one.' Dan ignored him. His head was still ringing. Blood flowed into his eyes.

The wife of *The Courant*'s foreign editor stumbled through the wreckage calling out, 'Larry, Larry . . . has anyone seen my husband?' She saw Dan. 'Where is he? Have you seen him, Dan? We were separated.'

'No, Jill. Sorry. What about Jim? Have you seen him?' Jill pointed towards the wrecked ballroom stage as she ran off, calling her husband's name.

Jim Slight was by the stage, trapped beneath broken beams. Only his head was visible. Dirt and blood covered his face, but he was conscious. His small eyes looked peaceful, without any sign of pain or alarm or any sense of occasion at all, as though he had woken up from a night's sleep.

Dan knelt and lifted a wide beam from across Slight's body; the chest beneath was crushed. He could not shift the heavy timber trapping his legs. Dan moved closer and saw in Slight's eyes that he recognised him. His mouth opened into the smallest smile and his eyes looked almost tender. Dan put a hand on his cheek and Slight tried to speak. At first there was only gurgling and bloody bubbles that became a watery red flow down his face. Then a weak fit of coughing.

'Shhh,' Dan said. 'Don't worry, boss, take it easy. They'll be here soon to help you.'

Slight tried again. 'Danny ... oh ... Danny ... my boy ... you're my boy.'

'Quiet down now. Be still until they get here.'

Dan stroked his face and Slight returned to staring upwards. It was a gentle gaze and he couldn't have been looking at anything, but his eyes seemed alive somehow with recognition, or readiness. After a few minutes, when his eyes closed, Dan knew he was gone. He sat there looking at Slight's voided face, its memories and feelings extinguished, left behind in the wreckage with no further purpose.

The tears down Dan's cheeks felt hot.

Chapter Three

Jessica Hunter leapt the white marble steps two at a time towards the entrance. At the top, there as usual to greet her, was the life-size bronze statue of Albert Porter. He was stepping forward, eyes narrow and truculent, hands placed purposefully on his hips. When Albert became a viscount after acquiring and reviving the ailing *Daily Courant,* he had changed his name to the 'more aristocratic' Chatstone and commissioned this statue as a tribute to himself. He'd stipulated in his will it should stand for all time outside the company's headquarters, there to bless its employees through the ages with his immortal inspiration.

This worked for Jess; for her, arriving at the world headquarters of the celebrated Chatstone Corporation was still like walking into a temple. Sometimes she would smile at the statue and tell it *Good morning* or *Good evening,* but tonight she was running late.

Jess had first climbed those steps eighteen months before, looking for a job. Her interview in *The Daily Courant* newsroom went well and soon she was back for casual work: three shifts a week for twelve weeks, no guarantees beyond that.

Six weeks later, the careless confessions of an ancient former deputy prime minister had presented Jess with the biggest story of her short career. The old man's tales of 'harmless fun' with young female staffers – revealed to Jess over late drinks at a party conference – led quickly to his disgrace and the resignations of numerous MPs.

The result of this triumph for Jess was to become a full-fledged staff reporter on *The Courant*, aged twenty-four. This early success did not, however, save her from the overnight shift, the slot most dreaded by ambitious reporters. They could spend hours waiting for something to happen, in the way firefighters might long for raging flames. There was time to write emails, loiter on chat sites, dream up witty messages on TikTok or X. Or dash to the pub, leaving behind jackets strategically placed on chairbacks at desks covered with important-looking clutter.

'You're late, Miss Hunter, very late,' Mustafa 'Moose' Abass called across the newsroom. 'Please pay me a visit when you can find the time.'

A couple of sub-editors looked up at Jess, frowning with mock reproof. Roy Jory, the deputy editor, was standing with Moose. He gave her a secret wink and Jess winked back. Jory was a large man with pushed-back coppery hair, red braces, khaki trousers that surrendered at the foothills of his distended stomach, and heavy glasses that always seemed about to slip off the tip of his rose-red nose. He was Jess's favourite exec. She had grown to recognise the look on his face: it represented the weary-wise demeanour old news pros adopted to give the impression there was nothing in the world left to shock them.

Jess called back to Abass, 'Many apologies, Mr Abass, I'm sure you must have a pile of work just waiting there for me.'

She put her overnight sugar boosts on a desk – a large bag of Maltesers and two Gatorades – tied back her long black hair, and walked to the news desk.

'Yes, sir, reporting for duty,' she said. Jess landed on a chair and wheeled it close to Abass with her legs.

Abass had been number three on the dayside desk until two days ago, when he was promoted to night news editor. His appointment had astonished everyone except those who knew the reason.

He was taking his new job very seriously, but he was only a year or so older than Jess and she was having trouble showing him the necessary respect.

'What are you doing here?' Jess said to him. 'I thought you had a date at the big summer party.'

Abass ignored her, leafing through that morning's *Courant* and stopping at page fourteen to prod his finger at the single-column story with Jess's byline.

'The editor is on another crusade against clichés,' he said. 'And you have been awarded the gold medal for your piece this morning.'

'Oh, terrific,' she said. 'What crime did I commit?'

She snatched the newspaper from Abass. It was not good to be singled out among the hundreds of *Courant* journalists for the criticism of Jim Slight himself. She had never even met him, only seen him leaning through the newsroom in fast, angry paces while everyone looked down, avoiding eye contact as if he were the emperor of Japan.

There were gashes of red pen through her story. She knew they were Jim Slight gashes. Abass pointed over her shoulder at the page.

'Nothing ever sparks fear in the pages of *The Courant*,' he said, raising his voice for the words *sparks fear*. 'We do not spark panic, either. Or hope, or rows, or crises. By and large, the only legitimate use of the word *spark* requires the existence of an actual spark. Otherwise it's tabloid talk – redtop slang – and this, Miss Hunter, is *The Daily Courant*.'

'Mustafa, I—'

'Wait, I'm not finished. You are a multiple offender.' He straightened himself, pointing again at the damning evidence. 'Nor do we like the word *plot*. The editor says the newspaper has become infested with the word *plot*. Above all, we do not like secret plots. So, your sentence this morning about something that sparked fears of a secret plot has won today's prize.'

'Moose . . .'

'Get a job on *The Sun* and I'm sure you can spark fears of as many secret plots as you like, but on no account can they happen in *The Courant*. Your crimes have been erased online, but they will live forever in these pages . . .'

'Moose, mate, listen to me – I'm not guilty. I did not write that line. Go check with the subs desk and give someone over there a bollocking for rewriting my copy. Maybe we should stop giving casual shifts to redtop subs.'

She stopped talking, staring at Moose, and began to laugh.

'What?' he said. His shiny hair was glued into a spiky black crest, like a tropical bird, a style Jess often warned him was way out of date.

'Mustafa! Mr Abass. You're wearing a tie? I didn't know you even owned one. Is this a sign of your elevated new rank?'

She leaned forward and grabbed Moose's bright yellow neckwear with both hands.

'Here, that knot looks dodgy. You need more practice. Let me put it straight.'

He snatched the tie away from her and wheeled back his chair.

'Cut it out, Jess.'

Jory laughed. 'Okay, children,' he said. 'Let's behave.'

'Seriously, Moose,' Jess said. 'I thought Leila was taking you to the party tonight. What happened to your big date with the boss's daughter?'

'She's out of town. I only found out a while ago,' Abass said. 'I was all ready and dressed for it.'

Jory was at the back bench, where he had been putting the print edition to bed before heading for the party himself. He had put on his suit jacket, and a blue polka-dot tie hung round his neck as he struggled to do up the top button of his shirt.

The news desk phone rang. 'I'll get it,' Abass said.

As he did, another desk assistant leaned across to Jess, gleaming with interest. 'What was that about?'

'You know he's dating Leila Chatstone?' Jess said.

'Really? You don't find out anything on nights.'

'Word is Leila got him the job,' she said.

Jess was heading back to her desk when Moose, still holding the phone, shot to his feet with his arm in the air like a cop halting traffic.

'Right . . . Okay . . . Wait,' he said, his voice louder with each word. Jess stopped walking.

'Roy,' Abass said. 'Can you pick up? Something bad's happened at Chat House. It's Perry Ainsworth. He wants to talk to you.'

As he listened, Jory began pacing back and forth as far as the phone cord would stretch. His mouth was wide but for a moment he didn't speak.

Jess looked at Moose. 'There's been an explosion,' he said. 'It sounds awful.'

'Hang on,' Jory said into the phone. 'Moose. You need to make some calls and get more people out there. And get someone to pick up this call and take what copy Perry's got.' He turned to Jess. 'Head for Chat House, fast as you can. There's a car downstairs waiting for me. You take it.'

Chapter Four

Chatstone House

At first, as Jess ran through the drizzle up the narrow lane, the big house looked festive, bright with floodlights and blue lights that flashed through the woods like nightclub strobes.

By the time she reached the roadblock, a helicopter had arrived, its beam like a giant's torch searching the grounds. People in hi-vis jackets dashed round the house. Ambulances and fire engines were parked at all angles on the hill.

A police officer pushed her roughly into a wet hedge as the roadblock opened and two ambulances raced past with their sirens. On a rise by the road, a police sergeant was surrounded by a crush of media. His face flickered with camera flashes as he read mechanically from his phone.

There had been a 'serious incident' – *no shit*, someone muttered – and 'some casualties'. He promised more detail as soon as it was available. Reporters held out their phones in the officer's direction, asking dutiful questions.

'How many people were there?'

'Was it a terrorist attack?'

'Has anyone claimed responsibility?'

They didn't seem surprised upon receiving no useful answers.

The journalists milled around murmuring to each other, exchanging pieces of information, and acting calm in a way

Jess was still too new at the job to imitate. She left the pack and confronted an officer manning the roadblock.

'I work in communications for ChatCorp and I need to get through. My boss told me to get here urgently,' she said. Deceptive, but not strictly untruthful.

'Hang on,' the man from *The Daily Telegraph* protested. 'She's a reporter from *The Courant*.'

The officer removed his chequered cap and wiped the rain from his face with a handkerchief. He gave Jess a 'nice try' smile. 'Sorry, darling,' he said. 'Emergency services only.'

The woman from the *Daily Mail* said to Jess, 'We're wasting our time hanging around here. That party's teeming with the bosses of every news outfit in the country.' She was browsing through her phone. 'They're filing to their offices right now and sending pictures. It's hopeless. Look at this.'

She showed Jess photos of wreckage and bloodied bodies.

'Christ,' Jess said.

The lane was lined with limousines and drivers waiting for their bosses – Mercedes and BMWs and a couple of Rolls-Royces. Jim Slight's driver was on her phone. In the back seat of Slight's car, an iPad and a water bottle sat on a pile of newspapers.

'He's not answering,' she said in tears. 'I keep ringing but it goes straight to voicemail. I heard the explosion a mile away while I was getting something to eat. The police were already here when I got back. People were screaming.'

It was pointless staying trapped down here waiting for the police to hand out a few thought-out morsels. Jess remembered advice from her night-shift pub sessions; pub nights in the company of wise old hands had often doubled as barstool tutorials. *On a really big story, don't hang around with the pack.*

Everyone sticks together for fear of missing something, but that way you get nothing special.

Down the lane a few hundred yards, she reached woods that hid a stile. She'd been here in the spring for the annual staff open day and remembered a path that led to the lake by the big house.

She ran through the darkness, rain rattling on the leaves, and froze behind some bushes at the sight of two police officers, one leading a dog. When they passed she ran up the hill towards the house.

'Hey, you're not allowed up there,' one of them called when she was already well past them. The mud sucked off one of her trainers. She picked it up and kept going.

Through the open doors of an ambulance, a body was covered with a grey blanket. Fiona Chester sat nearby, head against the terrace wall. Her eyes were closed and her body shuddering as though electricity were running through it. A woman in a yellow vis jacket put a dressing on her legs and shouted for a stretcher.

In the ballroom, two paramedics wheeling a stretcher ducked as part of the chandelier broke away. The young man they were transporting did not react when glass rained down on him.

Abandoned mobile phones flashed and buzzed with calls. Shoes and handbags were scattered among spoons and forks and pieces of china painted with blue and pink flowers. Chicken wings and shrimp were flattened underfoot. A toppled statue had split into three large fragments; it might have been the Duke of Wellington. Next to it was a strip of ripped pinstripe material. A hand wearing a thick gold ring protruded from it, its fingers curled into a claw.

Jess couldn't breathe. She turned away and staggered across the terrace, tripping and falling to her hands and knees, cutting her palms on the debris. Pieces of glass around her dazzled happily in the blinking blue lights as if there were something to celebrate. She grabbed the bottom of her T-shirt to wipe away the blood.

'Hey, you okay?' It was a man's soft voice. A hand touched her shoulder, but she didn't look up.

'I can't bear it,' she murmured. 'I can't go in there. I can't. It's awful.'

'You're from general news, aren't you?' he said. 'I'm Dan Brasher.'

Jess looked up with a start and forced herself to stand.

'Oh, hello, I didn't recognise you. I'm Jess.'

Dan's face was sliced all over with cuts. His right eye was swollen and almost closed and his head was wrapped in a bandage.

'You're hurt,' Jess said.

'The medics have treated me a little,' he said. 'There's much worse than me. Jim Slight is dead.'

'Oh, no, I'm so sorry.'

Dan gave a little nod. 'A lot of people are dead,' he said.

'Does the news desk know about Mr Slight?'

'Only Roy Jory knows, but he won't tell the others until he's sure the family's been told. They'll need to hurry getting hold of them before the others put it out.'

Jess had only seen Dan from a distance, ambling scruffily through the office to and from his big assignments. He was the star of the newsroom, the editor's favourite – like father and son, his newsroom rivals complained.

Dan took hold of her bleeding hands. She was covered in dirt from her fall. 'You sure you're okay? Get one of these paramedics to check these cuts. They look pretty bad.'

'They're busy enough. Don't worry about me,' she said. 'I better get to work.'

'Well done you, getting past the police. No one else seems to have managed it. You look like a survivor.'

'Was it definitely a bomb?'

'No one is saying on the record, but the police I've spoken to don't seem in any doubt. It must've been a botched attempt to kill the PM. I've filed a lot of descriptive stuff. Send them everything you get – photos and video. Let them work out what's fit to use. And best talk to Roy Jory. Moose is a good man, but he's very fresh and Perry could hear him getting shaky.'

'Is that Perry Ainsworth over there?' Jess said.

Perry was sitting on the terrace against a wall, naked from the waist up and holding a white wad to his head.

'Yes . . . he's pretty banged up. I thought he might be dead when I found him.'

'I'm going to talk to him,' she said.

'Good luck. He seems a bit delirious,' Dan said.

'Does he know about Jim Slight?'

'Not yet, and he's got enough to worry about right now.'

Jess kicked aside some glass on the terrace and crouched beside Perry. He stared up at her through half-closed eyes.

'Hi, I'm—'

'I know who you are,' he said, and turned to the medic treating him. 'You see, I told you there's some things I can remember.' He was slurring. Cuts covered the top of his body. The medic was treating his left hand. 'You are Jessica Hunter, one of *The Courant*'s brightest young things,' he said, with a smile of woozy satisfaction. 'You're the young star who ruined a few political careers not long ago – and quite right too.'

Perry's head rocked and his eyelids drooped.

'We gave him something for the pain,' the medic said. 'I think he was already very drunk.'

'Mr Ainsworth, can you tell me what happened, what you saw?'

'Not bloody much, I'm afraid. I remember getting here and that's about all.'

A stretcher arrived beside them.

'That'll have to wait, love,' the medic said. 'We need to get him to hospital.'

Jess walked alongside as the stretcher rattled unsteadily over the timber and glass and straight over a large, torn piece of landscape art.

'Have you ever seen a dead body before?' Perry asked her.

'Only my mum,' Jess said quietly. 'I was very young. Nothing like this.'

'There's a few dead bodies here I think.'

'Yes.'

'You know, when I was a young man travelling everywhere, I saw earthquakes and famine and civil war. Thousands – millions – will have died. But the office would always lose interest in these stories after a while. I'm not blaming them. Truth is, most people don't care much about the suffering of distant people in countries they know bugger all about.'

Perry was disappearing into the back of the ambulance next to an elderly woman in a sleeveless red dress. One of her arms was bandaged and the other attached to a drip. She was propped up, sobbing softly and clutching a Chanel bag so hard her knuckles were white.

'But this lot – they're rich and powerful and famous. Millions will eat up this story for weeks and weeks. But it doesn't mean much in the scale of human suffering.'

Perry squinted at the elderly lady. 'Lady Courtney? . . . Good evening to you,' he said, but the woman didn't seem to hear. He leaned closer. 'Don't you think I'm right, m'lady? That the events here tonight will echo round the world? That we care too much about the wrong kind of people?'

She gave Perry a mystified look and raised her handbag protectively to her chest.

Perry's head fell back. He laughed, then winced at some resulting pain. 'I'm just as bad, lying here seriously pissed off because I haven't been able to give them more than a couple of hundred words.'

A police officer cleared the way as the ambulance backed through the wounded and the ruins as its unfeeling, robotic warning kept repeating itself: *Stand well clear, vehicle reversing.*

Jess found Dan speaking to a police officer in a chief superintendent's uniform. The superintendent made notes while Dan talked. He closed his notebook as Jess arrived, telling Dan before departing: 'Thanks, mate. Very grateful.'

'How's the old man?' Dan asked Jess.

'A bit delirious, but talking some sense. I think I can guess the theme of his next column.'

Chapter Five

The *Daily Courant* newsroom

There was only one way to break the news, and Roy Jory could feel his thumping heart quicken. The families had been told and it was time to tell the newsroom. He stood and looked around. There must have been a hundred people by now, and he was struck again by the weird silence of modern newsrooms, no matter how calamitous the news. Once, excitement and anger had been hurled around by the old-fashioned medium of the human tongue. Now it was transmitted mutely, to people only feet way, by the dull nudging of keyboards, all the urgency hidden by mysterious technology – mysterious at least to Roy Jory, who liked black-and-white newspaper films to relive the clattering chaos.

He knew the newsroom would not be silent for long as he sat and swung his legs onto the top of the desk. Some traditions would never die. Some information was so big it had to be delivered the time-honoured way.

Time was he would have leapt onto his desk to address the newsroom. Tonight he did not refuse the helping hands that reached out as he stood to reveal the awful news.

He didn't need to call for silence, only for everyone's attention, whereupon even the nudging of keyboards ceased. Jory made himself stand unusually upright, but he couldn't conceal the quiver in his voice, or the tremble of his lower lip.

'There's very tragic news, I'm afraid, and the families of Jim Slight and Larry Shepherd have now been informed.'

Everyone rose at once behind their desks.

'Jim and Larry were both killed tonight in the explosion at Chat House.'

Gasps and little sounds of shock went in a wave across the newsroom.

'We know no more about Cressida Chatstone, except she's in hospital and her injuries appear serious. There are other casualties among our people, but that's all we can say for now.'

People cried and embraced each other, for once naked to the news they had to cover, stripped of the detachment that guarded them through the routine horrors that visited the newsroom every day of the year.

Jory coughed to free his tightening throat, but it made no difference.

'Okay, everyone,' he said. 'We have a lot to do.'

He dropped his head and folded his arms, unsure what to say next. Everyone was looking to him, waiting. The editor and the foreign editor had been murdered; Jim Slight was the best-known editor in the country – a Fleet Street landmark for more than a quarter of a century.

Jory made himself stand straight again and this time his voice was strong.

'Okay, people, listen up. Let's get back to work . . . let's make them proud.'

He called to Abass on the news desk, 'We'll need enough for a two-page obit on Jim, and a page for Larry. And let's use some of those photos in Jim's office he was so proud of.' Then he put his hand on the shoulder of the man in front of him. 'Call production and stop them running while we replate. We can't be out there without this.'

Once Jory was sitting back at his desk, a young sub-editor approached with a box of tissues, but Jory wiped his cheeks with the cuff of his shirt.

He turned to the man from circulation. 'Keep them running tonight when we get back up. As many copies as we can manage. And do me a favour. Marketing needs to know we're canning that summer weekend pull-out, so they should yank the advertising and scrap any promos on our websites.'

Then he called to the chief sub-editor, 'Take a look at Brasher's colour stuff. It's good. Be sure it's prominent on the home page and start it as a single on one in the paper.' For Jory, it seemed academic now that Brasher had quit after attacking him in front of the entire staff, unhappy with the cuts to one of his stories. His filing tonight was redemption enough. And it wasn't entirely Dan's fault Jory hadn't been able to keep his balance in the face of a hard push. He decided then to call Dan and offer him his job back.

The chief leader writer, Betty Adler, arrived at Jory's side to check he was happy with her editorial before it went online.

'You're going too hard that it was an attempt to murder the PM,' he told her.

'It certainly looks like it,' she said. 'Brasher says that's the big theory.'

Jory pressed his hands impatiently on the arms of his chair, pushing himself up and down a couple of times.

'I'm not disagreeing, but still . . . be firm on the possibility, that's all for now. It's okay to speculate who might want him dead – the Islamists, or some whacko new IRA faction, or that ex-wife who hates him so much. Leave a little room for doubt in case it's something else.'

'The BBC are going pretty hard on it.'

Jory shouted, 'I don't give a shit what the BBC says. They know as much as we do.'

Adler stormed off, holding her open laptop so precariously in one hand Jory thought she might be about to hurl it across the room.

He called after her, 'Also, you need a leader on Jim and Larry, okay?'

She gave a wave as she strode away, which Jory knew he could accept as an acknowledgement. Off to her cloisters, where leader writers got special space and quiet to develop their fine thoughts. Betty Adler could be hard to handle, but her brilliance made it worth the effort.

Jory had been at the night editor's desk on the back bench since news of the explosion first broke. He hadn't sat here for years, not since his younger days on *The Times*, but everyone else was at the party. Long ago, the night editor's desk had been the centre of gravity for all news. Every news story, every head-line, every word had passed this way before being released to the world aboard a fleet of trundling lorries. These days, the news flew out the building at the speed of light. The breaking news crew across the room was pumping it out now, bit by bit, and it was already flashing and buzzing on smartphones across the country, across the world. And sub-editors had become multi-taskers, feeding the hungry web even as they worked on headlines to fit the page and trimmed copy according to its allotted space. Maybe newspaper titles would outlive the printing press, maybe not. It was up to the digital whizzes to reimagine things.

But right now, Jim was gone and Jory's newspaper was the bullseye of a stupendous story. His hands were shaking above the keyboard.

Across the newsroom, Abass sat at his desk, looking like he was staring into the eyes of his own firing squad. He'd been like that since the news broke, sweaty-faced, bouncing his left knee and muttering to himself. Abass was in his mid-twenties, a downtable news desk man at the Press Association until six months ago, and promoted beyond his ability due to his link with the Chatstones. Two news desk assistants seemed to be doing most of the work. Jory walked over, stretching his braces, and put a calming arm around Moose. 'You okay, mate?' he said.

'Fuck, Roy, I can't fucking believe this,' he said.

'Just make sure we're well covered. It'll work out.'

'We've got more than a dozen people there by now,' Abass said. 'Plus Brasher and anyone else who's well enough to file. Dan says Jess Hunter managed to get inside the house – no idea how.'

Another news desk man interrupted. 'Jess filed some useful stuff and we have plenty of agency copy and the TV. We've called in good people who can pull things together in the office. We're in good shape.'

Jory squeezed Moose's forearm. 'Good man,' he said. 'It's going to be fine.'

Chapter Six

Chatstone House

Jess sat on a damp, grassy slope away from the house, in a pool of light from what looked like a transplanted street lamp. The trees were silhouettes against the clear, starry sky. It would be sunrise soon and Jess could hear the oblivious lilting of a bird, a robin, she was pretty sure; she listened to them in the mornings at home in Brixton with her dad.

After filing for hours, she was exhausted. She had felt like an intruder, guilty just for being there, watching helplessly as the police and paramedics dealt with all the blood and pain.

When Jess had forced herself to go back into the ballroom, a woman in a mask and white forensic suit was holding in her purple-gloved hand long white hair attached to a man's dangling head. The woman had lowered the head into a plastic bag and told Jess in the calmest voice, 'You don't want to be in here, love. Go outside with the others. This area should be sealed off by now.'

Jess's only experience of death was her mum lying in her hospital bed, still and pale, her hair combed, and her face soft, finally, after all she had been through. She was wearing a pink nightgown with frills round the neck, and her bedclothes were so peacefully neat. Even though Jess was only eight and she'd cried and cried, she knew it was good for her mother. She knew from her dad her mother wouldn't suffer anymore.

He'd held Jess so tight against his chest she could feel him crying. 'She's safe now, baby, she'll be safe,' he told her. Then, holding her straight in front of him in his strong arms, his face crinkled into a glassy-eyed smile, he'd said, 'You and I will make her proud. Is that a deal? Let's make her proud.'

Ever since, every time she did well at anything – the scholarship to Cambridge, her full blue in taekwondo, a job so soon at *The Daily Courant* – her dad told her the same thing. 'Your mum's up there,' he would say, smiling at the sky, 'and she's feelin' proud.'

Making her dead mother proud might have been a deal between Jess and her dad, but really, after all these years, it was him she wanted to please.

Dan landed on the grass next to her without a word. There were tears on his cheeks. Jess wasn't sure what she should say so she said nothing. He lit a cigarette and inhaled so deeply and for so long Jess thought he might not stop. When he did, the breeze swept a long trail of his smoke through the street lamp's yellow beam.

'I thought that was you,' he said after a moment. 'The cops are giving briefings now and it looks like *The Courant* has a dozen people at least. I'm knackered. We've done enough.'

'I know this has been awful for you.'

'You bet. Fucking awful for lots of people.'

'I feel like I shouldn't be here,' she told him. 'They think I'm a victim.'

'Office says your copy's looking great.'

'Right.' How little she cared right now how 'great' her copy might be. 'I always dreamed of being a war correspondent,' she said, 'filing dramatic stories from dangerous places. I don't think I've got the stomach anymore. Dreaming about it is nothing like witnessing the horrible reality.'

'No need to be ashamed of that. Most people don't. Others get addicted to it. This isn't like a war zone though. War is far worse.'

It was quieter now, no more noise to indicate the horrors and drama that had taken place; no desperate shouts or sirens or clattering helicopter, only the blinking blue rhythm of the remaining vehicles – and that was almost soothing.

'What's the worst that's happened to you?' she asked Dan. 'Don't count tonight. Don't count Jim Slight – that's got to be the worst.'

'There was a wedding outside Kabul,' he said. 'The bride, the groom, the families – all blown to bits by a drone hitting the wrong target. Everyone left alive was wailing. I saw it happen, but no one in this country cared. They buried my story in the foreign pages. That's all they thought it deserved.'

He checked his phone and sounded surprised.

'Look what just dropped from the Press Association,' he said, 'Someone has claimed responsibility. God! *Claimed responsibility.* I fucking loathe that phrase. Makes them sound so proud of themselves.'

He handed Jess the phone and she read aloud: '*As the criminal armies of the West have invaded our lands and killed our people, so the leaders of the West and the iniquitous propaganda of their puppet media have poisoned the world against our righteous struggle.*'

'Is this real?' she said. 'Where's it come from?'

'There's more,' Dan said, and Jess scrolled down.

'*No heed is paid to the barbarity we have suffered and they scorn the justice of our cause. But our jihad has begun and these messengers of hate will pay with their blood. Wrath of God will strike again and again and again.*'

'What? This is nuts,' Jess said. 'It's got to be the trick of some lunatic hoaxer.'

'Well, it's a bomb all right. Our friendly superintendent told me the explosives people are saying it was Semtex.'

'Who are these people? Have you ever heard of a group called Wrath of God?'

Dan shook his head.

Chapter Seven

New York, two days later

Jacob Abrams was very late. He was also stuck in traffic, sitting alone behind his driver in an old and stationary Mercedes. He had been in possession of this vehicle for fifteen years, but refused to replace it. These were hard times for newspapers, and the publisher had to set an example.

Spectacular summer storms in New York, with their sky-splitting lightning and saturating rain, were glorious to witness but also tended to flood the Franklin Delano Roosevelt Drive that ran along the river on the east side of Manhattan. That was where Abrams sat helplessly, holding the speech he was now unlikely to deliver on time at the opening of the annual gala of the Press Freedom Association.

The gala was an important date for American journalism, but this year's gathering had been given special gravity by the recent tragedy in Britain. Five people had been killed in the attack at Cressida Chatstone's Gloucestershire mansion. As well as Abrams's dear friend Jim Slight, the explosion had killed Slight's foreign editor, the French ambassador, the Hungarian commercial attaché, and a Portuguese waiter who had been standing near Slight with a tray of cocktails. Cressida Chatstone was one of fifteen seriously injured and her condition was grave.

After its gloating statement a few hours after the bomb, the mysterious Wrath of God – an organisation no one had heard of – had issued another, insisting the prime minister was never its target.

Our vengeance was directed at the vile merchants of deceit in the media. Those who would seek to destroy us, first Wrath of God will destroy, it had said.

Abrams would fly with his wife to London next week to speak at Jim Slight's funeral. Abrams and Slight had been close since Slight was *The Courant*'s young rising star, and Abrams London bureau chief of *The New York World*. In France last summer they had wandered the Normandy beaches talking about the book they would write when they retired. He would do it alone now, but Jim would be named co-author because it had been Jim's idea. They'd planned to make trips across the world to the sites of historic battles – Austerlitz, Antietam, El-Alamein, Iwo Jima, Waterloo, Hastings, all the way back to the wars of the Romans, Greeks, and Persians – and write a book telling the stories of these battles through the eyes of the lowliest fighters. Abrams and Slight had already written a bestselling book together.

He'd called Slight just hours before his death, after hearing that Dan Brasher had resigned from *The Daily Courant*. Abrams had given Dan his first job on *The New York World*, straight out of university. He'd been annoyed when Slight poached Dan to work in *The Courant*'s New York bureau.

'What's the score with Brasher this time?' he'd asked Slight on the phone.

'The usual, except it got out of hand. He sent poor Roy Jory flying in front of the whole newsroom. He's properly off the rails since his wife left him. He was never much of a drinker, but lately . . .'

'Would I be nuts to hire him back here?'

Slight paused and sighed. 'He's a good man with a great heart and he cares a lot. Maybe he cares too much. There's definitely some struggle going on in him, always was. He's a handful, but you know well enough how good he is when he's on his game. Go for it – can't promise, though, that I won't steal him back one day.'

Abrams had called Dan straight away and invited him to New York to talk. Dan had said he wanted time to think about it.

The downpour clattered on the roof of Abrams's car, and he looked east towards the open sky and the white, fracturing flashes. He wanted to lower the car window for a moment to feel the storm's power, but the switch on his door wasn't working.

His face was tanned and weather-worn and criss-crossed with deep lines. After all his years locked in the office, he missed the bliss of being far away on the road: waking to a hot tropical breeze, or the screech of gulls on a craggy coast, or even the howling horns of a Bangkok traffic jam or the flesh-drying cold of a Moscow winter. But most of all he missed the inexplicable pleasure of waking up in a strange town, certain that on that day he would not meet a single person he knew. He was a wanderer – not like the late, great Jim Slight. Slight had always lusted for the editor's chair and was sitting in one by his thirties.

After the Chatstone attack, Abrams's newspaper was unhesitating in its condemnation. A lead editorial in that morning's *New York World*, headlined *THE SWORD AND THE PEN*, had declared: 'If this group's target truly was the media, we have a message for them: they can slaughter individuals, but they can never murder the truth; and the truth is that the savages responsible for Chatstone are the great blasphemers of our age. They are barbarians who must never triumph.'

Abrams had written the editorial himself, and knew many of his employees were uneasy with the force of it. For once, he'd offered his chairman, Howard Wyler, an advance look. Wyler had sat in silence for a long time upon reading it, before saying, 'If you're sure.'

He had been absolutely sure, even though the editorials in other newspapers were less strident and many avoided all comment in their opinion pages. He knew that his industry must present a unified resistance to the life-and-death ultimatum it faced. Weakness would only embolden the killers.

As this year's president of the Press Freedom Association, that was the message Abrams was on his way to deliver to one thousand people in the grand ballroom of the Plaza-Asturias Hotel on Park Avenue. But he was late, and in the last fifteen minutes his car had moved uptown fewer than one hundred yards. He would have walked, but for the lashing rain.

The delay gave him time to reconsider every line of his speech, however, and Abrams began scribbling changes, mouthing the words, underscoring passages that needed extra emphasis, and marking additional points where he should pause for effect. The music in the car was turned up loud, playing Chopin nocturnes; they helped him think. After years of having to do it, Abrams still dreaded public speaking. He was too tense and absorbed to respond to the phone vibrating in the pocket of his tuxedo jacket.

When Abrams looked up, his car was approaching the 42nd Street exit. The traffic was still slow and some passengers were abandoning their yellow cabs and cars and running through the storm.

His driver had been browsing his phone in the standstill. 'Excuse me, Jake,' he said, turning down the music. 'I don't think it's just the rain. Something has happened. There's stuff online about an explosion.'

Abrams seized his own phone, and the screen came alive with news alerts, text messages and missed calls. When he opened his door, a man ran past shouting into his phone, 'They've blown up the Plaza-Asturias.'

The city wailed with sirens.

. . .

The storm quickly soaked his tuxedo. The pages of his speech spilled out the open door of his car onto the rain-washed FDR Drive.

On Park Avenue, police barriers were being set up a few blocks from the hotel, but years of practice made it easy for the old reporter to talk his way through. The hotel entrance swarmed with police, paramedics and victims. A group of men rushed out, virtually carrying the New York governor, almost throwing him into the back of a black limousine. The governor's chief of staff was on the sidewalk watching as the limousine sped away.

'Hey, Peggy,' Abrams shouted to her. 'Is the governor injured?'

'He's okay, a few cuts. He's just crapping himself.'

No one stopped Abrams from pushing through the hotel's revolving doors and running towards the ballroom, where a thousand people had gathered to hear him. The injured were wheeled on gurneys towards the exit. Many passing faces were familiar. A young woman from the office walked by unsteadily with a white bandage covering both her eyes. A paramedic was guiding her, talking quietly.

Against the wall of the wide corridor, a large man in a tuxedo was weeping. It was Chuck Healy. Abrams and Healy had been in the hotel together earlier that day, with Healy outlining the security following the Chatstone House attack. Abrams knew him well from when Healy was a New York City deputy police commissioner, before he quit and became head of security for the Plaza-Asturias hotel chain.

'Chuck, are you okay?' Abrams said.

Healy's eyes were raw. 'It's terrible. What a fucking mess,' he said. 'I let this happen. I wish I'd been killed.' He staggered away, shaking with sobs.

In the ballroom, Abrams's deputy knelt beside a capsized dining table. He was holding the hand of an unconscious woman. Her black dress was torn and her right arm looked badly injured. It was his deputy editor's wife.

'Nate, Nate,' Abrams called, and Nate turned towards him.

'Get the hell away from me,' he told Abrams. 'You couldn't help yourself, could you? You had to go with that insane editorial. How can you be surprised?'

'What are you talking about?'

'For fuck's sake, check your phone. Look at my wife here, will you. This is because of you. It was you they wanted dead.'

Abrams walked away and took out his phone.

The breaking news alert had dropped minutes before. Wrath of God had issued another statement: *Jacob Abrams was lucky tonight, but he will not escape his punishment. We swear to our almighty God that we will find him and make him pay for his savage libels. The true barbarians are Abrams, the billionaire family that enables his hideous lies, and all the media who would see us destroyed. Our revenge is not yet complete.*

The storm was still heavy as Abrams ran up Park Avenue on the phone to his wife.

'We've got no time, honey,' he said. 'We need to leave straight away. Bring your debit cards. Pack one bag for the two of us and get the doormen to bring the car to the front.'

. . .

Abrams's car turned on to Third Avenue and headed north. His wife was next to him, dragging on a cigarette and quietly crying.

'What are we going to do?' she said. 'Where are you taking us?'

Abrams didn't answer. He didn't know yet where they were going. He only knew they had to run and hide.

How had a bomb – a bomb intended to kill him – been planted in the hotel through all that security, less than twenty-four hours after his editorial went online? He knew how tight security had been; he'd seen it for himself. After the attack in England, the hotel had teemed with cops and security people. Every entrance was locked and guarded, or fitted with screening machines. There were sniffer dogs everywhere. Air-conditioning conduits were searched. It was like a fort. How the hell could a bomber have got into that place? There was only one answer: the nightmare of every law enforcement agency in the country must have come true. Somehow, terrorists had infiltrated the New York Police Department or the FBI. That was the only way it could have happened.

'The police or the Feds must be involved, Di,' he said to his wife. 'They tried to murder me. We can't trust any of them. We'll find somewhere to hide, somewhere no one can trace us through our phones or this car, somewhere we'll be safe.'

'But what happens to us then?'

Later, they pulled off the road in Westchester County, stopping at ATMs and using their cards to withdraw the maximum amounts of cash. As they headed north on the Taconic State Parkway, Abrams was thinking more clearly.

'Call a cab company in Poughkeepsie and tell them to be at the Todd Hill park-and-ride half an hour from now, and to wait for us.'

His wife made the call.

'We'll abandon the car, go to Hudson in the cab and find a motel,' Abrams said. 'We'll shop for some food and supplies and buy a burner phone no one can trace.'

The hard part would be finding someone to rent them a place without asking too many questions. Tomorrow he would contact Howard Wyler. He had worked thirty years for Wyler and risked his life for him in war zones. As editor, he had won award after award for the newspaper. Abrams and Wyler had been friends for years, visiting each other's homes and spending vacations together. He could count on Howie Wyler.

Chapter Eight

Tower Hamlets, London

It was late afternoon and the pub was empty, except for Alina behind the bar and an old couple side by side on a bench against the wall. The King's Head was one of a dying breed in Dan's gentrifying East London neighbourhood – a simple, old-fashioned, shabbily authentic public house. He enjoyed luring Fleet Street friends here. They would sit around for hours, hacks in a bar telling harmless lies to each other. It was the most familiar place in the world to him after his own house. One day, he would arrive to find it boarded up, with cheerful *Coming Soon* signs promising a *New Experience* in drinking and dining. It would be renamed the Intoxicated Turnip or Group Therapy and offer food architecturally arranged on square plates, with a blackboard promoting weirdly named micro beers and cocktails so complicated it would take forever to buy a pint.

Alina, the tiny, slender Romanian who worked from four through to closing time, was wide-eyed when he spoke. It wasn't just Dan's bandages and bruises; it was also the drink he'd ordered.

'No gin today, with your special slice of lime?'

'Just a Diet Coke if you please. I'm taking too many pills right now,' he said, then added, 'Might as well have the lime.'

Each day, with his lunchtime gin and tonic, Dan took a ceremonial bite into a big slice of lime; he liked the jolt of sourness. It was a habit he'd learned as a boy, watching his father. Dan had wanted to grow up to be like his dad, until he'd changed his mind.

The TV suspended above him was telling the same story he'd woken up to hours ago. The white-on-red message at the bottom of the screen gave the latest count: *THREE DEAD, 21 INJURED IN NEW YORK HOTEL ATTACK.* The bomb had exploded directly under the stage where Jake Abrams of *The New York World* should have been speaking. There had been minor injuries at the nearby VIP table, where guests included the New York governor and the presidents of two TV news networks, plus Abrams's empty chair.

The *New York World* editorial that appeared to have provoked the attack carried no byline, but Abrams had been widely identified online as its author. Dan suspected his name had been leaked in an effort by others on the newspaper to distance themselves.

Dan's mobile lit up with a video call. It was Siobhan Mac Stiofain calling from New York. Her face was so close to the screen, Dan could only see a tight shot of her green-ish eyes, her long, noble nose, and the smile he knew was a special effort to cheer him up. Siobhan had planned to visit Dan in London, but the bomb at the Plaza-Asturias would make that impossible. As an FBI agent, counterterrorism was her speciality.

'Hey, boy, how you been?' she said, and kept talking without waiting for an answer. 'It's wild here. No one knows what's going on. The Plaza-Asturias, for Christ's sake! There's been a massive screw-up at that hotel. Someone's getting fired, for sure.'

Dan looked back at the television while Siobhan talked. He liked the sound of her voice. It wasn't a soft voice. She had too much energy for a soft voice and too much to say to speak slowly. Siobhan was his oldest and best friend in the world.

On the TV, New York City's mayor had begun a press conference. Crowded restlessly behind him were the police commissioner, the fire chief, and the governor, with a bandaged hand. They all looked impatient for their moment to speak, relishing the limelight in a way that didn't look quite decent.

A new headline crept across the bottom of the screen: *NEW YORK MAYOR VOWS: WE WILL HUNT DOWN AND DESTROY THESE ANIMALS.*

Siobhan was still talking. 'Your pal Jake was so lucky. Some poor woman who owned the HearItHereFirst website was at the podium apologising for the delay when the bomb went off. Meanwhile, Abrams has vanished. He and his wife left their apartment building just gone midnight. No one knows where they are.'

'Have you guys any clue who's doing this?' Dan asked.

'Not yet, but there'll be plenty of suspects. The Mideast isn't short of people who hate the Western media.'

A man's urgent voice sounded off screen. 'Siobhan, you're needed now. They're waiting.'

'Got to go,' Siobhan said. 'There's a meeting starting. The director's flown in from DC.'

'Wait a minute. Where are you?' he said.

'At the Federal Plaza field office. I was at the hotel ten hours straight. It's very bad. I'll try calling tomorrow. Love you.'

Dan sipped his Coke and looked again at the old couple sitting in silence on the bench. They looked so content, with nothing left to say to each other, most of their lives behind them and all their worries and angers tidied away. Either that, or they could no longer stand the fucking sight of each other.

When Laura had asked for a divorce, Dan refused, but within a month of her departure California attorneys had sent a list of the grounds they would pursue if his resistance continued. They included seeking sole custody of Harriet, who was seven, and Amy, who had turned four on the day her mother took her away.

Laura's grounds boiled down to his 'emotional neglect' as a father and husband, his long absences, his 'uncommunicative' personality, his reluctance to 'share his feelings', and a 'lack of physical intimacy'.

On most of these charges, Dan bore some of the guilt, but the 'physical intimacy' allegation was harsh. It was Laura who'd started turning her head to dodge eye contact, who'd roll away each night at his touch and go to bed without a word, to be found upstairs already asleep. These symptoms had only developed in the six months before she left. It must have been about the time the affair with Charlie Dugdale began.

That she'd found someone else was tough enough. But it really hurt that Dugdale was a good friend. He was an American investment banker, and Laura had departed with him when he went back to his firm's Los Angeles office.

Dan lit a cigarette, showing some consideration for the rules by blowing his smoke in the approximate direction of the open doors beside him.

This family crisis had not improved Dan's performance at work; nor had his career prospects been enhanced by the fact he had been introduced to his runaway wife by her godfather, Jim Slight. Dan had never been much good at keeping in touch with his feelings; not unless they bulldozed their way through in a crisis like this. He couldn't believe how empty life had become since his family left him. He was such a mess that only a couple of weeks ago he had walked into a busy road without looking. That was impossible to explain, even to himself. Two vehicles had braked to avoid him; one went into a sideways skid on the wet surface. When it happened, and he imagined dying, the thought had sent such a wave of calm over Dan that for an instant he could see how a person might view their death as a solution. And that feeling terrified him; he knew he had gone momentarily nuts.

All the memories they shared were haunting him. The perfect, uncomplicated, unquestioning early years had become so clear and fresh and agonising to remember. Laura had been on her first visit to New York from California when Jim Slight gave her Dan's number. She was with a friend and Dan invited them to a party in Tribeca. They turned up late and Laura found him in the crowd. She held up her phone showing his photo and laughed. 'You are Dan Brasher,' she said, 'and I claim my free drink.'

He remembered her shining face as she'd looked at him, and how, all that night, as they wandered separately among the guests, they kept catching each other's eye, neither of them wanting to look away. He invited her for a drink the next night, and they talked until the bartender threw them out gone four o'clock in the morning. It was like that for three nights until, to his surprise, she reached under the table for his hand and placed it inside her unfastened jeans. After that, they left for his apartment for their first happy, hurried sex.

Laura moved from Santa Monica to Manhattan within five weeks, and within six months they were married. They made up their minds to wed when Jim Slight asked Dan to move from New York to the London head office. It had never been the same with any other woman, and Dan was thrilled, as well as a little mystified, that she saw something in him. If it was the glamour of his job, she must have soon realised her big mistake. He'd uprooted Laura from her home town, taken her to a strange country, then left her alone while he roamed the world.

For years, he spent weeks at a time on the road. It remained the same after the girls were born. He would promise to video of an evening and they would wait for his call; but often he didn't make the time. The excitement of whatever job he was on absorbed him too much. He had only himself to blame.

For weeks after Laura left, he slept in the same sheets to smell her, and the fading traces of fragrance she would spray on the pillows. Downstairs at night, he kept imagining the sound of the girls' soft, illicit footsteps when they were supposed to be asleep. In the morning, he would walk into their room and be surprised at the sight of their neat, abandoned beds. Every few weeks since they'd gone away, Laura put them on the phone from Santa Monica. Their English accents were fading a little with every call.

Alina slammed a glass on the bar in front of Dan. 'Come on, Danny, put it out or go outside. There's a love.' Alina worked hard at the local vernacular, but the strong Romanian accent remained. 'The after-work people are coming in,' she said. 'You'll get me in trouble.'

For someone so young and slight, Alina spoke with surprising authority, and Dan straight away stubbed his cigarette out in the glass.

He had never in his life been lost in such a deep gloom. He was boozy and unreliable and angrier than ever. All the drinking did was store up the pain, then ambush him later in a hangover of misery and despair. When he got into that stupid argument with Roy Jory and pushed him over, Jim Slight and a couple of others had intervened and marched Dan out of the office.

He'd called the next day to apologise. 'Mate, I'm ashamed,' he told Jory. 'That was disgraceful.'

'It wasn't your finest moment,' Jory said. 'I've got a huge bruise on my arse. Let's forget it, but you need to get yourself sorted, okay?'

Human Resources had got involved, even though Jory had declined to make a complaint, and Dan knew Slight was going to sack him.

His mother, Rachel, was a psychologist who thought her son needed help. But Dan didn't need cognitive behavioural therapy, or whatever his mother called it. He was a man who loved his wife and children and had been sent a little mad by the loss of them, and who deserved too much of the blame to feel sorry for himself. He was a neglectful father, an unreliable husband and, even at the best of times, a pretty impossible friend. That was as much self-recognition as he could handle. If there were explanations hidden away in him, so far unreachable, they were best left in peace.

Dan's mother liked telling him, 'You're too much like your father, wrapped up in yourself.' His father had started with nothing – Dan remembered his grandmother's modest terrace in Sheffield – and to him money had seemed to matter more than anything. By that measure, his dad's life was a phenomenal success.

His father had never been home either; Dan remembered his father kissing him only once and the brush on his cheek of the moustache he'd once worn.

His mother liked to say, 'I sometimes wish I'd married a truck driver,' though she would be speaking from the comfort of a Fifth Avenue penthouse or an oceanfront villa in the Hamptons. She had also stuck with her husband for nearly half a century.

It hadn't gone well when Dan, as a fresh graduate, refused to join his father's business. Their relationship had never completely recovered. It was only years later, when Dan had earned a few journalism awards and a small amount of fame, that his father had at last shown some pride in his son.

The King's Head was becoming noisy as more regulars crowded in. People Dan knew had arrived and he was in no mood for company. He headed to a nook at the end of the bar and wedged his foot against the door. Alina put a fresh Diet Coke and lime on the counter next to him and blew a kiss. 'On me,' she mouthed.

The best therapy for Dan wasn't a shrink's couch. Maybe his work was part of the problem, but it was work that made him feel best. Meanwhile, mysterious people were in the process of destroying newspapers where he had spent his working life. Sure, *The Courant* and *The World* had their faults, and their owners their eccentricities, but they were great newspapers that had done good work for many years. Jim Slight – dear, loyal Jim – was gone, just like that, before they could rebuild their bridges, and Jake Abrams, his first mentor, was running for his life.

Dan was serious about his work, but never romantic. Journalism was an untidy struggle; its 'truth' came shaded by the vehicle through which it arrived, most often a vehicle controlled by rich families and corporations with their own secrets and biases. There were plenty of fakes and liars in every line of work. In the news business, things had to be done in a hurry and journalists were more often guilty of honest mistakes than deliberate deceit. He could live with that. Right now, what mattered was helping along the destruction of these miserable killers.

Dan had quickly decided to accept after Jake Abrams called with a job offer, but events had prevented him from calling back to say so. *The World* wouldn't be the same without Abrams, but he couldn't stay in hiding forever.

Dan emailed the newspaper's editor-in-chief to be sure the offer still stood. In a few minutes, a reply arrived inviting Dan to meet in Manhattan. The editor-in-chief was Francis Wyler, the company chairman's son and heir. Dan was no fan of Wyler, but at least he would be back in the US and closer to his girls.

Chapter Nine

Jess was having a whirl of emotions. She was still haunted by the death and ugly wounds, the uncomprehending faces of the victims, how helpless they had looked, and how inhuman the people who did this to them were. The weird thing was she was also missing the rush of that night, and feeling guilty about that.

Dan Brasher had told her war correspondents could become addicted. A few days ago she'd been sure it would never happen to her, but already she was beginning to wonder. Everything seemed so dull and unimportant.

It was her lucky break to have been working the night of the bomb. Wrath of God was still the big story, but the office heavy-weights were handling that. And the big news had switched to New York.

Now she was back to everyday crap stories. An email dropped assigning her one of those fluffy human interest features she hated. It was also about the boss's daughter.

'Please, Roy, please don't let them make me do this,' Jess begged Jory. Jory's email ordering up the story had been forwarded to her and Jess knew he was impressed with her Chat House material. 'Leila Chatstone? Really? I won't be able to say anything even mildly critical about her, or the family, or the company. It'll have to read like a piece out of *Hello!*'

Jory wasn't in a sympathetic mood, dealing as he was with the pressure of filling the vacuum left by Jim Slight. He was too old and out of date to get the top job, and was only filling in until they found a suitable tech-savvy replacement.

'I know, Jess,' he said. 'But that's what they've asked for and sometimes we have to do things like this.'

'Who's *they*?'

'Sit down,' Jory said, shooting a finger towards the seat at his desk.

He lowered his voice. 'Fiona Chester is trying to raise Leila's profile. Cressida is in bad shape and investors are nervous. She needs to show the company has depth without her.'

'Fiona runs PR. Why doesn't she write it herself?'

'Jessica,' Jory said, with his stern voice. 'She's the director of communications, one of the most powerful people in ChatCorp, Cressida Chatstone's most trusted friend, and Leila's godmother. Would you care to pop upstairs and give her that message yourself?'

She didn't answer. Jess had met Fiona at Cambridge when she'd come to give a talk on the media. Chester had also arranged Jess's job interview at *The Courant*. She was the closest Jess had to a mentor.

'Leila's got a long way to go from being a junior in marketing to running the company,' Jess said.

'That's not what they're talking about,' Jory said. 'Not for a long time, anyway. She's being groomed for that, but this piece is part of a bigger picture. The business section chaps are working on other things, including a major profile of Ambrose Cracknell.' Ambrose Q. Cracknell Jr was ChatCorp's new chief operating officer, an American tech whiz hired from Meta to lead the company's reinvention. With Cressida Chatstone gravely ill, Cracknell was acting CEO after less than a month with the company.

'How do I make Leila look good when she's publicly attacked the company's newspapers and she goes around acting like a raving left-wing radical?'

Jory threw himself back in his chair and looked at the ceiling, making a growling sound.

'Skate over the radical stuff,' he said. 'Find a relative who'll dismiss it as the misguided idealism of youth. Drop it in that Rupert Murdoch put a bust of Lenin in his room at Oxford.'

'He did?'

'Yes, and it's fair to point out he didn't grow up to be a wild-eyed communist.'

Jess knew she was trying her luck, but couldn't resist pushing back one more time. 'Can I get something serious to do after this, *pleeeeease*?'

'Go away now, Hunter, and do your job,' he said, but with a smile.

Jess smiled back and retreated. She knew there was no escape. She would get this Leila puff piece out of the way and keep pestering for something decent. The buzz was that Dan Brasher might be coming back to *The Courant*. Maybe she could work with him.

She was glad about Jory's elevation, however temporary. He was planning retirement in a couple of years and a retreat to bucolic Essex, where he and his wife bred red setters. Cressida Chatstone was his favourite customer; one of his dogs had been the least significant victim of the Chat House bomb.

· · ·

The archives supplied enough of Leila's friends to fill out eight hundred words or so, but the best direct contact Jess had was

Leila's current date. She called Moose Abass to fix a meeting before his evening shift.

'I can't make it. Too busy,' he said.

'Mate, I need your help. I only need a few stories, some stuff about what she's like to be around. Her favourite films, books, music. I don't need to use your name. Do me a favour.'

'I can't. She's a friend. She wouldn't like it.'

'What am I missing here? The newspaper her family controls wants to run a soft piece about her. Fiona Chester – her godmother, Moose – her godmother has asked for the piece. What's the problem?'

'Fiona Chester is not Leila's godmother.'

'What are you talking about?'

'I'm not saying any more,' he said.

'How is she not her godmother? Everyone knows that. You can't just sack your godmother.'

'Leila doesn't want anyone to know why. It's no one's business but hers,' he said, and hung up.

What the hell was that about?

Ten minutes before Abass's shift began, Jess waited at the entrance to the cul-de-sac leading to ChatCorp HQ. Abass was always on time. She kept out of sight on the corner, knowing he would be coming from the Knightsbridge Underground.

'Leave me alone, Jess,' Abass said, brushing past her.

'Moose, stop,' she shouted and, somewhat to her surprise, that's what Abass did.

'You can't unsay what you said to me on the phone,' she said.

'I didn't say anything.'

'Why are you acting so weird? We're going somewhere now for a drink and you're going to explain. If you don't, I swear I'm going to tell the office what you said. How the hell can Fiona Chester suddenly cease to be Leila's godmother?'

Abass flapped his arms in surrender. 'Okay, okay. I can see you're never going to let this go. I shouldn't have said anything.'

In a pub down the road, Abass picked the ice out of his orange juice and Jess sat listening with both hands on a pint of Pilsner.

'If I tell you this and anyone finds out, I'm done for at ChatCorp,' Abass said. 'Leila would never forgive me if she knew.' He sipped his juice, looking pained. 'It's no use to you anyway. They'll never run it in the paper. Not even her mother knows.'

Jess gave an exasperated laugh. 'Please, Moose, you're doing my nut here. Are you going to tell me or what?'

Moose's face clenched and he looked hard at Jess.

'All right, I'm going to trust you,' he said. 'A few years back, without her mother knowing, without telling anyone, she decided to convert to Islam, and Muslims don't have godparents.'

'Oh,' Jess said.

'That's it, that's all.'

'But that's not such a big deal. Why has she kept it secret?'

'She knew it would make her mother furious,' Abass answered. 'It's all because of her father. He's a Pakistani Muslim. She studied his religion and decided to convert.'

'I've never seen her father identified. Only that he's a Pakistani her mother met after she quit university and went travelling the world. They had a fling and she came home pregnant and her mum refuses ever to talk about him.' She took a large swallow of her pint. 'Now I wish you hadn't told me.'

'You should forget it,' Abass said. 'She made me swear not to say anything. For sure, the paper will want to stay away from it with Cressida so ill and not knowing. No one else is going to tell you.'

After Abass's revelation, Jess started calling Leila's friends – and that's when she thought her story might be turning into more than a puff-piece feature. After speaking to half a dozen who knew her well, things weren't adding up. All of them believed Leila had left for a two-day trip to Venice five days before the Chatstone attack. But, in the three days before the bomb, when she was supposed to be home, none of them could get in touch with her. One friend had invited her to a party the day after she was due back, but Leila never turned up, or explained her absence. Another had arrived in London from New York, but Leila didn't answer her calls or messages. Some tried calling her after the bomb without success.

Abass didn't seem surprised. 'She can be a real loner – a bit all over the place. We'd go out a couple of times in a week, then she'd just vanish off the radar. She's like that.'

'So what happened the night you were supposed to be taking her to the party and she cancelled at the last minute?'

'I called her mobile, but she didn't answer. I was all ready to go. When I called the house, they told me she was in Venice, which was news to me. I didn't think a lot of it. I just came to work in my suit and tie.'

Jess tried contacting the friend Leila was supposed to have been visiting in Venice, but her phone and email responded with messages she was in Bhutan and out of touch. She was due back tomorrow. Jess would keep trying.

Chapter Ten

A lorry piled with gravel blocked the street to ChatCorp's head office. Met Police officers with submachine guns and handguns down their legs guarded the steps to the main entrance. A dozen others were dressed in grey with Kevlar combat helmets and fearsome assault rifles of the kind Dan saw mostly in war zones; a counterterrorist unit.

Dan presented his ID to an officer. 'I've an appointment with Roy Jory,' he said, and the officer waved him up the marble steps with his weapon.

A black band of mourning wrapped the left arm of the first Viscount Chatstone's statue. Inside, Harry the doorman sat redundantly on a stool, one foot on the ground, studying his phone, not far from the line of employees and visitors lining up to pass through two newly arrived body-screening devices. In more prosperous times, Harry Odhams would have been at the bottom of the steps each morning to open limousine doors for chauffeured executives and editors, ready with his large umbrella in the event of rain. Now they arrived prosaically in black cabs or vehicles summoned by mobile apps. Only Cressida Chatstone and Jim Slight arrived by chauffeur; now Jim was gone and no one was sure if Cressida would ever come to the office again.

Dan was at *The Courant* to tell Jory he didn't want his job back, and that he was on his way to the airport to meet the editor-in-chief of *The New York World*.

Upstairs, he headed without thinking to his old newsroom desk and felt a territorial twinge at the sight of someone sitting there. It was Jess Hunter. Jess stood, smiling at him as she removed a pair of glasses with red frames. Her hair was tied back with what looked like a thick green elastic band. She was wearing an Arsenal sweatshirt and jeans, and, it seemed to Dan, although he was no expert, absolutely no make-up. Her left hand was bandaged.

'Hello!' Jess said, and shot out her other hand to shake his. Dan took it with a large smile.

'You're looking much better than the last time we met,' he said, then pointed to his lacerated face. 'I'm still pretty sore.'

'Are you coming back?' Jess said. 'Everyone's talking about it.'

He looked around the newsroom at all the empty chairs.

'Everyone? Where are they all?'

'Not many of us are actually coming into the building. People's nerves are in shreds.'

'I'm here to see Mr Jory,' Dan said. He didn't want the truth around the newsroom before speaking to Roy.

'A lot of people wish you'd never left,' Jess said. 'I'm told they want you to work on these bombings. I'd really like to work with you if you're going to be here.'

Dan liked how Jess maintained her easy, open smile even as her eyes turned sharp and inquiring.

'What are you working on now?' he asked.

'A profile of Leila Chatstone. It's part of a corporate effort to show the depth of management without Cressida Chatstone. They want to show how Leila's being groomed for the future when she'll take over from her mum. Business is working on other things, including a major piece on Ambrose Cracknell.'

Dan grimaced. 'Count yourself lucky you didn't get the Abe Cracknell job. I've known him for years. That's like putting lipstick on a . . . on a plonker.'

Jess laughed. 'Actually, the Leila thing might be interesting. None of her friends seem to know where she was in the days before the bomb.'

'Italy, I thought,' Dan said.

'That's what everyone seems to think, but things aren't making sense. I tried calling her but she's never available. I should be able to sort it when I contact the friend in Venice she was supposed to have stayed with. She's due back today from a holiday.'

Jess smiled to herself as Dan walked towards the editor's office. She had deliberately sat herself at Dan's old desk to be sure he noticed her.

· · ·

Jory was inside the glass-walled editor's office, perched on the corner of the desk. The chair was occupied by Ambrose Cracknell and his sneakered feet were on the desktop. He was wearing a black T-shirt and faded blue jeans, the classless couture of Silicon Valley; though perhaps not so classless with that gigantic gold watch and the T-shirt most likely being a Brunello Cucinelli that sold for going on five hundred quid, plus those high-end Golden Goose sneakers that seemed old and battered but came new that way for people like Ambrose Cracknell who thought shabby was chic.

Cracknell waved as Dan approached the open office door. Dan and Cracknell had known each other since they were teenagers, but this would be their first meeting since Cracknell had started his new job.

'Daniel! What a treat,' he said, swinging his feet to the floor. He walked towards Dan and embraced him with both arms. Dan knew the greeting was phony. 'You didn't answer my email.'

'Sorry,' Dan responded. 'I've had a few things going on. Welcome aboard. You've sure walked right into a pile of trouble.'

Cracknell smiled at the mystified look on Jory's face. 'We grew up neighbours in Manhattan,' he explained. 'The same apartment building on Fifth Avenue. He was good with words and I was good at numbers. I helped Dan's father make a few million a couple of years ago. Isn't that right, Daniel?'

'It certainly is, Abe,' Dan said, 'and he'll be forever grateful.' Cracknell's face twitched; Dan knew he hated his childhood nickname. They'd attended the same school, before Cracknell went to Princeton to study electrical engineering and computer science and Dan headed for New York University. Cracknell had been a timid nerd as a kid, but Dan had watched him transform to become a rising star, moving from Microsoft to eBay to Google to Meta, making fortunes on the way. The nerd was by now well hidden beneath that look of invincible self-approval. His ChatCorp deal wouldn't be public until the annual report, but it was no doubt astronomical.

Cracknell knew zero about journalism, but only the company's news people worried about that. Cracknell was here to ensure the company kept pace in the new world of artificial intelligence and machine learning, virtual reality and ever-evolving methods of advertising, and on and on. ChatCorp had already moved into television and film production and launched its own streaming service, Worldflix. These days newspapers earned a fraction of the company's revenue; ChatCorp hung on to *The Courant* for its prestige and the subtle influence that came with owning it.

'First time I've set foot in this office,' Cracknell said. 'Cressie told me to leave the newspapers alone, that she'd take care of them. Guess it's going to be a while before she makes it back.' He stared at the disintegrating papier-mâché model of a man that was perched in a corner on a bentwood chair. 'What the hell is that?' he asked.

'It's Albert Porter, ChatCorp's founder,' Jory said. 'Made by pupils of the Limehouse School for Poor Children and Orphans. Albert was by far their most successful pupil. It was presented to him almost a century ago and it's sat in the editor's office for decades.'

Albert's effigy was dressed in the full scarlet and white plumage of a viscount. A gold-painted coronet was dislodged and hanging on the side of Porter's head, its fall halted by Albert's right ear.

'Jeez,' Cracknell muttered. 'Talk about living in the past.'

He then turned to a wall of framed photographs. Jory walked to be beside him. 'And that,' Jory said, 'is Jim's wall of fame.'

They were all photos of Slight in the company of famous people: Blair, Clinton, Obama, Trump, Thatcher, both the Bushes, Mother Teresa, Princess Diana, the Dalai Lama, Jeff Bezos, and, incongruously, Taylor Swift. Slight had had a weakness for pictures of himself with the rich and famous. A small photo of Dan with Slight was still on a corner table, the two of them celebrating Dan's Journalist of the Year award after a string of stories out of the United States and the Middle East.

Cracknell scanned the wall. 'Jeff Bezos!' he said, reaching for the photo. 'What's he doing on one of our walls?' He snatched the photo and dropped it into a large bin next to the desk. 'That man's a dick.'

Jory and Dan looked at each other and Dan reached into the bin to retrieve the photo. 'Come off it, Ambrose,' he said. 'That's Jim Slight's life in pictures and he was proud of it. The people here are grieving for him. Show some respect for fuck's sake.'

Cracknell looked hard at Dan. The counterfeit friendliness had vanished. 'So, you've come here in the hope of getting your job back ... is that right, old pal?'

'We're not exactly pals, Abe,' Dan said, 'and furthermore—'

Jory interrupted. 'Okay, gentlemen, let's not get out of hand here. And Ambrose, you're well aware it's the sole right of the editor who gets hired and fired on this newspaper, as well as what stories it does and does not publish.'

Cracknell shrugged. 'So I've heard. It's a strange rule, if you want to know what I think.' He turned to Dan. 'So – it looks like you're safe ... fired and rehired in the space of a couple of weeks. That's got to be some kind of record – all thanks to the man you sent flying in front of the entire newsroom. Gotta say, I could never be so forgiving.'

Jory reached out his hand to Dan, beaming with generosity. 'Delighted to have you back.'

Fuck, now what do I do? But Dan knew he had no choice.

'I'm really sorry, Roy – really, really sorry, but I've been offered a job at *The New York World*. That's what I came here to tell you. They called me before the bomb.' He pointed to his bag. 'I'm off to New York today to meet them.'

Jory went pale. Even the tip of his rose-red nose might have lost colour. 'Okay, okay. Please, let's talk this over,' Jory said, and turned to Cracknell. 'Ambrose, please feel free to leave us while we sort this out.'

'Don't worry about me,' Cracknell said. 'Happy to stay. There's a lot I have to learn.' He took a seat on the leather sofa.

'Dammit, Dan,' Jory said, lowering his voice. 'I'm sticking my neck out bringing you back. Can't you see that?' He pointed to Cracknell, who was punching a message into his phone.

'I've got to speak with them. Francis Wyler called—'

'Francis Wyler! I'd forgotten he just got that job. Good lord, you're not going to work for that imbecile. Without Jake Abrams that place will be adrift in no time. I need you here. Look at how many people are running for the hills.'

'I've already promised to go to New York,' Dan said.

'But, Dan, you've got to think ahead, think about your future,' Jory said. 'I won't be hanging around for long. This job could be yours one day.'

Dan smiled and pointed over his shoulder. 'What, with people like him running the show?'

Cracknell spoke without looking up from his phone. 'You guys do know I can hear what you're saying, right?'

Dan ignored him. 'Anyway, I'd sooner boil my balls in lava than ever become a newspaper editor, let alone try to fill Jim Slight's boots. I'm sorry, Roy, but I've got to go see them. They bought me a plane ticket and I promised.'

Jory threw his pen on the desk and it bounced to the floor. 'Take the trip then, and decide whether you'd sooner work with me, or that . . . that total fuckwit Francis Wyler. Think of the newspaper. Think of Jim. What would he want you to do? I guarantee you'll have far more free rein from me than he ever gave you.'

Jory's assistant put his head around the door. 'Jess Hunter wants to see you, says it's very urgent.' Jess was standing outside with the news editor.

'It better be,' Jory said, and waved for them to come in. 'What's so important?' he asked them.

'I've just found out something very, very weird,' Jess said. 'Leila Chatstone never went to Venice. She wasn't there the night of the bomb.'

'But her mother told everyone that's where she was.'

'Well, she was wrong. I just spoke to the friend she was meant to meet there and she told me Leila never turned up. Leila sent a text saying she couldn't make it.'

'Where's Leila now?' Dan said, but Jess hadn't finished.

'There's more,' she said. 'Leila was supposed to have flown to Venice five days before the attack and told her friends she would only be gone two days. When she didn't turn up back here, these friends assumed she'd decided to stay longer in Venice. But since she never went in the first place, that's five missing days when she wasn't in Venice or back home.'

'We need to speak to Leila, pronto,' Jory said, and turned to Jess. 'She's back at Chat House I think.'

'Go easy on her, Jess,' Dan said. 'Her mum's in a very bad way.'

Chapter Eleven

Fiona Chester's angry voice was so loud Jess could hear the muffled sound of it at the other end of the newsroom. She was in a wheelchair facing Jory behind the editor's desk; they were sitting knee to knee looking fiercely at each other. Dan was in the office picking up his bags, and as he walked out, Jess stepped in front of him. 'What are they arguing about?'

'Chester doesn't think you should be probing into the affairs of the Chatstones, which is total bollocks.'

'What's she even doing in the office so soon?'

'Good question. She checked herself out of the hospital. Tough lady – and she's really on a roll in there. But it's none of my business. I don't even work here. I've got a plane to JFK to catch.'

'Aren't you coming back?'

Dan ignored the question. 'It's your story. You should get back in there and see for yourself.'

'I better not. A bit out of my league with that lot.'

'Don't be a wimp,' he said over his shoulder as he headed for the exit.

Jess knocked on the door to the editor's office. When no one responded, she walked in and listened to the argument.

'I'm the acting editor, Fiona, and I've a contract protecting me against interference from people like you' . . . 'You're a damned employee, Roy, and you don't have the freedom to intrude on the people who employ you' . . . 'I refuse to turn a blind eye just because a Chatstone is involved. If this turns into a story and the others found out we sat on it, that would be catastrophic for the newspaper and for my personal credibility'. . . 'Oh, please! Go to hell with your personal credibility' . . . 'Enough, Fiona, it's already decided. We absolutely need to talk to her about this.'

Ambrose Cracknell was still on the sofa looking confused. 'I don't get it,' he said to Chester. 'I'm the acting CEO. Can't I just fire him for gross misconduct?'

'Please, Ambrose. Let me handle this. It's not that simple.'

'It's a newspaper, Ambrose,' Jory said. 'And it's *The Daily Courant*. A lot of editors do exactly as they're told, but not at *The Courant*.'

'This is no ordinary editorial decision, Roy,' Chester said. 'We've never challenged the family about their personal lives. Let's leave that to the others. They're ready all the time to jump on us. God knows they make life difficult enough for the Chatstones without our own newspapers piling it on. She's a wayward young woman, always has been. She's driven her mother mad for years going places without letting her know. Not only that, the girl's in a state of shock. Her mother might never recover.'

Fiona caught sight of Jess and swung her chair round. 'Ah, Miss Hunter. It has been decided the issue of Leila's whereabouts will not be the subject of any further inquiries.'

Jory came out from behind his desk, hands on his head gripping tufts of his coppery hair. 'Stop, Fiona, please. You know that's not for you to decide.'

Chester spun her chair back to face him, gripping at the wheels, looking ready to run him over.

'My job is to represent the interests of this family and this company, and the two are inextricably woven together. Leila is also my goddaughter, so of course I confess some personal feelings. But we'd be intruding on someone's grief and distress. *The Courant* gets precious whenever the *Worldly News* or the other redtops intrude on people's privacy. Now look at you. Jim Slight would be disgusted.'

Jess said nothing. She hadn't told anyone yet about Leila converting to Islam. She wanted to give Abass the chance to reveal Leila's secret, but he wasn't answering her texts. Jess didn't want to land Abass in it, but she had to say something now.

'I have more important information I wanted to check first with Leila before sharing,' she said. 'But I think I need to tell you now.'

'What could possibly make a difference?' Chester said.

'Ms Chester,' Jess began. 'I believe Leila no longer considers you to be her godmother.'

'What in God's name are you talking about?'

'I've been told Leila has secretly converted to Islam.'

Fiona's anger surrendered to wide-eyed shock. She released her grip on the wheels. 'Who on earth told you that?'

'I heard it from one of her very good friends. She seems to have converted because of her father. It didn't seem relevant at first. She's a grown woman entitled to keep it secret if she wants. But with the bomb and the fact she vanished for five days . . .'

Fiona looked hurt and mystified, and angry again, all at once.

'Unbelievable!' she said finally. 'She's never known what to believe in. I would take her to Sunday school, but I don't think she ever went to church as an adult. At Cambridge, she joined the Conservative association. By the time she left, she'd turned into a radical socialist. She was always a hard girl to fathom.'

'I don't think even her mother knows she's become a Muslim,' Jess said.

'I'm sure of that,' Chester replied. 'Cressie would have told me right away.'

Jory turned to Chester. 'If this is true, we have no choice. And I promise you, without the tiniest shadow of a doubt, Jim would follow through on it. There's no other way. When the police find out, you can be sure they'll make her give an explanation.'

Chester didn't answer.

Jory went on. 'Look at what we've got here – a woman who secretly converted to Islam has disappeared at the same time terrorists bombed her home. These people murdered Jim and Larry and the others. To say the very least, Fiona, it's an interesting set of circumstances.'

'I don't believe there's any way she's connected with what happened.'

'I'm sorry, Fiona, but we need answers to some straightforward questions. Of course we won't go near it if it turns out she was . . . I dunno . . . off on some tryst with a married man.' He nodded towards Jess. 'And Miss Hunter here knows to treat her very gently.'

'I'm going with them. I'm going to make sure she's treated properly,' Chester said. 'If you won't let me, I'm going to tell her they're on the way and she'll just hide somewhere.'

She cast a wounded stare towards Jess as she wheeled away. Jess decided it was a look of disappointment in the young graduate whose career she'd launched at *The Daily Courant*.

It was a bad day for someone whose job, above all, was protecting the Chatstones. The flagship of the mighty Chatstone empire was staging a mutiny, guaranteeing glee among its enemies.

Chapter Twelve

Chatstone House

They drove clear of a patch of woodland, and Chatstone House appeared on a distant hill, the colour of dirty gold. Jess was with Fiona Chester and Moose Abass in the back of the ancient Chatstone family Rolls-Royce. When she'd told Abass she had revealed his big secret, he'd looked like he would collapse. He was still in a panic on the journey to confront Leila. 'Oh, God, save me,' he kept saying, his eyes closed like he might actually be praying. 'You promised – you promised me you wouldn't say anything.'

'I'm sorry, mate, but her disappearance and the Muslim thing put together made it impossible.'

'Leila said she'd told no one else but me.'

'That's nonsense,' Chester interjected. 'You can't change your religion without anyone knowing.' She was clutching an overhead strap and gazing through the window. Every now and then she grimaced and repositioned herself. At the start of the journey, she'd washed down a couple of tablets. Her wheelchair was in the boot.

'If Leila's got an innocent explanation, I'm stuffed,' Abass said.

'Don't be dramatic,' Jess said. 'You'll have Jory on your side.'

Abass gave a weak laugh. 'Right – that's sure to fireproof me when the entire family hates my guts.' He ran his hand across the red leather seats of the old car, cracked and curling in multiple places. 'Maybe she went away somewhere on a religious retreat. She wouldn't tell anyone about that.'

'If religion was the reason, why wouldn't she tell you?' Jess said. 'And if she knew she'd be away, why invite you to go to the party with her?'

Abass shrugged.

Jess knew they were treading on sensitive territory. Most newspapers dodged delicate coverage of its proprietors. Even the name ChatCorp hardly appeared in its own titles, except when the corporate earnings were released and only then with the most positive possible spin on its performance. But Roy Jory had sent Jess away with good advice: 'Cover it like you would any other job. I'll catch what you write if it goes too far.'

Jess decided that covering it like any other job also permitted her to coax whatever useful information she could from Cressida Chatstone's dearest friend.

Chester was struggling out of her seat and stretching for a water bottle in the walnut partition ahead of them. Jess reached to get it for her. Chester was a slender woman, always in a tight-waisted business suit, black or grey pinstripe, with the same necklace of silver beads, and dark stockings with perilously high heels, though since her injuries she had abandoned the heels for blue running shoes.

'This car is so huge,' Jess said, handing Chester the water. 'I've never been inside a Roller before. Can I send my dad a picture?'

'Be my guest. Long ago, Cressie's grandfather was sitting right here.' Chester raised her voice. 'And Teddy was a young lad at the wheel even then.'

The white-haired chauffeur chuckled. 'Now we're just two

old bangers,' he said, smiling at her in the rear-view mirror. 'I don't mean you, darling – me and this steam engine.'

'Keep your eyes on the road, old man,' Chester said, looking at Jess and raising her eyebrows. It sounded like Teddy and Chester had spent their working lives employed by the same family; it didn't appeal to Jess, a whole career trapped in orbit around the Chatstones.

'Leila's spending a lot of time with her mum, right?' Jess said as she took photos with her phone.

'She's often at the hospital, but Cressie's not conscious much of the time. Even awake, she's mostly incoherent. Leila and I are the only two people whose presence she'll tolerate. Visitors make her hysterical. When the police came to ask some questions, she got so upset the doctors made them leave.'

'It is strange Leila never told anyone about cancelling Venice except the friend who was expecting her.'

'On the night after the bomb, she left me a voicemail,' Chester said. 'She said she'd just got back from Venice. I didn't hear it until I was in hospital. I haven't seen her since I got out. She's living in the gatehouse because everywhere else is such a mess from the bomb.'

'What reason would she have to lie to you?' Jess asked.

'I keep telling people – she's not someone who's easy to understand.'

Jess had been at Cambridge the same time as Leila, but they'd never met. Jess was a scholarship girl, a plumber's daughter, with the same mixed-up accent as the other Brixton kids she grew up with. She didn't spend much time with rich students.

Abass had fallen asleep, resting his head against the window, letting out irregular snorts and mumbling as though he were having a bad dream.

'You know Cressida Chatstone really well,' Jess said.

'We were at school together. She's always enjoyed herself, loves a crowd, but she ended up hating university. Every little thing she did or said seemed to end up in a gossip column. She dropped out after eighteen months. Without telling anyone but me, she went off by herself to travel the world. She was in Pakistan the longest. When Cress got home from Punjab, she was four months pregnant.'

'Is it right she didn't even tell Leila's father he had a child?'

'Cressie hardly knew him. They'd only met a couple of times. She wouldn't get rid of the baby, but she didn't want anything to do with the father. He was a poor social sciences lecturer at the local university, a total stranger she knew nothing about. She thought a clean break was best for her and Leila. She wanted to erase him. That's caused plenty of family friction over the years. Cressie wouldn't even know now if he's dead or alive.'

'He's obviously educated. If he's alive, he must know he has a daughter.'

'Years ago, Cress said he sent some letters and postcards, but she ignored them.'

'Didn't Leila change her name when she was in her teens?'

'There was a huge fuss over that,' Chester said. 'She was named Alexandra after Cressie's mother, but she went on and on about wanting a Pakistani name. Cressie gave up in the end.' Chester took another pill, then laughed. 'I remember one weekend sitting with Leila when we still called her Alex. She was only seven or eight and she was looking at the pictures in some glossy magazine – *Vogue* or *Elle*. There was a story in it about the family. "Auntie Fi," she said. "What's a golden girl? It says here I'm a golden girl."'

They both laughed. Jess made discreet notes on her phone.

'She always hated the idea of spending her life working for ChatCorp. She'd complain about having to sit through long dinners next to famous people pretending to be interested in her. During holidays from university, she would have to sit in the corner of her mother's office. Her mother would tell people, "Oh, this is Leila, my daughter. I hope you won't mind if she sits there quietly while we talk." I'd see her sat there like an ornament, poor thing. She loathed being groomed for the top. "Everyone will be tiptoeing around me because I'm the boss's daughter," she'd say. "They'll see me pushed up the ranks over the heads of people far smarter than I am."

'I tried to comfort her. "Your mum's only young," I'd tell her. "She enjoys the life. She'll be doing it in her eighties. What've you got to worry about? You'll be like Prince Charles." She gave up in the end and took a job with the company, but she's still got the rebel in her. This recent business of attacking the newspapers in public – it's made Cress very unhappy.'

The car slowed to pass through the tall gates leading into the grounds of Chatstone House. It passed a small stone gatehouse and headed up the yellow gravel drive. Chat House was among the largest private residences in the country, set in five hundred acres of the rolling wolds of Gloucestershire and surrounded by parklands landscaped by Capability Brown.

The brakes squeaked, bringing the car to a halt at the front entrance. A large part of the façade was covered with scaffolding and white sheeting. The sight of it gave Jess the same rush of panic from that night outside the ballroom.

Abass stirred from his nap and Chester reached for her walking cane.

'This place has suffered through a few dramas over the years,' she said. 'Albert Porter, the first viscount – he was a bit of a wild man. I think the whole family's got that in their genes. He crashed his plane here. And poor Neal only lasted six months in the job.'

The stories of both men were famous. Cressida Chatstone's great-grandfather had been sixty-two when he crashed his biplane through the roof of Chatstone House, killing himself, his twenty-five-year-old mistress, and the family butler who was bringing breakfast in bed to the doomed proprietor's wife. The manner of the viscount's death surprised no one. For years, he had enjoyed impressing lovers with his reckless cockpit manoeuvres. Usually, his well-practised aerial loop came within a hundred feet of the Chat House roof, but not on that occasion.

And Cressida had been forced into the top job when her brother, Neal, killed himself early one autumn morning as he lay on the lawn beside the serpentine lake. The blast of his shotgun had also killed one of the four resident swans.

'Neal was always troubled,' Chester said. 'I think he was pushed over the edge by the grief of his dad's death and all the responsibility that landed on him. Cressie was happy until then running the family's charitable foundation.'

Jess walked quickly around the car to Chester's door. She reached for her hands to help her stand, while Teddy the chauffeur delivered the wheelchair.

'This place attracted some notoriety in the sixties too. The tabloids ran sneaky pieces about parties here involving drugs, and what they used to call show girls.'

Jess laughed.

'That seemed to stop when the Chatstones acquired their own tabloid and the power to strike back,' Chester said.

Teddy placed Chester's handbag in her lap and Abass began pushing the wheelchair across the gravel until she made him stop.

'I'll do it myself. I'll be doing it a while yet,' she said. She could walk a few yards with a stick, but needed the wheelchair for more.

'Oh, come on, Ms Chester,' Jess said. 'We know you're tough, but no one gets a wheelchair through gravel without a push.' She took hold of the chair herself and wheeled it inside the house. 'You've been very loyal to the family all these years,' Jess continued.

'Don't ask me to explain it. My ex couldn't stand them. He said I was the victim of a cult. He told me, "It's either them, or me." That was ten years ago.'

They stopped in the ballroom, near where the bomb exploded. Much of the destruction had yet to be cleared. Workers were carrying away pieces of timber and broken furniture.

'The police haven't let anyone else in here until this morning,' Chester said, swinging around to see the devastation she'd survived.

The explosion had blown a deep hole through the floor, and the wooden walls were scorched and splintered. Remnants of the chandelier still hung above fragments of furniture.

'They say the bomb was placed at the bottom of the podium,' Chester said. 'It was packed with random nuts and bolts, even glass marbles and shards of ceramic, apparently. They were all crowded so close to hear Jim.' She looked up. 'That chandelier looks like it could fall at any moment.' Then she pushed away, waving at Jess and Abass to follow. 'They looked for fingerprints on what was left of the podium and the package, but there were none they couldn't identify – Cressie, Jim Slight, one of the security people, a few workmen who helped set up the party. All interviewed except for Cressie. And Jim, obviously.'

'How close were you when the bomb went off?' Abass asked.

'About fifty feet. I stayed off the stage when Cressida and Jim went up. Cress was back by the piano when it happened. She wasn't herself that night. She was in tears telling me Leila had gone to Venice. They must have had an argument, but I don't know why.'

'Do they fight often?' said Jess.

'They don't see eye to eye on lots of things. They're very different people. Leila says the newspapers are too conservative and that the *Worldly News* is cruel. It's a fair point about the *Worldly News*, to be honest, but it was very profitable for a long time.'

Chester propelled her chair away from the wreckage onto the terrace. This was where Dan had found her after she fell and cut herself on broken glass. The French windows were boarded up. The long lawn down to the lake was still churned and muddy from the emergency vehicles. A woman in jeans and red shirt was stretched out in the sun just beyond the shade of a wide willow at the lake's edge. Three swans were out of the water close to her, like guards.

'There's Leila,' said Chester. 'That spot's been her safe place since she was tiny. Chat House used to terrify her. When she was about five, she got lost, it's so massive. She was running through the house in a total panic – all those paintings of dead people along the walls with their eyes following her and knights in armour waving swords and spiky clubs.'

'Let's go and see her,' Jess said.

'We'll all three go together, but please, do go easy on her,' Chester said, adding with a smile, 'Jess – best you wheel me down the grass.'

Leila seemed asleep as they came near, on her back with her face to the sun, arms stretched to make the shape of a cross, long hair spread across the grass like a big black fan. The swans hissed when they arrived.

Chester leaned from her wheelchair. 'Leila, darling, are you awake?' she whispered.

Leila opened her eyes and smiled. 'Auntie Fi,' she said, pushing up on one elbow and rubbing her face. 'What a nice surprise.'

She looked at Abass quizzically. 'Mustafa. What are you doing here?'

Then she looked at Jess. 'Who are you?'

'I'm a reporter at *The Courant*. Jess . . . Jess Hunter. We want to ask you some questions.'

Leila stumbled as she jumped to her feet.

'What questions? I'm not answering any of your questions. Get away. Please go away.'

Chester took her by the hand, but Leila pulled away.

'I'm sorry,' Chester said. 'We didn't mean to surprise you. They only want a few minutes.'

Abass approached. 'There's nothing to be scared of. Some things have come up. They need explaining, that's all.'

Leila moved backwards away from him with her arms tight around her body.

'You've no right being here,' she said. 'This is private property. You're harassing me.' Then she turned to Chester. 'Why are you doing this to me? You know Mum's very ill, she might be dying.' Her deep, dark eyes looked more afraid than angry as she walked rapidly away.

Chester said to Jess and Moose, 'That's enough, you two, let's go. The poor girl is devastated.'

'No,' Jess said. 'Something's wrong here.'

She ran after Leila.

'Please, let me ask a few questions. Everyone thought you had flown to Venice. But that isn't true, is it? Your friend in Italy told me you cancelled at the last minute. Why did you lie about being there?'

Leila stopped and turned. 'Leave me alone,' she shouted.

'And why did you convert to Islam and not even tell your own mother?'

'I'm not speaking to you.'

'Does it have something to do with your Pakistani father? Does he know?'

Leila lunged forward and slapped Jess across the face.

'How dare you. I don't even know who my father is,' Leila said, and called to Moose. 'Mustafa, what have you told them? I trusted you. You were the only one I trusted.'

Then she ran away along the driveway, beneath the columns of cedar trees towards the gatehouse.

'Fuck,' Jess said to herself as she walked back towards Chester and Moose.

Chester looked angry. 'I'd have smacked you myself,' she said. 'You had no right chasing her like that. She's distraught.'

'I'm not sorry. I know she's upset, but that was way over the top. There's no good reason to be that scared of us. She went crazy the instant she knew we had questions. She knew what we wanted to know and it terrified her. She's definitely hiding something.'

. . .

Leila watched from between the flowered curtains of a small window as the Rolls-Royce moved past the gatehouse. The young woman she'd run away from lowered the car window to give Leila an unsmiling nod.

They know about Venice. They were bound to find out. They're going to find out everything. I can't talk to them, I can't talk to anyone, but they're going to find out the truth about what happened. What will they do to me then?

She stood in the living room. It was alive with animal trophies, all of them glaring at her: a jaguar crouched to pounce; a buffalo head with long horns peered from the wall; a ferret on the fireplace mantel showed its needle-sharp teeth; at her feet were the gaping jaws of a tiger-skin rug. *Those animals look like they hate me. When it all comes out, everyone will hate me. It will destroy us. It will destroy the whole family.*

Lying still on the floor was an Irish setter, both its front legs wrapped in bandages. Leila sat on the rug to stroke the dog's fur and began to cry.

Chapter Thirteen

HEIRESS LEILA SUSPECT IN BOMB HORROR ATTACK
The Sun

RIDDLE OF CHATSTONE BEAUTY'S LOST DAYS
Daily Mail

It was before six o'clock the next morning when plainclothes officers marched Leila from the gatehouse with three ChatCorp lawyers following. Every step she took looked reluctant, with the officers holding tight to her arms and almost lifting her along. She was crying and her face was streaked with long strands of hair. The police said they had handcuffed Leila because she refused to come quietly.

Leila caught Jess's eye as her head was pressed down into a car and a line of yellow-jacketed police held back the crowd of media. Television reporters shouted silly questions they knew Leila would never answer, all to add drama to their footage – 'Tell us what you're hiding Leila . . . Do you know who these killers are? . . . Do you think these terrorists are fighting for a righteous cause?'

They had been staking out the gatehouse since the middle of the night, when Jess's story had broken online. All *The Courant*'s rivals had picked it up on their websites and front pages.

Back in the newsroom after witnessing Leila's arrest, Jess was talking to Jory. They were heading for a briefing for editors at Scotland Yard.

'It's supposed to be off the record,' Jory told her. 'I fear it'll be a lot of waffle, but I better be there. They must be praying Leila can lead them somewhere.'

'Don't you think they're getting ahead of themselves, hauling her in like this and leaking she's a suspect?' Jess said. 'It's hard to imagine a young woman in a family worth billions has turned into a mad terrorist bomber.'

'They're desperate to show some progress. And who knows? She's hiding something, that's for certain. She's an impressionable young woman. Maybe someone has manipulated her.'

'You think some extremist mullah has radicalised her and she's blown up her own mother?'

As she was speaking, Jess recognised three smart-suited lawyers – two men and a woman – heading for Jory's office. They'd been with Leila when the police took her from the gatehouse.

'Can I stay?' Jess said.

'Sure, they might have some questions for you. You'll be kicked out if you're not welcome.'

Jory introduced Jess and the lawyers looked wary. 'Hold on,' said the woman. 'This isn't a bloody press conference.'

'It's okay,' Jory said. 'Jess here broke the story. She knows what happens here is strictly for internal consumption.'

'It doesn't matter,' another lawyer said. 'We've got little to report, except that she didn't tell them a damn thing. She didn't even tell us anything, except that she wasn't going to speak to anyone. The whole time, she either ignored the questions or said "no comment". They kept asking about her father, but she just sat there, dumb, staring over their heads and every now and then breaking into tears.'

'What happens now?' Jory asked.

'The Met have no option – they have to at least treat her with suspicion.'

'But they don't have anything to charge her with, right?' Jess asked. 'There's no law against keeping your mouth shut.'

'There can't be any doubt she's withholding something,' the woman lawyer said. 'Under the Terrorism Act, they can hold her fourteen days without charge. They'll keep her a few days at least, in the hope of wearing her down, but we should expect her at least to face an initial charge of obstruction of justice. They're very agitated she's failed to produce a mobile or a laptop. They've got warrants to search the gatehouse and Chatstone House.'

· · ·

About forty people were milling around the briefing room at New Scotland Yard, or seated in lines of chairs, murmuring to each other. The Metropolitan police commissioner, Daneen Hassan, was sitting at a table flanked by an array of others wearing uniforms or simple suits. Among them was the chief superintendent who had spoken to Dan on the night of the bomb. Jess knew she recognised her.

In the rows of seats were executives and editors representing national and regional newspapers, as well as the BBC, ITN, Sky, GB News, and several websites. Everyone was acting friendly towards everyone else, but Jess wasn't sure about the level of sincerity. She sat between Jory and the editor of the *Daily Express*.

The commissioner walked to a podium and tugged the microphone towards her. She began with a slight smile. 'I hope it's not in vain to begin with this plea,' she said. 'Your industry appears to be the prime target of these atrocities and we feel we have no option but to share with you as much information as possible. It might be a lot to ask of a group such as this, but we implore you to keep whatever we say within these four walls.'

Commissioner Hassan paused for a reaction and the same words rippled through the room: *Of course, of course.*

'Also,' she continued, 'to pre-empt any questions about Leila Chatstone, all we can say is that our inquiries are continuing.'

Hassan picked up a small device, and when she prodded it a large screen behind her lit up with a split image of the bombed ballrooms of Chatstone House and the Plaza-Asturias Hotel in New York.

'These explosive devices were skilfully made and, as you can see, very destructive. Chatstone House was a surprise. There were a number of security people at the event, but nothing sufficient to guard against an attack like this. But after Chatstone House, the Plaza-Asturias Hotel was made doubly secure with highly sophisticated systems and trusted security experts and armed police ...'

She stopped as Jory raised his arm.

'You still have no suspects at all? Scores of people here and in the States have been brought in for questioning. Have you nothing to show for it?'

'None of the obvious suspects has yet been eliminated. It seems clear that one of them, or a breakaway group, is responsible.'

The audience rumbled with discontent and the commissioner raised her hands.

'Please, rest assured we will find these people and bring them to justice. The people with me today, and our associates at the

Secret Intelligence Service and GCHQ, have spent many hours with our colleagues in the United States pooling our knowledge. We have yet to develop any definitive leads, but it is only a matter of time.'

Hassan pushed at her remote device again and a world map appeared, with red arrows pointing at countries in the Middle East, Africa and the Far East.

'We have yet to trace any evidence of a group called Wrath of God,' she said. 'Our relations with the security services of Russia, Iran and China are not ideal, to say the least, but they claim to be as confused as we are.'

She gestured to the world map and its red arrows. 'Our intelligence in other areas where Islamists are most active – Iraq, Yemen, Somalia, Pakistan, Nigeria, Afghanistan, and elsewhere – has so far failed to provide any useful information. The same is true of other European countries where there have been attacks in the past, such as France and Belgium.

'Therefore, we need to keep an open mind about who the culprits might be. We should not rule out the possibility this is the work of a foreign state, and possibly the first part of a mission to disrupt and intimidate our free media. We already know certain nations have flooded the digital world with false news.'

Gasps and seat-shuffling swept the room. The *Mail* boss spilled some of the water he was on the point of drinking. 'Oh, come on,' he said, patting his wet tie with a handkerchief. 'Are you telling us Russia or some other country might be out to murder the free world's media?'

Commissioner Hassan sounded irritated. 'My point is, we have yet to discover who is responsible. We're not saying it is Russia, or China, or Iran, or the regimes in Iraq or Afghanistan, or Venezuela, or North Korea. But we would be foolish not to recognise there are a great many countries that feel ill will towards us. We know, don't we, of evidence some time ago that the Russians were willing to pay cash bounties to the Taliban for the murder of British and American troops?'

Everyone began talking, but the woman from *The Times* was loudest. 'Madness,' she cried. 'It would be suicidal for any of these countries to attack us like this.' The other executives became even noisier agreeing with her.

Hassan walked out from behind the podium. 'Ladies and gentlemen, please,' she said. 'Right now, we cannot rule out any possibility. We can only promise to do all in our power to help you and your entire industry stay safe. These two attacks came in quick succession and we must take seriously the threat that there will be more. We will continue to provide protection for your main premises, but we strongly recommend you take your own precautions.

'It is most important you cancel all public events that would be attended by large groups of media people. Awards ceremonies should be suspended until further notice, also events in support of good causes relating to journalism. We would also advise firmly against any gatherings in the most favoured bars and public houses, as well as restaurants and press clubs. As for the content of your newspapers, that is entirely a matter for yourselves, but there seems to be no doubt how they will react against any newspaper if they feel—'

'Wait a minute, please,' came a big voice from the front row.

The commissioner's face froze as everyone turned towards a man with a gigantic frame. It was Ben Tremblay, redtop proprietor and retail tycoon, who, judging from his pained face, was having to apply all his strength to the arms of his chair as he rose slowly above the gaping faces like a breaching whale.

He stood there, a shadow over the room, six foot four inches tall and more than twenty-five stone – according to *Private Eye*'s account of the unrestrained lifestyle of 'Big Ben'. Ever since he'd attempted to buy power and respect as owner of two redtops – *The Daylight* and *Sundaylight* – and the tabloid *New York Herald*, Tremblay had been mocked by the great and the good for his social ambitions and his rough Canadian country ways.

Tremblay, breathing heavily from the effort of getting to his feet, stared down at the diminutive commissioner. 'You're telling us the entire media industry in the United States and the United Kingdom should hide under a rock to make ourselves safe from these monsters? Isn't that exactly what they want? If they can smell our fear, they will never stop making demands.'

Hassan walked close to Tremblay and tilted her head so far back to meet his eye she might have been looking at a passing plane.

'You're entirely welcome to your journalistic ideals,' she said, 'but our job is to keep the citizens of this country safe. Right now, that's all we care about, and you need to remember your words and headlines risk getting people killed. You should let us find these terrorists first. They tried killing the publisher of *The New York World* after that editorial. That looks like a revenge attack, pure and simple.'

Tremblay held his arms wide and looked around at his colleagues. 'I'm sure we're all very grateful for your advice, Commissioner. But my recommendation to you is that you stick to your job of catching the bad guys, and you let us do ours.' Tremblay searched the room. 'Do we agree?' he asked. No one said a word.

The presentation continued, with unsettling information about how Islamist terrorist groups had established themselves in Britain and much of Europe and the United States, with accounts of terrifying-sounding attacks foiled at the last minute. Photos and video of sinister-looking men and women appeared on the screen. They had been taken from the air in Syria and Iraq and Afghanistan, or through long lenses down streets in Istanbul, Beirut, Brooklyn, Bradford and Detroit. They were fighters with Al-Qaeda and ISIS, or possibly dissidents who had defected to form their own groups, or homegrown extremists who might have returned to Britain or America after the collapse of the Islamic State, though no one was sure they were even still alive.

'Nothing but a lot of known unknowns,' Jory whispered to Jess.

The meeting was breaking up when Jess checked the news on her phone. The first headline was *POLICE FEAR FOREIGN STATE BEHIND BOMB ATTACKS*. It was from the *Daily Express.*

Jess frowned at the *Express* editor as she held her phone in front of him.

'News is news, young lady,' he said, and stood to walk quickly from the room.

As they were leaving, Jess felt a touch on her shoulder. It was the chief superintendent from the night of the bombing. He spoke without looking at her.

'They'll announce a couple of hours from now that we've identified Leila Chatstone's father,' he said. 'He's a social sciences professor at the University of the Punjab. We're told his daughter has visited him more than once. Apparently he's away on a sabbatical and no one knows where.'

'What's his name?' Jess said.

'That's all I've got,' he said, giving her a quick smile. 'Pass on my best to Mr Brasher.'

Jess felt no inclination to tell her informant Dan no longer worked for *The Courant*.

Chapter Fourteen

New York

Dan came on foot from his hotel to the Park Avenue apartment of Howard Wyler, chairman of the New York World Company. He enjoyed the massed anonymity of Manhattan's crowded avenues, seeing everything without anyone seeing him. On the way, he passed the former president's apartment building, where two groups of protesters – those who loved him and those who hated him – were squabbling on the sidewalk as a couple of cops warned them to behave.

This part of the city – the well-mannered blocks of the Upper East Side near Fifth and Park – was Dan's least favourite. It was old and rich and too pleased with itself. He knew it well: his parents lived on Fifth. It was a relief to Dan they were travelling in Asia; he wouldn't be obliged to visit, and listen to them worry, or hear his mother ask again and again whether he and Laura might get back together.

A doorman stood in front of the brass-framed entrance to the Wyler building. He was in a cornflower-blue cap and matching uniform with yellow piping. The entrance was closed and the doorman made no effort to open it as Dan approached. Two men in black suits with watchful expressions were nearby.

'How can I help?' the doorman said, without moving from his position.

Dan identified himself. 'I have a dinner appointment with Howard Wyler,' he said, whereupon the two suits walked towards him.

'We need to search you,' one said, and frisked him top to bottom before waving a handheld metal detector over his body and requiring Dan to turn out every pocket that set it off.

After that, and having inspected the contents of Dan's bag, the man spoke into his sleeve as he gave a thumbs-up to the doorman, who rapped on the glass of the entrance. Another doorman inside unlocked and tugged open the heavy door leading to the lobby.

The lobby was long and wide with a floor of black-and-white tiles so highly polished it played tricks with Dan's balance. His mild hangover might have been a contributing factor. In the distance, an elevator door of gilded silver slid open.

It was only a few years since Dan had last seen a slim, diminutive Francis Wyler, and at first Dan didn't recognise the short, round figure bounding towards him. But he recognised the bottle-bottom spectacles and the ugly, plump lips.

Francis was now *The World*'s editor-in-chief and Dan had known him since they'd sat at adjoining desks in the newsroom.

'Good evening, old chap,' Francis said, with a huge smile. 'Wonderful to see you, absolutely wonderful.' He leaned in for a quick, uncomfortable embrace while maintaining his huge smile. Dan remembered that smile and its overpowering lack of sincerity, and the way Francis's lifeless brown eyes always betrayed it. It was so wide and fierce he felt assaulted by it. Francis was one of those people with the habit of acting over-joyed at the sight of everyone he met.

He went on chattering inanities in the high-pitched half-English accent he'd picked up after a year at Oxford. Dan spoke a Mid-Atlantic mangle swinging between New York American and Yorkshire English, depending on which country he was in. Everyone agreed he sounded more Yorkshire after a few drinks.

In the years since they'd sat together in the newsroom, Francis's rise in the company had been dramatic. As soon as Howard Wyler felt inclined to yield power, Francis would inherit control of the New York World Company, publisher of the country's most prestigious newspaper. But Dan, and anyone who followed the business, knew Howard was hesitating, and that his hesitation was based entirely on the question of his only son's competence. Francis had survived catastrophes that would have ended the career of a mere mortal. Once, he had produced a story about brutality in the New York Police Department, naming an officer who was alleged to have beaten a Harvard graduate and raped his girlfriend. When the city desk expressed doubts about the story, Francis's rage so intimidated the duty editor, the story was published. It turned out Francis had been the victim of a complicated hoax perpetrated by a former Harvard classmate who didn't like him. The episode might have ruined another journalist, but Francis was absolved because of his 'inexperience', while the editor was dismissed for failing in his supervision of the company heir.

Francis stopped talking and peered at the cuts on his visitor's face. 'You look rather knocked about, Daniel.'

'I was lucky enough to be having a smoke outside the ballroom when the bomb went off,' Dan said. 'Were you at the Plaza-Asturias on the night it was attacked?'

'I didn't attend,' Francis said. 'That was Jake's affair. My goodness, does he have a lot to answer for.' He raised his arm to reach Dan's shoulders and shepherd him towards the elevator. 'It's extraordinary Leila Chatstone might be part of this terrorism business. Her father, too. She always was an unhappy girl. Do you expect her to be charged?'

'I've honestly no idea. She certainly has some questions to answer.'

'You can't imagine the high anxiety reigning in this company at the moment.'

'Oh, I think I can,' Dan said.

'Our reporters writing about these attacks are getting weird threats.'

Another man in a black suit was holding open the elevator door.

'You've even got a man with a gun operating the elevator?' Dan asked.

'Dad feels safer staying at home since the Plaza-Asturias. We're all dreading what will happen next. Everyone has to come here now from the office. Every night he's having an early exec supper for an update on the day. He wants to see you. He still insists on having control of everything. The meal will be a bit dreary. It's the same crowd – all those old farts he should've fired long ago.'

The elevator climbed non-stop to Howard Wyler's penthouse and opened directly into the hallway. Along the apartment gallery were portraits of *The New York World* publishers through the ages, a family parade of more than a century of power – from high starched collars, groomed beards, walrus moustaches, into the more clean-shaven twentieth century and beyond. Howard Wyler's portrait was casual and jacketless with a blue open-neck shirt, knee raised on a chair in an ever-so-mild nod in the direction of new-age billionaires in their jeans and T-shirts. But every portrait displayed the same firm-eyed entitlement that came from being a big-beast newspaper baron accustomed to the tributes of politicians and business executives and everyone else with a stake in what their almighty newspaper had to say. It wouldn't be long before these portraits belonged in the American Museum of Natural History ... in an exhibition of mammals rendered extinct by a changing world.

In the dining room, executives were lifting food onto their own plates from dishes laid out down a long narrow table. One person was already seated at the dining table, alone and ignored. It was Otis Jeremiah Wyler III, Howard Wyler's father and predecessor, and grandson of the newspaper's founder.

Otis was well over ninety, and all the stresses and dirty tricks of his long life were carved deep into his war-torn face. His unhappy, washed-out brown eyes still had the hint of permanent disapproval Dan remembered from a dozen years ago; but that was the last remaining evidence of the colossus who had towered over the American newspaper world in the sixties and seventies.

Behind him, a large oil painting showed a steamship ploughing past a limp-sailed schooner. Dan figured it had been in the family since the days the steamship was a metaphor for the brave new world of newspapers. It needed an update, with a fleet of algorithm-fuelled speedboats drowning that steamboat in its wash.

Howard Wyler and his wife, Cornelia, were together by a window. She was far taller than her husband and aiming an angry look at him. 'You could have sold it years ago for billions,' Dan heard her say. 'Look how smart the Bancrofts were. That man Murdoch paid them a fortune for *The Wall Street Journal*.'

Francis took Dan by the arm and led him away from his parents. 'For my father, keeping *The New York World* alive is a sacred duty. The only online spending he'll approve is on the website, but that'll never save our skin. He doesn't care about other things we're developing. He thinks it's all too boring.'

Dan moved with a plate along the buffet, spooning chicken and broccoli and French fries from silver dishes suspended above rows of candles.

Walter the butler directed Dan to his seat. When he'd first met Walter Kravits, Dan was a reporter at *The World*. Walter was a Ukrainian, who sent money home to his single sister and her two children in Kyiv. Since before Russia invaded, Howard Wyler had been helping Walter in his efforts to persuade the US authorities to allow her to immigrate; but the authorities had refused, citing a conviction for selling drugs when she was in her teens. On a couple of trips to Ukraine, Dan had carried gifts for Walter's family. Now the sister was a refugee in Poland, still trying to get to America.

'Nice to see you again, Walter,' Dan said, but Walter only nodded.

Everyone was ready to eat except for Howard and his wife. They were in the same place at the window, by the look of them still disagreeing. Walter walked over to them and gestured towards the table. Francis stood as his parents walked to their seats. 'Dad, you remember Dan Brasher from long ago. He's over from London to talk about coming back to us.'

'Yes, yes,' Howard said. He reached across the table to grip Dan's hand. Howard's hair was white, but he was slim and wiry. He was said never to miss his vigorous daily workout and was famous for experimenting with every new health-food fad. 'The three of us will have a talk after this,' he said. He paused, looking at Dan's cut face. 'I hope you're recovering. Tragic news about the poor Chatstones. Such a wonderful family. Poor Cressida – and this awful business with Leila must be shattering for them.

A lot of others have got to be behind these attacks. They need to find Leila's father.'

Howard tucked a white napkin into the collar of his shirt and folded his arms. He was the only person without a plate of food.

'Some things never change,' Francis whispered. 'He still eats his own special meals. Walter is always looking out for the latest wacky diet.'

Howard peered at his son. 'I heard that, young man,' he said. 'It pays to stay in shape. You should give it a try sometime.'

As everyone else waited to begin, Howard's meal arrived in a blue-and-white striped bowl. The butler placed it before his boss, took a spoon, and sprinkled the dish with what looked like brown sugar.

'Good grief, Howie, what the hell is that? It looks like human intestines,' said Klaus Weber. Weber was the company's chief financial officer and had worked forty years for the Wylers.

'Feel free to mock, Weber,' Howard said. 'But Walter assures me this meal contains a particular plant ingredient from some-where in the foothills of the Himalayas. The local inhabitants have consumed it for centuries and they've been rewarded with long and healthy lives. Isn't that right, Walter?'

Walter nodded seriously.

Upon taking the first taste of his magical meal, Howard paused and frowned, but then, with a look of determination, took another substantial spoonful. Klaus Weber looked amused as he cut himself a generous slice of rare steak.

'Did you speak to Jake Abrams yet?' Weber said to his boss.

Howard put his spoon into his bowl of food. 'I have no interest in making contact with Abrams,' he said. 'He has put all our lives in danger.'

'He must have called three times by now,' Weber said. 'Your assistant says he sounded frantic.'

'Does anyone know where Jake is?' Dan asked.

'We don't know and we don't care,' Francis said.

Weber looked at Dan. 'Jake told the chairman's assistant he needed our protection. He said he's afraid to trust anyone, even the police or the FBI. He's sure the attack on him was an inside job at the hotel.'

Howard raised another spoonful of his meal. 'Abrams has gone mad,' he said. 'That was an insanely reckless editorial. It was asking for trouble. I knew it was wrong, I knew it, and allowing him to run it was the biggest mistake of my life. I believe in a newspaper's right to independence, but not in its right to get us all killed.'

Dan interjected, 'Hang on, am I understanding this? Jake Abrams has reached out to you for help and you're ignoring him? How can you do that?'

Klaus Weber nodded while swallowing a large mouthful of his steak. 'Listen to what he's saying, Howard. Jake's worked thirty years for us. He's reached out to us – to you. We owe him something.'

Howard looked angry and anxious at the same time. The vein on his forehead inflated and he was clenching his teeth so hard his jaw muscles began to spasm. But Dan wasn't in a sympathetic mood.

'I can't believe any worthwhile media company would abandon someone in this way,' he said. 'Certainly, the Chatstones never would.'

Otis Wyler made a growling sound and banged the table with his knife and fork.

'Awful fucking family, the Chatstones. A load of cunts,' he said, then sat in silence.

Everyone looked at everyone else.

Cornelia Wyler, on Otis's right, put a gentle hand on her father-in-law's arm. 'Language, Otis, please.'

Otis leaned away from her. 'I've known that family more than sixty years. They're snakes, every last one of them.'

'Dad, you're fighting old wars,' said Howard. 'They're our friends now. It's only been a matter of months since they helped us bring down Gene Applegate and win a Pulitzer.'

Otis's face took on a look of futile concentration.

'The president, Dad. Don't you remember?'

'Don't give a shit,' Otis said. 'The Chatstones are a gang of treacherous bastards. Thugs – skewering us in that trashy tabloid of theirs. And that Viscount Chatstone who just died. Good fucking riddance to him. He double-crossed me again and again. But I got the evil old cocksucker in the end.'

The old man stopped speaking and everyone kept looking at him. His face creased into a vaguely sadistic smile. Dan thought he must have stumbled in his head on some attic of forgotten things and found a happy memory – some act of cruel reprisal against the loathsome Chatstones.

'Here we go,' Francis whispered. 'Grandpa's train of thought has gone flying off the rails again.'

'Come on, Dad, that's history,' said Howard softly, looking into his meal and swirling it with his spoon. 'That viscount's been dead for years and the family's having a terrible time. His daughter was running the company until that bomb.'

Dan didn't want to hear any more about Otis's forgotten wars. 'What's happening to Jake?' he said. 'How could you turn your backs on him after all he's done for you, after all the accolades he earned for you as editor-in-chief, and the profits, and all the risks he took as a correspondent? Are you afraid of helping him?'

'Screw Abrams,' Francis said. 'We owe him nothing. He's created a calamity for us.'

Dan pushed back his chair and turned to Francis. 'It's a crime to leave him out in the cold like this, it's a sin. If these people find him, he'll be a dead man. What about your duty of care? You're a huge corporation.'

Klaus Weber was nodding vigorously as he kept chewing. Dan felt a rush of disgust looking round the silent table: at the almighty chairman, feeling indestructible with his life-extending diet and daily self-devotions in the gym; the prim wife and her ridiculous lineless face, quibbling over their dwindling billions; the fat-faced dope of a son who'd never had a single struggle to get where he was; the deranged patriarch, sitting there half-comatose with his death-mask face, reliving pointless triumphs and treacheries. What vacuum-packed lives of privilege they enjoyed and how heartless they were, sitting here in their private fortress while Jake was out there somewhere begging for their help.

'When this is over, Jake will disgrace you all,' Dan found himself saying. 'He's going to have a world-beating story about the mighty media empire that left him stranded.'

Howard Wyler gave Dan a cold glare. Otis fixed his angry old eyes on him. 'You can fuck off,' he said.

Howard turned with his plate to Walter. 'Thanks for this,' he said. 'I don't think I can finish it all. I'm sure it's very good for me, but I'm not fond of the taste – a little bitter.'

The butler looked distressed as he took the plate.

'Please don't worry about it, Walter,' Howard said. 'I'm always willing to try something new.'

Howard sat sipping a glass of water while everyone else continued eating. Dan asked where the bathroom was and excused himself. He walked to the elevator and left the building. He couldn't think of a better means of escape.

Back at his hotel bar, Dan sat in a corner with his laptop and messaged Roy Jory: *I've decided to accept your job offer, talk terms later. My first piece for you will arrive within the hour. It's an opinion piece, five hundred words max.*

Dan wasn't going to wait for poor abandoned Jake Abrams to drop a bucket of shit over that foul Wyler family. He would do it himself.

After that, he called his best friend.

Chapter Fifteen

Siobhan Mac Stiofain was at the open door when Dan arrived at her six-flight walk-up. She leaned against the wall, her long arms folded across an oversized red T-shirt, bare feet below her blue tracksuit pants.

'Hey, boy,' she said. 'How you been?'

'Have you been waiting there for me?' Dan said.

'Not for long. I was watching from the fire escape. How's it going, boy from Sheffield?'

Just the sight of her made him feel better. The fond angle of her face, the twitchy spasm of her nose when she smiled, blonde hair always snatched back in a ponytail, those eyes that could see right through him. She felt like a sanctuary.

'Ah, you know – one thing and another,' he said.

Siobhan wrapped her arms gently around his neck and put her cheek against his. Then she held him at arm's length, looked him up and down, and laughed.

'What's happening to you, boy?' She patted his stomach. 'Getting to look middle-aged here. You're out of breath from those stairs, admit it. I remember you jumping them two at a time. You need to cut down and get back to the gym.'

'Fuck off,' he said, and embraced her again.

She took Dan by the hand and led him into the apartment. 'There's someone I've been wanting you to meet,' she said.

A young woman was lying on a sofa in jeans and a blue shirt.

She was wearing a red-billed Atlanta Braves baseball cap pushed back on her long, flaxen hair. Siobhan's tortoiseshell cat was stretched out beside her.

She jumped up at the sight of Dan. He knew instantly who she was.

'Don't tell me, let me guess.' Dan closed his eyes and put his fingers on his temples. 'You are ... Bridget ... er ... Bridget Kenny.'

They laughed and Dan reached out and kissed the woman on both cheeks. 'I've heard plenty about you and seen lots of photos.'

'Okay, Danny, you can shut up now,' Siobhan said as she opened the refrigerator to bring out a bottle of white wine. 'You drinking?' she asked him.

'You bet.'

'Aren't you still on meds?'

He smiled. 'I promise to drink slowly.'

'What about the cigarettes?'

He looked sheepish and took out a Marlboro pack.

'Not in here,' she said.

'I know, I know.' He put the cigarettes back in his pocket.

Kenny sat cross-legged, looking at Dan from the sofa. Her big Audrey Hepburn eyes seemed unsure; so did her smile. Dan got the impression she was waiting to be judged, or trusted.

'You haven't been at the FBI so long as the boss here,' Dan said, pointing with his glass at Siobhan.

'Four years,' she said, smiling at Siobhan. 'I'm still a rookie beside her.' She had a soft, southern voice.

'Will you be a better FBI contact for me than Miss Mac Stiofain? I'm her oldest friend and she won't tell me a thing, not unless there's something in it for her.'

Kenny laughed as she stroked the cat, who was now curled up asleep in her crossed legs. 'She knows lots more than they ever tell me.'

'You people have got to find Jake Abrams,' Dan said. 'He's being stiffed by his employer of thirty years. He's begged them for help and they won't even take his calls.'

Siobhan nodded. 'We know. We'll protect him if we can find him, but he won't come willingly. Howard Wyler's office told us he's got it into his head the bombing was an inside job and he won't trust anyone.'

'I want to find him and run his story in *The Courant* about how the Wylers betrayed him. I've written something myself. Those people need to be shamed. Do you think it was an inside job?'

'For sure they got those explosives past incredibly intense security,' Siobhan said.

'If we find him, he'll be safe with us,' Kenny said. 'He's doomed if they get to him.'

Dan had finished his wine already and held the empty glass out to Siobhan. She gave him a reproving look. 'Not yet. Slowing down, remember?'

'Who is it wants to capture him?' he asked. 'Do you have any idea who these people are?'

'We've nothing to go on yet, except for these crazy claims of responsibility,' Siobhan said.

'Who else has a conceivable motive?' Kenny mused. 'It has all the hallmarks of Islamists. And the situation with that Chatstone heiress looks pretty incriminating.'

'Where do you think Abrams is hiding?' Dan asked. Siobhan and Kenny exchanged a quick smile.

'We promise to let you know,' Siobhan told him. 'As soon as we've got him somewhere safe. We think we're getting close.'

Kenny got up from the sofa and reached for the leather jacket hanging over a chair. 'If you happen to find him before we do, for God's sake make him get in touch.' She gave Dan a wary smile as she put on the jacket. 'I'm outta here. Better get going so you two can talk about me.'

She kissed the top of Siobhan's head and gave her shoulders a quick massage. The apartment door closed behind Kenny and Siobhan asked straight away, 'What do you think?'

'What do you care what I think?'

She pinched Dan hard on the painful underside of his arm. 'Ow!'

'I'm serious.'

'She made a reasonable first impression,' Dan said. 'She didn't seem very sure about me. You thinking of moving in with her?'

'Don't know yet. I like her a lot, but I haven't known her long.' She gave Dan a mischievous look. 'She's cute,' she said, and winked. 'But the sex is not so great.'

'Haven't you got to tell them if you're dating a subordinate?' Dan asked.

'Yes, and we will,' Siobhan said. 'She needs a couple of weeks to sort out a relationship back home in Augusta. We won't be able to keep working together.'

Siobhan poured them more wine and went with her own glass to the other end of the sofa from Dan. She stretched out to tuck her bare feet beneath his leg. Dan kicked off his trainers.

'Did you put that there because I was coming?' Dan said, nodding towards a photo of the two of them from years ago: college kids in blue denim shorts and baseball team T-shirts – his Yankees, hers Mets – standing together on top of a stone wall. They'd been juniors when Dan took her to Yorkshire to show her the Dales.

'It's always been here somewhere,' Siobhan said. 'You just never noticed.' Then she put on a glum face. 'So, you've blown a big job interview and you're not coming back to New York.'

'Not quite,' Dan said. 'I spoke to the new editor at *The Courant*. I've got my old job back and he's agreed I stay here on the bomb story. I want to find Abrams, even if you can't. The poor bastard is stranded. I made *The Courant* promise to help him. It's a madhouse at *The World*; I'd forgotten what a strange family they are. I just rattled off an angry piece about them for London. The Chatstones aren't quite so insane as the Wylers. That Francis is more of a creep than he ever was. These self-entitled mega-rich kids who never get pushed out the door and made to fend for themselves ... they drive me nuts. Great wealth – being born to unspendable riches – it's an emotional handicap, don't you think?'

Siobhan laughed. 'I don't know, Dan. Ask yourself.'

Dan shrugged.

'You seen Laura?' she asked.

'Nope.'

'You did mess her around pretty good.' Then she added, sounding strict: 'Play it cool now, don't go being stupid. You've at least got to make sure you get to see a lot of the kids.'

'She messaged me the other day for a video chat with the girls,' Dan said. 'But all she wanted was to check she's still the beneficiary of my life insurance. It was the first thing she asked. I think she's expecting me to get blown up.' He gave a long, defeated groan. 'She even took the dog. That guy she's run off with is such a goof. I was a total idiot.'

'The kids will still love you forever.'

Dan winced like those words had sent a shot of pain through him. 'If she stays with him they'll have a stepdad at home and I'll be this far-off father on the other side of the world. The kids are sounding less English already.'

Siobhan drank some wine but said nothing. Dan knew she wouldn't; and he'd only get annoyed if she tried some worn-out words of comfort.

They'd met as high-school sophomores. He would see Siobhan walking alone, always alone, along the sidewalk near their school, gangly and gorgeous and looking solemn, with music in her ears and a book. Dan was a new boy and as lonely in school as this enigmatic girl appeared to be. The other boys were friendly enough, but all he had in common with them was the English language, and even that similarity could be approximate. They knew nothing about English football or cricket, and he didn't know the rules of any American sport or the names of any sports stars, except Muhammad Ali, and Joe DiMaggio because of his appearance in a Simon & Garfunkel song and the fact he'd married Marilyn Monroe. The other boys were baffled to learn his favourite sports team was named after a day of the week – Sheffield Wednesday.

When Dan finally found the courage to speak to her, Siobhan was sitting on the school steps, out of the rain. 'What you listening to?'

She lifted her headset. 'What?'

'What's the music?'

'Kenny G,' she said, and walked inside without another word. The book was *A Clockwork Orange*, so Dan suspected she wasn't listening to Kenny G.

He tried again a week or so later. 'I don't believe you're listening to Kenny G.'

'What?'

'Don't tell me again that's Kenny G. You'd be lying.'

'Clever boy,' she said, popping out the cassette to hold it up to him.

'Pulp!' he said. 'Pulp! Love them. "Common People"! They're from a town called Sheffield in the English county of South Yorkshire.'

'I know that.'

'And Sheffield is the place where I was born. I've got loads of their tapes at home if you'd like to borrow them.'

That was when they decided to be friends. It wasn't a smooth friendship, not for a while, not until they grew to understand each other. She was a troubled girl and Dan's mother became her psychologist, but as Siobhan had told Dan years ago, 'Your mom helped me to be honest with myself and to be happy with the truth.'

Siobhan's truth had caused Dan to alter his view of how their friendship might develop, but still it went on to become durable and trusting in a way they would sometimes laugh together trying to explain; they were misfits, they decided – two young misfits in an out-of-step world.

After Yale, then Yale Law, Siobhan's ambitious parents had been crushed when she decided to become a New York City cop. Their disappointment diminished only slightly when a recruiter persuaded Siobhan the FBI would be a higher calling. Ten years later, she was one of six senior special agents reporting to the FBI assistant director in the New York field office, the country's biggest.

Siobhan was well known for her tough-guy act. When she was on a tear, with her face crunched into furious folds and her jaw muscles clenching, Dan had seen men freeze. But he knew

the belligerence was a well-rehearsed act. Her deep-down softness was the real thing; even when she was acting truly pissed
off, Dan could see it in her eyes.

He could see it right now. Siobhan had gone quiet, and if he
spoke Dan knew she wouldn't hear a word.

She put her half-full glass on the table and pushed it away.
'This is a total shitshow, Danny. And I'm right in the middle of
it. We've hauled in dozens of people, and so far nothing. There's
no chatter we've picked up, no trails we can follow, no pattern
we can make out. It's very weird. We thought we had a pretty
good take on Islamist extremists operating here, but it's like
we're looking for ghosts.'

The TV was on mute, playing scenes of the bombings yet
again. A headline flashed on the screen: *MEDIA WORLD IN
TERROR OF MORE ATTACKS*.

'It's getting wild,' Siobhan continued. 'Every media outlet
in the country is demanding protection. Private security outfits
can't meet the demand.'

Dan reached for the remote and turned the TV off. 'Okay,
enough of that for now. There'll be plenty of this for weeks to
come. Let's talk about something else.'

But Siobhan kept talking. 'Why are you even doing this
when others are running away? It's not like a war zone. The
biggest chance of getting killed in a war is by accident. But
these people will take aim at you. I hope you're not looking to
get yourself killed.'

'Don't be daft.'

'Well, you did walk straight into a busy road. That was insane.'

'I wish I never told you that. I lost it, I admit, but I can
promise you I'm not looking to get killed.' He stood and
reached to pull Siobhan to her feet. 'Let's get some air.'

Dan opened the fire escape window and they sat on the ledge, looking down on the treetops lining the street. The smell of cooking cabbage drifted from the window below, and from above them came the tuneless soothing of a wind chime. Three young women tumbled noisily out of the corner bar and an electric DoorDash bike swished by. Further off, a few sounds rose above the background growl of Manhattan: a chopper fluttering along the river; a faraway siren.

Dan lit a cigarette. 'You forget how loud this town is when you're not here all the time.'

Siobhan wrapped herself tightly around his arm and pressed her head into him. 'So, go on with what you were saying – exactly what's the point of exposing yourself like this?'

'I'm fucking angry, Siobhan, and it's getting personal,' he said. 'Poor Jim. He could be an awful bastard, but he did everything for me. He put up with me for years. I watched him die. He just faded away right in front of me. I forget he's gone sometimes. I keep wanting to call and tell him things. Of all the perils of his life on the road – Vietnam, Ireland, Sri Lanka, the Balkans, the Middle East again and again – after all that, he had to get blown up at the Chatstone fucking House summer party. And Jake Abrams is out there now, shitting himself, with no one to turn to. They want to kill him, they want to wipe out their critics. What are we supposed to do – put our arms in the air and surrender?'

Siobhan took the cigarette from Dan's hand and took a drag. Dan looked reprimanding as she handed it back.

'Anyway, Mac Stiofain,' he said. 'Your job can be pretty scary. What is it that drives you?'

'I like catching bad guys. Also, it beats sitting in some fancy law office, which is what my folks wanted. I enjoyed the shock value, though, seeing their faces when I told them I wanted to be a New York City beat cop.'

She reached again for his cigarette but he moved it away, shaking his head. 'Don't – you'll regret it and then I'll have to blame myself.'

Siobhan stood and leaned so far forward on the fire escape railing her legs left the ground and she was balanced horizontally, hanging high above the street like a circus acrobat, with her back arched and her arms spread in a perfect swallow dive.

'Shit, Siobhan, please stop,' Dan said. 'I hate you doing that.'

She laughed. 'I know,' she said, and sat again to lean against him.

'I think it's non-stop insecurity that drives you, Mr Brasher. That's a high-octane fuel, that is. You're trying to prove something to yourself, but you're not sure what. You do like impressing your dad, though. I've seen that proud twinkle in his eye when he introduces you to his big-time business pals. I think you like that.'

'Don't tell anyone, least of all him.'

'You could have gone to business school and been his partner, and rich.'

'Lucky for him, I refused. I'd be crap at it.'

Dan swung his feet back into the apartment.

'Anyway, I'm not completely alone doing this. A few at *The World* are still covering it and they're getting threats like the people at *The Courant*. Youngsters see a story like this as a chance to make a name. There's a young woman in London keeps emailing for some of the action. She got a great beat from a source about Leila Chatstone's secret meetings with her father. That was a belter of a story.'

They both crashed on the living-room sofa.

'I need the bathroom,' Dan said. 'Put some music on. I need cheering up.'

'What do you fancy?'

'"Good Vibrations".'

'Noooo! We weren't even born when that song came out – R.E.M.?'

'Whatever. Something to make me smile.'

In the toilet, Dan called Jake Abrams's mobile and left a voicemail: 'Get in touch. I know the Wylers have stiffed you. I know you don't trust anyone. Don't call me direct. Get a message to me some other way. I want to help you.'

It was a long shot, but Abrams might be desperate enough to risk it. He wouldn't have his phone with him, but might use a pay phone or a burner to check his messages.

'R.E.M. it is,' Siobhan said when Dan returned to the sofa.

She called up music on her phone and turned it loud through the speakers – 'It's the End of the World as We Know It'.

They laughed, and he kissed the top of her foot. Her toenails were painted midnight blue and the polish was peeling. She sprang up and pulled him from the sofa and they danced.

. . .

It was six in the morning when Siobhan woke him. She was naked out of the shower with a yellow towel draped over her shoulders, looking at her phone.

Dan sat up. 'What?'

'Something's happened to Howard Wyler and his butler,' she said. 'They're both in Lenox Hill Hospital. The doctors think they've been poisoned.'

PART TWO

The tennis ball bounced high down the long driveway and into the woods. The young border collie sprinted after it and ran back, holding the ball in its mouth, to drop it at the man's feet.

'They are listening to us now, my love,' the man said, bouncing the ball down the hill once more. 'Now they know true fear. They have tasted our anger and grief.'

He looked down from the hilltop as clouds crept low through the valley and the forest swayed to the rhythm of the morning wind. The collie returned again to deliver the tennis ball. The man picked up the dog. It licked his face as he ruffled its black-and-white head.

'Come on, Spike, let's eat,' he said, and the dog followed him up the stone steps towards the big front door. It stayed beside him as they ascended the wide luxurious staircase inside.

He had once loved this house and its memories and the happiness it held. When he was a boy, his was a poor and angry home, and when it was quiet, it was a brittle and unreliable quietness. Late on a Friday or Saturday, when his father and elder brother most often came to blows and their big bodies crashed around the tiny living room, he would run to the room where he slept, put his hands to his ears to block out the rage of his real world, and look from the small window at the miles and miles of glittering city far below. He would imagine all the places he would rather be, and wonder if his lost mother was somewhere down there, and whether, with the world's most powerful telescope, he might find her walking along a distant street. Every day, he hoped she would reappear in the apartment, in the same way it happened night after night in his dreams. He was seventy now; she had never come home.

The kitchen TV showed people talking urgently about the attacks. Former chiefs of the FBI and CIA, now earning a living as talking heads, expressed dismay at the unfathomable failure of their former agencies. TV reporters on the North Lawn of the White House revealed details of an overnight presidential crisis meeting and increasing speculation the FBI director was about to be fired.

The man smiled. There would soon be more news to report and to debate. He had made sure of it.

Chapter Sixteen

He had never before felt like a suspect, never been collared by the cops accused of 'fleeing the scene'. Within minutes of the news from Siobhan, Dan received his own call from the London news desk saying the New York police were looking for him.

He arrived downtown at One Police Plaza in the company of Siobhan. He thought they would clear him straight away. 'If I were running from the scene of a crime, would I head straight to the apartment of a senior FBI agent?' he asked them. Siobhan vouched for him, too, but they kept him most of the morning, sitting in a room while detectives visited intermittently to ask the same questions: 'What were you doing at the Wyler apartment?' *I was invited.* 'What did you eat?' *Tough chicken and broccoli.* 'Why did you disappear?' *Because there were too many freaks in the room.* 'Do you have a grudge against Howard Wyler?' *Yes, I do.*

That last answer required some explanation, but even when they let him go the cops didn't look convinced.

Siobhan was waiting for him. 'Relax, boy, they know it wasn't you,' she said, with a smile meant to reassure him. 'They'll do some background checks, going through the motions, but you'll be fine . . .'

She stopped to answer her mobile and her face turned anxious in an instant. She walked away, hand over the unused ear; her voice was loud, though Dan couldn't make out the words. She came back in a hurry, heading for the elevator.

'Got to go. It looks like someone tried to poison George Frobisher.'

'What?' Dan said, following her.

'A kitchen hand collapsed and died after helping prepare dinner at his apartment last night. Read this.'

She handed Dan her phone: '*Wyler and Frobisher have long been the hated enemies of our people. No one who insults us will go unpunished. Frobisher will be made to pay in the end.*'

'Good grief,' he said. Dan had known Frobisher for decades. He and Dan's father had been friends and business associates long before Frobisher's father-in-law, President Eugene Applegate, was hounded from office in a financial scandal. In the scandal's aftermath, Frobisher's own businesses had been devastated. He had been an unafraid critic of Islamist extremists even before he and his father-in-law escaped unharmed when a roadside bomb killed three members of their motorcade in Cairo.

'In other news,' Siobhan said, 'Wyler and Kravits are both gravely ill. They swallowed ricin. Apparently Wyler was the only one at dinner to eat some fancy health food.'

'Yeah, a vegetable from the Himalayas that promises everlasting life.'

'Well, it appears Kravits finished his boss's life-giving meal.' Siobhan kissed Dan's forehead. 'Talk soon,' she said and ran along the sidewalk, waving for a taxi.

The police had confiscated his phone and handed it back in a plastic bag. He turned it on to find eight messages from Perry Ainsworth. His tone became more urgent with each one. In the penultimate, he sounded desperate: 'For goodness' sake, man, will you please call me back.' Only the final message was softer: 'Sorry, dear boy, I hear you're in a spot of bother. Call as soon as you can.'

Perry was happy to hear from him when Dan called, by the sound of him a little drunk and in a pub. 'Are you back in action already?' Dan asked.

'Have you stopped reading the newspaper? I had a column in this morning. I'm fine, but listen, the most amazing thing happened – Jake Abrams called.'

'He called you?'

'Hang on – too many people in here.' The bar noise faded. 'That's better. Yes, he called me. I haven't spoken to Jake for years and he just called. I could hardly believe it was him. He was very mysterious. He didn't even name you — said, quote, *Your colleague in New York*, unquote, had sent him a message asking him to get in touch but on no account to call him direct. I knew it had to be you. Poor devil sounded petrified. I've no idea where he was calling from, but he said he would call again at eight New York time tomorrow morning. He's going to call my mobile and he wants you to be there as well as me.'

'Can you come?' Dan said. 'Best avoid telling anyone why.'

'Of course, I already told Roy I wanted to head over to write a few columns, but that's all. I'm here with a bag and booked on the last flight this evening. I need to hurry.' Dan heard him shouting for a taxi, then a car door slamming. 'See you on the morrow, young Daniel. And here was I, thinking my days of living dangerously were far behind me.' Dan could hear Perry's smile.

Dan called George Frobisher next. There was no answer.

Chapter Seventeen

Dan drank his morning coffee and looked out at Lexington Avenue from the window of his once favourite diner. It was seven thirty and Perry, who should have reached his Manhattan hotel before midnight, was half an hour late.

The morning newspapers were stacked beside him, unopened; Dan had bought them reflexively, telling himself he still enjoyed the feel and smell of paper and the un-electronic random access provided by the simple turning of pages. Truth was he screen-read them most of the time.

He had been up much of the night filing the latest news to London: Howard Wyler and his butler had died and George Frobisher's Turkish chef had been detained for questioning. Big media was even louder in clamouring for protection, the president had ordered the FBI director for New York to take charge of the investigation, and the city police chief was blaming budget cuts for a manpower shortage, a charge that naturally led to the mayor threatening to fire the chief for incompetence. Siobhan's shitshow had truly hit the fan.

The main news from London was Leila Chatstone still refusing to talk and charged, as expected, with obstruction of justice. She had been released on bail with stiff conditions: she had to wear an ankle tag with a GPS locator and could not be more than two hundred yards from the Chatstone gatehouse, except to attend group prayers at a mosque; she was allowed no visitors except healthcare workers, delivery people and her lawyers; and access to internet equipment or telephones was forbidden.

Dan texted Perry: *Where the hell are you?*

Having ordered without him, Dan turned away his first dish, complaining about cold eggs and burnt hash browns. The young server rolled her eyes and removed the plate with such irritation that two rigid bacon rashers bounced to the floor, where they were now being crushed beneath passing feet. He would have walked out right away if he hadn't been expecting company. He was definitely never coming back.

When Perry turned up, even the morning diners of the Upper East Side, who were not easily impressed, glanced up at his arrival. He was impeccable as usual, and so out of date he might have emerged through a time warp – his fedora at a jaunty tilt, double-breasted three-piece pinstripes, gold-clipped collar, blinding yellow kipper tie, shillelagh over his shoulder, its black handle big as a clenched fist.

Perry scanned the diner with a scowl. 'My God, old chum, what kind of place do you call this?' he said. He studied the torn covering of the bench across the table from Dan and flicked away some bread crumbs.

Dan grinned as Perry slid gingerly along the bench to sit opposite him. 'This place may have seen better days, but it'd still earn five stars back in Wigan,' he said.

Perry, having composed himself, spread his arms and beamed at Dan. 'Well, here we both are, in the thick of it again. Delighted to have you back in the fold, dear Dan, and sorry to be late. The hotel took a jolly long time pressing my suit.'

The angry server's arm shot in front of Perry and not all her coffee pot's discharged contents made it into his cup. 'Don't complain,' Dan said, loudly enough for her to hear. 'She gets very angry when her customers complain.' He wiped the table with a paper napkin as the server stormed off muttering.

Perry shuddered in reaction to a sip of the coffee and pushed it aside. 'Things are in bad shape back home,' he said. 'Very sad to say, Cressie's demise would appear to be imminent. The doctors say she's developed sepsis and it doesn't look hopeful.'

'What will happen without her? No one in the family has a prayer of filling her boots – they couldn't care less except for their dividends. Ambrose in charge? . . . My God.'

'That's the big question. No one seems to be manning the bridge on the corporate floor, not unless you count Cracknell. If it wasn't for Jory and Moose and a few others, the newsroom would be headless. The place hasn't been so quiet since Covid. I know Jory always said he didn't want the top job at his age, but I think he's enjoying it. He's shown a lot of pluck while so many of them are skulking at home on their laptops. I must say it was very big of him giving you a job after the reprehensible way you behaved.'

Perry looked at the time on his phone. 'Abrams should call in ten minutes.' He placed the phone between them on the table and pulled a spiral notebook from his inside pocket. 'Look, you know this Abrams fellow well, correct?' he asked, flipping through the notebook.

Dan was about to remind him, but Perry didn't wait for his answer. 'I spent a bit of time with him in Belfast and Bosnia, way back,' Perry said. 'The poor boy sounded truly desperate. It wasn't easy to understand him, but he did use the word *doomed* a number of times. I told him to call the police for protection, but he said it was too dangerous. He kept going on about these bombers having inside help, that there was no other explanation. He saw the security chief at the scene and apparently the poor chap was destroyed with guilt and having a total nervous breakdown.'

'That bomb went off less than twenty-four hours after Abrams's editorial went online,' Dan said. 'How the hell did they accomplish that? These people have to be bloody well organised.'

Perry looked at the menu and Dan pushed his cold toast across the table. 'Play it safe. Have this.'

Perry broke apart a brittle slice.

'This is a very weird business,' Dan said as Perry crunched on the toast. 'I don't get why they're trying to scare off the media. These people are proud of their butchery. They enjoy headlines. It's how they scare the shit out of everyone. Why try to behead the messengers? It's not logical.'

'It worked for the *Charlie Hebdo* killers,' Perry said. 'You never see images of Muhammad on front pages, or anywhere else.'

Perry's phone lit up and buzzed. 'It must be him,' he said, picking up the phone and listening. 'Yes, this is Perry Ainsworth . . . Hello, Jake. Tell me where you are.'

It was only about a minute, with Perry scribbling in his notebook, before the phone call ended. Perry's only other words, at the end of the call, were: 'We need time to hire a car, but we'll be there as quickly as we can.'

Perry put the phone back on the table. 'Goodness, he wanted off that call fast as he could,' he said, looking at his notes. 'Where is Chatham in Columbia County?'

'That's upstate, a hundred and twenty miles or so north, going on three hours away I guess.'

'He appears to be hiding away in an abandoned house a few miles north of there.'

'We got him . . . Fucking brilliant,' Dan said.

'He was very specific about hiring a car with my credit card and a car that's not fitted with satnav. We've also got to turn off our phones and avoid roads with tolls, and I've got to do all the driving.'

The angry server loomed again, wielding her steaming coffee pot like a weapon. Dan shrank away, arms up defensively. 'Just the check, please,' he said.

'My buy,' Perry said.

The server pulled the check from her apron pocket and Perry handed over his credit card.

'How much should I tip?' he asked Dan.

'You're joking.'

Perry folded a twenty-dollar note and placed it under his coffee cup. 'Mustn't be cold-hearted. She might hate her job, but the young woman has a living to earn. She might have hungry children at home.'

. . .

Bridget Kenny had prayed for the information she'd just received. The pressure to find Jake Abrams was becoming unbearable.

'Hey, Kenny, where's the boss?' an eager-faced young agent had called across the room in the FBI's downtown field office, waving a phone receiver in the air. 'The surveillance techs need her urgently. Looks like they've located him.'

Thank you, God, Kenny said to herself.

Kenny was at her desk outside Siobhan's empty office. 'Siobhan's out,' she said. 'Let me pick up.'

'We got him,' an excited voice told her. 'He called the same UK number as yesterday, but this time with an exact location.'

'Who was he speaking to?'

'Same English guy, name of Perry Ainsworth. He's on the way now to meet Abrams. Should be there in the next few hours. Abrams was very agitated, just rattled off directions and disconnected.'

'Is he still upstate where he bought the phone?' Kenny asked. The FBI had already found Abrams's abandoned car and the cabbie who'd driven him to Hudson, and had picked up video of him in a local store buying a burner phone.

'Yup. He called from Albany again – about thirty miles from the location. He's hiding deep in the woods near the town of Chatham. From what he told the English guy, he's living in an isolated shack with his wife. The conversation was brief, but we'll email the recording to Mac Stiofain now.'

'No, better send it to me,' Kenny said. 'She's out of action for the next few hours. We need to move fast before these people get to him.'

Chapter Eighteen

Perry turned off the main highway and Dan ran his index finger over the unfolded map he had purchased in place of the forbidden satnav. 'It's a long time since I used one of these. Very primitive,' he said. 'We're getting close, I think.'

'This is so insane,' Perry said, with a grim laugh. 'Think of it – one of America's most respected editors is out here hiding somewhere, scared half to death. It's like we're in some failed state in the Mideast or Africa.'

They turned onto an unfinished road that curled through sloping fields with a few grazing cattle and into hilly woodland. Perry slowed the car and Dan put down his window. Wisps of low cloud slipped through the hills like a waving veil. A deer in the woods gave them a long, dumb stare, and as it fled three others materialised as if by magic from the shadows, then disappeared in gliding leaps over the rocks and fallen trees and through the ferns.

'This country is properly wild,' Dan said. 'England can be so man-made and manicured – crops, neat fields, planted hedgerows, trees in perfectly measured lines. Listen to the wind through the trees. It sounds like they're whispering to each other.'

Perry sighed. 'Is that so, old boy. And what do you suppose these chatty trees are whispering to each other?'

'No fucking clue, but their grammar's perfect.'

They carried on, looking for Jake Abrams's marker: a red shirt tied to a tree next to a narrow downhill trail.

Perry sat up sharply, looking into the rear-view mirror. 'What's this idiot behind us up to?' he said. Dan turned to see a large white pickup inches from their tail. The truck's driver began leaning on his horn.

'He's in one hell of a hurry,' Dan said.

'Well, this track's too narrow to pull over, so he can jolly well wait.'

At that moment, the truck lunged forward and crashed hard into their car.

'Christ, what's he up to,' Perry shouted, braking.

As he did, the truck hit the back of their car again and began pushing it along the track.

Dan shouted, 'Just take off and get away. Something's wrong.'

Perry picked up speed, bouncing and skidding along the rocky, rutted trail with the truck crashing into them again and again.

'There it is,' Dan said, pointing towards the red shirt hanging from the branch of a silver birch. 'Turn right here.'

Perry swung hard, sending the car into a sideways skid until it came to a halt facing down an even narrower track. Before Perry could get moving again, the truck slammed hard in the driver's side of the car and pushed it off the path. The pickup then took off towards Jake Abrams's hideout.

Perry was leaning forward, still against the steering wheel.

'Are you hurt?' Dan said.

'I'm okay, I think,' he said. 'What the hell is happening?'

Dan leapt from the car. 'Get out of there and hide in the woods,' he said to Perry, and he ran down the winding trail.

He knew from Abrams's directions the house was about three hundred yards off the road. He heard two gunshots as he ran, and soon after the pickup came speeding back up the trail. Dan ran into the woods and lay in the deep ferns as the truck passed. When it had gone, he followed the trail towards a clearing and a clapboard shack with parts of its roof missing and windows mostly covered with board. When he reached the shack, its door was swinging open. He called out a few times, but there was no reply.

Jake Abrams's abandoned hideout was a single room with two worn-out leather armchairs, a square table with three bent-wood chairs, a wooden bench, and an unmade bed with a bright quilted cover. On the table was a lit cigarette in a metal ashtray. A pan of water was still boiling on the stovetop next to a small refrigerator. A double-barrelled shotgun on the floor was hot. He turned off the gas ring and sank into a leather chair. *What the hell's happened to them?*

Outside came the sounds of a car, shouts and running feet. Dan went to the door to see Bridget Kenny and three others. Perry was walking behind them towards the shack.

'Where are they?' Kenny said.

'They've been taken, I think,' he said. 'Moments ago in a white pickup.'

'They might have wanted to kill us,' Perry said, leaning against the doorway.

Another car sped down the narrow trail. A woman, with a man holding a camera, ran towards the shack.

'Hey,' the woman said. 'I'm Steph Dunleavy from the *New York Post*.'

'What the fuck! What are you doing here?' Kenny shouted.

'We got a tip-off Jake Abrams was hiding here.'

'Well, you're too fucking late. We're all too late.'

'Someone called our city desk,' Dunleavy said.

'You two need to get out of here,' Kenny told her and the photographer. 'This is a crime scene.'

'What about them?' Dunleavy protested, pointing at Dan and Perry.

'They're witnesses,' Kenny said. She turned to another agent, pointing at the journalist and her photographer. 'Get them out of here,' she said. 'And we need an APB for a damaged white pickup truck.'

'Already done. It's sure to be stolen,' the agent said.

'Fuck, fuck, fuck,' she said. 'How the hell did they beat us to it?'

'We certainly didn't tell anyone,' Perry said. 'But it can't have been much of a secret if the entire *New York Post* city room knew about it.'

'Anyway, how did you discover this place?' Dan asked.

'Don't go worrying yourself about that,' Kenny said. 'I could ask the same question of you, but you're never going to tell me.' She gave Dan a glare. Was this the same apprehensive blonde he last saw stroking a tortoiseshell cat on Siobhan's sofa?

'We've got nothing to hide,' Perry said. 'He called and invited us.'

An agent interrupted. 'Abrams's wife has just been picked up. A driver found her sitting in the middle of the road a couple of miles away. She called the police and she's being brought in to the Chatham police department.'

The FBI took statements from Dan and Perry then drove them to Main Street in Chatham, where they found a place called the People's Pub; Perry said it sounded comfortingly English. Dan ordered a pint and turned on his phone; it had been off for hours, according to Abrams's instructions. He filed an account of the drama that had taken place, adding Perry as the second byline.

Later, in a taxi heading to Manhattan, a text arrived on Dan's phone. It showed a screenshot of a map, with a blue dot pinpointing his exact location. They would have led them the whole way had Jake not told them to shut down their phones; yet they'd somehow found him anyway. He looked again at his phone. There was another text:

Mr Abrams is no longer available. He's safe. For now. We will be in touch with you. There is work we must do together. Tell no one about this message, not even your travelling companion. If you do, Mr Abrams will die.

Chapter Nineteen

The yellow cab from JFK was sucked along with the impatient torrent of traffic streaming towards the Midtown Tunnel. The Manhattan skyline came into view and Jess could see all those famous shapes standing in a jagged line along the horizon, lit up by the afternoon sun, stood there like a welcoming committee.

Jess had been pestering the news desk for better assignments, and now New York had become the centre of the Wrath of God story with the death of Howard Wyler and his butler, the attack on an ex-president's son-in-law, and the abduction of Jake Abrams. Dan had made the news round the world with his story of Jake Abrams's abandoned hideout and the speeding pickup that had rammed him and Perry off the road.

There had been sympathetic looks when news spread she was going to New York as Dan Brasher's back-up, but Jess couldn't believe her luck. She didn't know Dan well enough to be afraid of him.

Roy Jory, the part-time dog breeder, had given her the best advice: 'He's like a golden retriever with a personality disorder. Every now and then he thinks he's a pit bull. Make sure to stand up to him and you'll be fine.'

Jess checked in to the celebrated Plaza-Asturias Hotel and stood beneath the grand lobby clock. It towered above her, its bronze curlicues, soaring eagles and gilded miniature Statue of Liberty shimmering in the beams of four spotlights. It was like an object of worship, an altar to time at the heart of fast-moving Manhattan. Jess hated that she couldn't help feeling intimidated by places like this.

She wanted to send her father a selfie, imagining his delight seeing her at such a famous place, but that was impossible. Dan had been emphatic. No one, absolutely no one, must know she was checked in to the hotel.

He had insisted on an entire backstory to explain why a single young woman was staying alone at the Plaza-Asturias. She should tell everyone at the hotel she was here for a few days seeing friends, visiting museums, and going to Broadway shows and jazz clubs. The trip, she should say, was a birthday gift from her father. Her dad would think it hilarious he could afford to make New York City a birthday gift for his only child.

Jess had no idea what she might find, but Dan's directions had been clear: 'Talk to people. The cleaners, the barmen, the concierge. Find out what they know. Take a ride somewhere in the hotel limo, sit up front with the driver. Get along with everyone.'

She was surprised how unscathed the hotel seemed until trying to visit the grand ballroom where the bomb had exploded. The entrance was sealed off with big black boarding and yards of yellow tape warning *CRIME SCENE – DO NOT CROSS*.

. . .

'Hey, Jess. Have you ever been in a home that cost eighty million dollars?'

She laughed down the hotel phone at Dan. 'Not unless you count bombed-out Chat House and the time my dad took me to see Buckingham Palace.'

Dan couldn't help laughing too. He needed happy company. After receiving that anonymous text, he'd been awake much of last night with the dread these Wrath of God killers in some way wanted to use him. He was keeping his phone turned off as much as possible.

But the sound of Jess's voice, its eagerness and innocence, also reminded him how inexperienced she was. He worried whether he had done the right thing bringing her to Manhattan for an assignment that was turning so dangerous and messy. If these people were stalking him, they were bound at some point to find out about her. But this was her first foreign assignment. He remembered how exciting that had been for him. He would make sure she was careful.

'Ben Tremblay's called me,' he said. 'He's at his New York penthouse and wants to meet. He's invited me for afternoon drinks. Come along – you'll get an astronaut's view of Manhattan.'

Dan was worried Tremblay wanted to recruit him to work for one of his rowdy redtops, as he wasn't interested. He could have declined the invitation, but the prospect of Tremblay's company always held a grisly fascination. Having Jess along might distract him.

Tremblay was a caricature of his own bawdy newspapers. He was like an alien life form, unreached by everyone else's agreed ideas of civility and social convention. He dwelled behind a sociopathic shield of mad self-belief, immune to all mockery – unable even to interpret the way people reacted to him. Dan could never decide whether to hate him or envy him.

'He's sending his car,' Dan told Jess. 'I'll pick you up in twenty minutes.'

It was a stretch Bentley, two-tone blue with a ceiling and seats of quilt-stitched leather and a floor of deep lambswool. There was walnut panel everywhere, and baffling rows of colourful screens and switches and buttons to press. Dan saw Jess take a long look at the chauffeur as he opened the car door for her. He was a good-looking guy and he gave Jess a huge smile. She was smiling herself as she sat to face Dan in the four-seat rear cabin. The driver turned to speak to them. 'Hi, I'm Mike, Mr Tremblay's bodyguard and driver. We'll be there in about ten minutes or so. The boss says help yourself to the champagne.' They grinned at each other. Half-bottles of champagne and glasses were in a low-lit shelf inside one of the doors. Dan popped and poured.

'Tremblay must be a real character,' Jess said. 'He made quite a scene at the Met commissioner's briefing.'

'You've never in your life met anyone like him,' Dan said. 'You'll see. He's kind of creepy, but in the end just another unscrupulous rich guy picking off fading print products with famous names so he can hijack their prestige and what's left of their influence, and milk them dry with cost cuts. He'd be a nightmare to work for. He's a sadist, the way he treats people.'

Jess pointed to the driver. 'Shh. He can hear us.'

'Who cares? He'd probably agree with every word.'

Mike smiled into the rear-view mirror. 'Don't worry about me, folks,' he said. 'I hear much worse.'

'See?' Dan said and they both laughed. 'Tremblay works hard at being a total jerk – it's how he intimidates people. He likes acting the good guy as well, playing the guitar with superstars at charity concerts so everyone gets to see the soft side of the rock-hard tycoon. The closest to Tremblay I can think of is Robert Maxwell. He's long dead. He was a total crook who—'

'I know who Robert Maxwell was, thank you,' Jess interrupted, having finished her champagne with surprising speed. 'I read books and everything.'

'Of course you do,' Dan said. He deserved the rebuke and refilled her glass, smiling at her until she smiled back.

The elevator shot them to the top of the high, skinny tower. It looked like a giant silver toothpick in the muscular Manhattan skyline.

From the wall-to-floor windows of Tremblay's high perch, Manhattan was so far away it seemed unreal to Dan – detached and bloodless, like a computer graphic, with Central Park, Manhattan's vast lung, reduced to the size of a ragged green rug.

But Jess's eyes lit up. 'Whoa!' She laughed. 'It's like an image from that Google Earth 3D site. You'd never dare walk naked in this place. You'd be exposing yourself literally to all of New York City.'

They were waiting for their host.

The apartment had floors of green marble, with mirrored walls and golden door handles. Lurid painted statuettes of semi-nude women and erotically entangled couples stood in a row with their mirrored reflections, beneath wall lights dripping with purple crystal.

When Tremblay arrived, Jess was standing at the painting of a lily pond inside a golden frame. She pointed at the painting. 'Is that a Monet?'

'Indeed, it is, sweetheart,' Tremblay said.

Tremblay went over to a guitar with a black-and-white body, leaning in a corner between two speakers. 'And that's a Fender Stratocaster,' he said. 'Eric Clapton played it at the Royal Albert Hall.'

Dan could see Tremblay studying Jess as she smiled at the Clapton guitar and touched it lightly, like a holy object; he hadn't said she was coming.

Dan put a hand briefly on her shoulder. 'Jess and I are working for *The Courant* on the US side of this story. She's one of our brightest, so don't you go poaching her. We're not for hire.'

There was no one else in the room, apart from a tall man in a high-buttoned green jacket and white gloves. He was standing in a far corner, having delivered a tray with champagne in a bucket, three glass flutes rimmed with gold, and a well-arranged plate of tiny crackers spread with caviar and smoked salmon.

'Who else are we expecting?' asked Dan.

'Sue's joining us,' Trembley said, and called to the man in the green jacket. 'Hey, Juan – tell Sue to quit beautifying herself and get in here. And we need another glass for this young lady.'

He sank into a large lavender sofa and pointed Dan and Jess to chairs either side of him. When he leaned back, his belly unfolded out of his T-shirt and over his pink capris. The T-shirt was either a proud self-assessment, or his idea of a joke: *ALL I KNOW IS I'M A MOTHERFUCKING DELIGHT.*

Sue hurried into the room murmuring apologetically. She poured champagne into each of the glasses before sitting on the sofa close to Tremblay, and handed him a note, which he read and placed on the sofa next to him.

Tremblay smiled at Sue and his eyes disappeared into his Dizzy Gillespie cheeks. 'Don't worry about it, darling,' he said. 'It'll be fine.'

Sue didn't look reassured and he put his hand on her knee. She was in her thirties and her long red hair was wild with curls. She couldn't have been much more than five feet tall. Her chest and hips were enhanced by the perspective of her tiny waist. Sitting beside her, Tremblay looked like a hazardous companion.

'She's worried,' he said, patting Sue's leg. 'Some of my friends are getting anxious about me sticking my neck out.'

That morning's London newspapers were spread before Tremblay across a glass coffee table. He was on every front page following his appearance on BBC *Question Time*. Tremblay's own newspaper *The Daylight* had the boldest presentation. He held it up to Dan and Jess:

BIG BEN STRIKES
'These monsters will never beat us'

Tremblay smiled as he placed his newspaper back on the table and stroked smooth the front page with the palms of his hands.

'Well, you've refused my job offer before I even had a chance to make it,' he said to Dan. 'I wasn't sure you'd locked yourself back in with the Chatstones.'

'I decided that was the best thing.'

'So, tell me what you think is going on here. I hear you have contacts in the right places. My guys at the *Herald* are jealous. You've got a friend who's a big-shot FBI agent.'

'She's a very old friend. Unfortunately, not very forthcoming about her work.'

'We can't let these people shut us up, right? We've got to face up to them, or soon enough they'll be telling us what to put in our newspapers.'

Sue cast a fearful glance at Jess, shaking her head very slightly.

'You're right, up to a point, Mr Tremblay,' Dan said. 'In the long run they can't win, but there's real danger until they're caught or killed. It's not easy fighting with words against an adversary with the humanitarian instincts of Vlad the Impaler. Every employee in the news business is in danger, but most of all high-profile leaders like yourself. Jake Abrams is only the latest, and it doesn't look like they're planning to stop.'

Tremblay folded his arms tightly and his little eyes grew smaller.

'What's happened to that guy?'

'No one knows if he's even alive, but it all started for him when he attacked these people in his newspaper.'

Tremblay scanned the newspapers in front of them. Every front page was covered with his photo and bold words. He sat back in his sofa and deflated, as if his huge frame had sprung a puncture.

'But whoever these people are and whatever the fuck they want, we can't be showing weakness. Don't you think? We've got to speak up.'

'I admire your courage, sir,' Dan said. 'But you need to be very careful. If they want to hurt you, there doesn't seem to be much right now that can stop them.'

Tremblay frowned and waved at the man in the green jacket to clear the coffee table. They were being dismissed.

'That didn't last long,' Jess said as the elevator hurtled downwards.

'He's getting scared,' Dan said.

'Who's Sue?

'Definitely not Mrs Tremblay. That man is such a tosser, but I wasn't kidding. He needs to shut up.'

Outside, away from the refrigerated otherworld of Tremblay's building, it was a still and steamy late afternoon. Dan had turned on his phone. 'Perry wants to talk. Important news from London, he says.'

Dan's call went straight to voicemail and he punched in a text message. 'I've told him to meet in an Irish bar near here,' he told Jess. He looked skywards towards Tremblay's penthouse and smiled.

'After that place, I need a real-world Irish bar.' Dan pulled out his sunglasses and hooked his jacket over his shoulder. 'You knackered after the flight, or do you want to join us?'

Chapter Twenty

At Dan's suggestion, Jess was sipping Old Crow bourbon from Kentucky. He could see she was unsure of the taste. They were in an Irish place on Second Avenue with a blinking neon green clover outside. Rows of liquor bottles glittered behind the long, otherwise dimly lit bar. Billy Joel was coming through the speakers singing 'Piano Man'; another decent song tortured to death through repetition.

'Roy Jory is proud of you,' Dan told Jess. 'You've delivered two great stories in a couple of days. You put the newspaper ahead of the police. That doesn't happen often.'

'I was lucky.'

Dan wagged his finger. 'Never credit luck for your success. Never admit that to the desk. If they think you're a genius, just nod and take it. Trust me, you'll need the high points to balance out the disasters.'

'I've got to confess, the lead on Leila's dad I got from that superintendent you helped after the bomb. He told me to send you his best. I think that tip was a favour to you.'

Dan laughed. 'Well, I hope you didn't tell anyone. Take all the credit you can get.'

'I'm not sure how popular it's made me, landing Leila behind bars.'

'Don't worry about that, either. I was impressed how Jory stood up like he did, to get it in the paper. Never mind the editor's guarantee of independence – others would have quaked under the pressure.'

Jess had taken another sip of Old Crow and looked in pain. 'Gimme that,' Dan said, taking the glass. 'It's like watching someone swallow medicine. Let's get you a bottle of beer.'

She looked grateful. 'I need something to cool me down in this weather.' When her beer arrived, Jess took three long swallows.

'How come everyone turned up at Abrams's shack at the exact same time?' she asked. 'You and Perry, the FBI, the bad guys – and the *New York Post*, for goodness' sake.'

'Someone told the bad guys, or they're sophisticated enough to track him down themselves,' Dan said 'The FBI were close to finding Jake before this happened. They located him the same time as us. If the FBI were tracking his comms already, they could have picked up Perry's conversation with Jake. It's my bet the terrorists are sophisticated enough to have located him themselves. The *New York Post* tip-off? The *Post* people have strong contacts, especially Dunleavy. She'll have heard it from inside the Bureau.'

'What do you think's happened to Jake Abrams?'

'They certainly meant to kill him with that bomb, and they had a second chance in the woods. If they still wanted him dead, it's hard to figure why they went to the trouble of running off with him.'

Jess had finished her beer with speed and held up the empty bottle to the bartender. 'My shout,' she said.

'No more for me,' Dan said.

'Make mine a gin martini,' said another voice. It was Perry. 'Sorry I'm late. I had a rather interesting phone call and had to file a few words to London. God, it's hot out there.' He gave

Dan an inquiring look. 'I tried calling you, but your phone went straight to voicemail.'

'It's on plane mode,' Dan said, and Perry's big eyebrows rose in surprise.

Perry lifted a stool to sit at the bar between Dan and Jess. His fedora was tipped back and the sweat on his face sparkled in the light from the liquor line-up. Also, his tie was loosened, which was very un-Perry. They waited while he inhaled half his gin martini.

'I've been told by a completely reliable source that they've found Leila's iPhone,' he said. 'It was in one of the big rubbish bins at Chat House, smashed to smithereens by a hammer or something. The police are rather irritated about this, to say the least, and they're talking about revoking her bail.'

'I guess she's still refusing to say a word,' Dan said.

'Not a dicky bird. The Met want her passwords, but naturally she's refusing to provide them. They've also been searching for past signals from her phone – from cell towers, or however that's done. The curious thing is they can't find any trace of it for the five days before the bombing. It wasn't detected again until late on the night of the Chat House attack. That was in Gloucester, but after an hour or so it vanished again. My man says they're using some technology to try to access her iPhone data, but it's apparently difficult . . . At this point, I rather lost track of what he was saying.'

'They'll get the data eventually,' Jess said. 'It might take a while.'

'Whatever she's hiding, it must be mighty important to her,' Dan said.

A lone guitarist appeared in a corner. He tied his white hair in a ponytail that reached to his waist, and began tuning up.

Perry stood. 'Sorry to rush, but I've got a column to file.' He finished off his martini. 'Talk tomorrow.'

Jess got up too. 'I need to get back to the hotel and speak to some people before it gets too quiet.'

'Hang on a minute,' Dan said as Jess threw her bag over her shoulder. 'You be careful, okay?'

'Please, Dan. You've already given me a lecture about staying undercover.'

'Well, I'm giving it again now. We know these people are ruthless killers, but they're clever too. We need to assume they've had inside help and that they're tech-savvy. In case anyone connected with that hotel is involved, you need to make fucking sure they don't tumble you. Understood?'

'Yes, boss,' Jess said, with a quick mock salute.

Dan was by himself now, and the old musician smiled and nodded as he sent random, whiny chords through the bar. Left alone, Dan felt his guard deserting him. Being with people helped him feel the strength he tried to project. Seeing them believe it helped him believe it too. But his fearlessness was just for show. It was in solitary moments like this that the truth came knocking and all the stored-up dread arrived. He had been on the edge of it from the moment he saw that text.

These killers would know where he was whenever he turned on his phone. They were taunting him as well as tracking him. He didn't know why they'd picked him, what he might have done, but he had written dozens of stories about Islamist extremists, and if they were the people doing this, and revenge was their motive, he had given them every reason to kill him. But they could have killed him and Jake in the woods. And why had they said they would be in touch?

The guitarist flicked his ponytail back over his shoulder, plucked a little to find the tune, and began his first song. It was 'Yesterday'.

Dan groaned and left the bar, his drink unfinished.

Chapter Twenty-One

'Where you from?' Gilda asked Jess. 'I *love* your accent.' She said *love* in a long, deep way, like it belonged in a song. The hotel was already quiet when Jess had got back. Bombs were not good for business. Guests strolled occasionally through the lobby; the concierge sat alone with a crossword; a man with a managerial voice reprimanded three reception-desk attendants for playing Mortal Kombat on their phones; and, with only a couple of customers, the bartender wanted to chat.

She was a large Black woman with a bright smile and an experienced face. She wore a white shirt, a bow tie, and a badge saying *GILDA*.

'My grandaddy visited London in the war,' she said, 'but he never came back. Killed right at the end in Belgium, January 1945, at the Battle of the Bulge. His last letter home said if he wasn't shot, he was gonna freeze to death. All the way from the Mississippi Delta to die in the freezing cold in Belgium. My mom was only three.'

'My parents came from Jamaica,' Jess said.

'Beautiful place.'

The bar was clean, but still Gilda was wiping it in broad sweeps with a damp red cloth.

'I was in the ballroom when that bomb went off,' she said. 'I thought the world was coming to an end. I said to my mom I guess I got some idea how scared Grandpa must've been.'

'That must have been awful. Were you hurt?' Jess said, show-ing more concern, she hoped, than professional interest.

'No, just couldn't hear right for a while. But there was so much blood, and people crying out. And that poor website woman at the podium, she was right on top of the bomb. She shouldn't even have been stood there. She was only saying sorry for the guy being late – then boom. She didn't stand a chance, God rest her soul.'

'Isn't the security here famous for being tight?'

'Tight?' Gilda laughed. 'On a big night like that it was. With all those high-flying types, with the governor and the mayor and the famous media people, getting to work here is like getting into the White House. They search everything. There are cops and security people, and dogs sniffing every-where. A plainclothes cop was right there in front of the podium when it happened. Killed instantly, they said. My man works in security here.'

Jess took a sip of her sparkling water and considered what to do next. Best not to seem eager to meet the boyfriend.

'He can't figure it out,' Gilda went on. 'He's seen presidents and kings visit, all kinds of folk a lot of crazy people want to kill, and nothing like this has ever happened.'

Jess chatted a while longer with Gilda and learned her shift ended at eleven every night, the same time as her boyfriend's.

Two middle-aged men in suits arrived at the end of the bar, ordered vodka tonics, and began talking loudly and incompre-hensibly about the business dinner they had just left. They kept glancing at Jess, and after a while waved for Gilda's attention.

'Honey,' Gilda said to Jess, smiling in a world-weary way and wiping the bar once more. 'Guys over there want to know if you'll join them for a nightcap.'

The two men leaned on the bar, smiling at her. It was nearly eleven o'clock. 'Not with them,' Jess said. 'I'm going for a stroll before bed. Is there a decent bar near here?'

'Sure there is.'

• • •

In a bar behind Grand Central station, a few people were watching the baseball – the Yankees were out of town and down against the LA Angels. A man with a neat beard, who had been shouting at the screen, beamed at the sight of Gilda.

'Hey, beautiful,' he said, and hugged her. Then he smiled a wide, hygienic white smile at Jess and gave her a long look.

'This here is my man's boss,' Gilda said. 'Ang – Angelo Caputo. Say hello to Jess, all the way from London. Some guys were hassling her at the hotel bar so I brought her along.'

He ignored the game and insisted on buying drinks. 'Ooh – buying a round for once, Mr Caputo,' said Gilda, flicking an eyebrow at Jess.

While Caputo was away getting the drinks, Gilda whispered to Jess, 'Careful what you say. He's the hotel security boss and he's under a lot of pressure. The police spent hours questioning him. Someone really messed up that night.'

With a beer in her hand, Jess accepted more compliments on her accent – it didn't get much admiration back home – and chose to ignore Gilda's warning and put some questions to Caputo.

'Were you there when the attack happened?'

'Sure – of course. Me and half the NYPD. They overran the place after what happened in England. I got sidelined that night. My boss arrived from HQ and took over the show. It was annoying as hell at the time, getting pushed aside. But after

London, they weren't taking any chances. I've got to admit it was kind of a relief. The cops have spent hours making me go over and over that night, but I wasn't even running things.'

Caputo's boss, Jess learned, was the man in charge of security for the entire Plaza-Asturias hotel chain – retired NYPD captain Charles Healy.

'Poor Chuck must wish he never set foot in the place,' Caputo said. 'He was a deputy commissioner, three stars on his shoulder. Seen it all – mass murders, the Mafia, 9/11. But he's cracked up over this. He went over everything himself just before the guests arrived; that's the kind of guy he is. He was sobbing and sobbing on the night. He's still home under sedation, can't talk to a soul, not even his friends or the NYPD.'

Jess made sure to remember the NYPD captain's name. It sounded like a feature she might sell to London if she could get him to talk. Here was a senior cop, toughened by years of death and mayhem, who finally cracked at the horror of what had happened on his watch at the Plaza-Asturias.

It was way past midnight now and Jess was getting tired. She hadn't slept for almost twenty-four hours. The game had finished by the time she left; the Yankees had lost. Angelo Caputo asked for her phone number and she obliged. Dan hadn't told her to flirt; she'd made that decision herself.

Chapter Twenty-Two

The house was a grey-painted clapboard colonial with black-shuttered windows and a straight stonework path leading through a lawn dying of neglect. A wilted rhododendron bush stood by the white front door. It was late morning but the curtains were still drawn.

Jess knew she was working against the odds knocking on Chuck Healy's door. She'd spent an hour reading about him online and knew he avoided publicity. His police career had ended suddenly three years ago, when he became embroiled in a corruption scandal exposed by *The New York World*. He was exonerated of wrongdoing, but never went back to the NYPD. Jess wouldn't be the first journalist to approach him, but she was good at getting people to talk. She'd travelled by train to the Westchester suburbs north of the city, and it was the sky there that struck her most. So much more of it, after all those shadowy ravines in the city; Manhattan was full of streets that never saw a sunny side.

She pulled back the screen door to bang on a large, unpolished brass knocker. A small woman, stooped and in her sixties, peered out of the gloom, clutching together the top of her pink dressing gown. Her eyes were suspicious.

'Yes?'

Jess introduced herself and her newspaper.

'No, no,' the woman said. 'You shouldn't be here. The police have asked for the media to leave my husband alone. He's not talking to any of you people. You need to leave.'

'I'm sorry. I didn't know,' said Jess. 'I only just arrived from London. I've come a very long way and I wonder if Mr Healy could spare me a few minutes to talk about that night at the Plaza-Asturias. I know it was a terrible, terrible time for him.'

'Who's that, honey?' a man's voice came from inside the house.

'It's a girl reporter from London.'

The man appeared and stepped in front of his wife, grabbing the door and telling her, 'Give the guys a call, right now.'

He was tall, more than six feet, with thick, tangled hair. He wore red Bermuda shorts and a blue tank top that clung to his large body.

'Are you Chuck Healy?' Jess asked.

'You heard what the lady said. Get outta here.' He was shouting. A gust of beery breath hit Jess in the face.

She didn't move. 'I've been speaking to your colleague at the Plaza-Asturias – Angelo Caputo. He's very worried about you. So are a lot of people there who know you. Can I just ask you—'

Healy pushed hard to open the screen door and Jess jumped backwards. His wife reappeared.

'Chuck, please don't. I've called them,' she said. 'Come back inside.'

When she tried to restrain her husband, he took hold of her with both hands and moved her effortlessly back into the house, almost lifting her off the ground. Then he twisted Jess round and pushed her off the steps with such force it felt like a punch. She fell hard onto the stone path. Healy stood over Jess, so close she could tell he needed to shower.

'Get out of here, lady, right now,' he said. 'Take yourself right down that path and don't you come back, or else you're going to be in a pile of trouble.'

Rather than intimidating Jess, this threat brought out the tough Brixton in her. She looked up at him with an angry, unafraid smile. 'Fuck you, mister. How dare you,' she said. 'You just assaulted me. I am perfectly entitled to ask you to speak. All you had to say was no.'

Healy's wife rushed out of the house again, wrapping both arms around her husband's large torso. She was too small to have any hope of holding him back. 'He's sorry, he's sorry,' she said to Jess. 'Please, darling, you need to leave.'

A police car with its lights flashing braked sharply outside the house, and an officer walked towards Jess as she sat on the path. Her tights were torn at the knees and her legs were bleeding.

'You okay, miss?' he said. 'You're on private property right here and it's sure looking like you're not welcome.' He held a hand out to her, but Jess ignored it. She jumped to her feet and pointed towards her attacker.

'That thug attacked me,' she said.

'Morning, Chuck. You okay?' the officer said.

'I assaulted no one, Jim,' Healy told the officer as he headed back to his front door. 'She got clumsy and fell. Tell her to get the hell out of here.'

'Don't worry, I'm leaving,' Jess said. But she wasn't going to be rushed. She brushed off her skirt and jacket and took plenty of time retrieving her shoes and her bag and its contents from across the dying lawn. She could tell by the aches there would soon be bruises everywhere.

Jess waved at the cop and the Healys, all standing on the front step looking down at her. 'You all have a good day now,' she said. 'And God bless America.'

Chapter Twenty-Three

Ben Tremblay's chauffeur, Mike, sprang from the big stretch Bentley when his boss's gigantic frame loomed into the rear-view mirror. He smiled, seeing Sue, his beautiful assistant, with him. She was wearing a tight white dress that finished an inch or so above her perfect tanned knees. Sue looked unhappy; even midday was too early for her.

'Morning, Mike,' Tremblay said as Mike opened the Bentley's wide back door and prepared for the daily feat of transferring Tremblay's massive frame into the luxurious back seat. First, with Mike's help, Tremblay shuffled his six-foot-four, twenty-five-stone bulk into the correct position. Tremblay's leg muscles had no hope of controlling his descent. It was a matter of aim and release, and Mike the chauffeur was the bombardier.

'Okay, sir, down you go,' Mike said, and down Ben Tremblay went, with the big Bentley, all two tons and more of it, shuddering at the impact of his arrival. That was how it happened on the fateful afternoon Mike set out to drive his boss to lunch at Ben Tremblay's favourite Manhattan venue, the Carlyle Hotel.

Mike put on his chauffeur's cap and started the engine. He guessed he was the last chauffeur in Manhattan required to wear an old-fashioned, shiny-peaked chauffeur's hat and white gloves. But Tremblay was a poor boy made good, and Mike knew looking the part was important to him. His boss, however, had relented recently on the matter of the white gloves. Mike had persuaded him, given the heightened security concerns, that he needed unhindered access to the gun in the holster tucked beneath his left arm. He was a retired New York police sergeant who had worked three years for Tremblay without ever using his weapon, except during the shooting-range practice Tremblay insisted upon. Until today, he had been his boss's sole protection, but from tomorrow a back-up car with two additional armed guards would travel everywhere with Tremblay. He'd been scared into it by those British journalists who'd visited last night. Mike was glad of that: he wouldn't stand a chance against a gang of terrorists.

In the back seat, Sue was protesting. 'I wish the hell you weren't dragging me along to this,' she said. 'Who is this guy we're seeing, anyway?' Mike liked the sound of Sue's voice even when she was really angry about something; it was a raw Brooklyn voice – tough and honest.

'He's the marketing chief of a huge Silicon Valley tech operation, my dear, and he's planning a massive advertising campaign.'

'It's going to be so boring and I've got a crushing headache. Can Mike just drive me back? I need some Advil.'

'You know I need you with me, my sweet,' Tremblay said. 'This guy likes a pretty face and we need his business. Be a good girl now and turn on the charm while I tell him what great publicity he's going to get in our newspapers.'

Mike could see Tremblay behind him stroking Sue's leg. He knew she hated that, just as Mike hated the thought of Sue spending her nights alongside that fat fucking barbarian. They would quit their jobs one day and head off together; Sue had promised they would – when the time was right.

'You're looking very hot his morning, by the way,' Tremblay told Sue in a loud whisper.

Mike and Sue caught each other's eye in the mirror. Sue made an angry shape with her mouth and looked away from Tremblay to study the back of her hand. 'It's the middle of the day and you're forcing me to flirt with some Silicon Valley geek,' she said.

Mike edged the Bentley up the car park ramp towards the street. At the top, he paused to look as usual into two mirrors positioned to view oncoming pedestrians on the sidewalk.

The street was quiet. A man in a hi-vis jacket and hard hat leaned against some scaffolding across the street and tossed his cigarette into the gutter. A blue van was double-parked with its engine running and would have to move to make way. The sidewalk was clear apart from a bent old man walking slowly with a walking frame. A young nurse was holding him by the elbow. Mike stopped to let them pass.

'Turn up the music, Mikey,' Tremblay said. 'I love this song.'

Mike looked down to turn up the volume and the speakers blasted out the Bee Gees singing 'Night Fever'. Sue put her hands to her ears in mock horror. 'Help! I'm being tortured,' she cried, and Mike looked over his shoulder to laugh. Sue was a fan of Lady Gaga and oldies like Streisand and Sinatra.

But when Mike turned, Tremblay wasn't laughing. He was looking straight ahead through the windshield, terrified.

'Mike!' he shrieked, pointing ahead.

Mike turned back to see the bent old man was now upright. He had pushed away his walking frame and pulled out a gun to aim it straight at the car, straight at him.

Two things then happened simultaneously. Mike pushed down hard on the accelerator and the man pulled the trigger. The Bentley lurched forward, sending the gunman flying as it careened across the side street and crashed into the side of a parked Volvo. The gunman's body bounced off the Bentley's roof before landing in the street. The 'nurse' and the man in the hi-vis jacket lifted the gunman into the back of the double-parked van and climbed aboard themselves as it took off towards Park Avenue.

. . .

Tremblay witnessed none of this, having dived onto the lambswool carpet of his car the moment he saw the gun. Now he could hear Sue screaming. He looked up to see her legs in the air. She was diving into the front of the car. Tremblay sat up and Sue was on the front passenger seat, leaning towards Mike and sobbing, with blood on her hands and face and her bright white dress. 'Mike, Mike . . . oh, Mike,' she kept crying.

Tremblay struggled out of the car and pulled open the driver's door. Sue's head was against Mike's shoulder. His peaked cap was in place and his foot still heavy on the accelerator. The engine was roaring and the Bee Gees were still singing.

Sue looked up at Tremblay and lunged towards him, battering his chest and shouting: 'I hate you . . . I hate you . . . you're a fucking monster.' Tremblay did nothing to prevent her. He sank to his knees, looking at Mike while Sue kept swinging at him. The single bullet had hit Ben Tremblay's chauffeur in the face above his right eye. The quilted leather headrest behind him was soaked with his blood.

Chapter Twenty-Four

Jess had been here only yesterday, driven by the murdered chauffeur. She had listened to Ben Tremblay's bluster and seen the face of his terrified girlfriend. Now the lobby of his building was teeming with media and cops. Outside, an ambulance weaved through a clutter of emergency vehicles and the street was blockaded between Park and Madison. Within an hour of the shooting, Wrath of God had taken credit: *Ben Tremblay was lucky this time, but he will soon pay for his reckless words.*

Jess was in a crowd of reporters and cameras behind a cluster of microphones. A reporter next to her shouted across the room. 'Hey, Sam. When's someone going to give us an idea what's going on here?'

An NYPD officer, wearing a cap with a gold band and three stars on the collar of his white shirt, waved dismissively in the reporter's direction. 'Gimme a minute,' he shouted back, and went on talking with a tall woman with a blonde ponytail.

'Who's Sam?' Jess asked the reporter.

'Chief of counterterrorism, but not for long the way things are looking.' The tall woman was leaning close to the terrorism chief, looking grim.

'Who's he talking to?'

'That's Siobhan Mac Stiofain, a big shot at the FBI in Manhattan.'

When they'd finished talking and Siobhan walked away, heading towards the bank of elevators, Jess ran towards her. 'Miss Mac Stiofain,' she said, doing her best to smile brightly. 'I'm Jessica Hunter. I work at *The Courant* in London with Dan Brasher.'

'Hey,' Siobhan said, 'I think he mentioned you. Are you the one who pestered him to come here from London?'

'I guess so.' Jess smiled. Siobhan caught sight of Jess's scuffed and bloody knees. 'You had an accident?'

'I tripped on the pavement running here from Grand Central.'

'Wow! They look sore,' Siobhan said. 'What can I do for you?'

'I'd really appreciate your help,' Jess said.

· · ·

Tremblay was on the sofa in his huge living room, a half-empty bottle of Glenmorangie on the table next to him. He needed both hands to keep his glass steady. Red polka-dot undershorts were visible beneath his loosely fastened bathrobe. Two women were sitting across the room making notes as they talked to his assistant Sue. They nodded in Siobhan's direction.

Siobhan took hold of Jess's arm. 'Remember what I told you. Write about the scene here as much as you like, but not a single word of what he says. Okay?'

'I promise,' said Jess, shocked and pleased with herself for talking Siobhan into bringing her to the apartment. Roy Jory had told her once: 'Never be afraid to ask, doesn't matter how crazy. They can only say no.'

Jess stayed back as Siobhan approached Tremblay, for fear he recognise her from the previous day. A blue-suited man with a shaved head sat next to Tremblay. He appeared to be reading aloud from a notebook, and Tremblay looked annoyed at whatever the man was saying.

Jess listened as Siobhan introduced herself. 'You're that man Brasher's friend,' Tremblay said.

Siobhan nodded. 'I know you've already been answering my colleagues' questions. But we'll need to spend more time with you to put together as much information as we can.'

'Sure, whatever, but you're wasting your time. I spoke out against these people and they tried to kill me. End of story.'

'Did you get a good look at the shooter? Did he look Middle Eastern?'

'Maybe. I couldn't tell. A little bony guy with gingery hair.' Tremblay put down his glass and licked spilt whisky from his fingers. 'You have absolutely no idea who these people are, am I right?'

'We're working on it, sir.'

He looked up at her. 'They're going to keep trying to kill me, aren't they? At this rate, we'll all be fucking dead before you work it out.'

Tremblay compressed himself tightly with his arms, pushing his stubbly chin into his chest. He nodded towards the man with the shaved head.

'This guy works for me and he's a complete fucking moron. This is all his fault. He's the one who's been telling me from the beginning to stand up to these headcases.'

The insult did not seem to surprise or upset the man, who smiled weakly at Siobhan and raised his eyebrows.

'He's the editor-in-chief of the *New York Herald* and he thinks he's a genius. All journalists are smartasses.'

'Please, Ben,' the man said. 'I'm only asking you to wait a while and think about it.'

'Think about it? Seriously? I'm sitting here with a dead man's blood all over me. He was murdered by someone who wanted to kill me – *me*, dickhead, they wanted to fucking kill *me*. What do you mean, think about it? Fuck the newspapers. Fuck them.'

He grabbed the man's notebook and held it up to Siobhan.

'I told this Einstein here I was going to sell the newspapers or shut them down if I can't find someone stupid enough to buy them. And he starts reading me an editorial he wants to run. He wants to quote . . .' He paused, 'Who's the guy?'

'John Milton,' the man said.

'Whoever the fuck he is,' Tremblay said, and began to read. '*He who destroys a newspaper kills reason itself. Give me the liberty to argue freely, above all liberties . . .*'

The man reached for the notebook. 'That's not the exact quote,' he said.

'Oh, fuck off,' Tremblay said, tossing the notebook at him. 'And fuck the newspapers. They're not worth the trouble. I thought they would be fun to own but it's been a shit experience, even before this. No one gave a stuff about me when I was nothing more to them than a glorified shopkeeper. They left me in peace. But, oh boy, did they pile in when I dared to buy some newspapers. Disgusting people, those Chatstones and Wylers. They're so fucking up themselves. Their papers have hounded me for years. Pieces of shit.

'They're not going to have me to kick around anymore, and I'm not going to get myself killed. We won't be running another word about this crap. I don't care what people think. They can stick the newspaper business. They've got no future anyway.'

Chapter Twenty-Five

Dan slammed his laptop shut. He'd been pecking at it, making small edits before sending Jess's update on the Tremblay shooting to London. They were in *The Courant*'s New York bureau, though the word *bureau* hadn't been an honest description for a long time. Once, *The Courant* had kept half a dozen or more journalists in Manhattan, but these days the 'bureau' was a room with space for one desk, a metal filing cabinet, and a corner table for making coffee. The single staffer had been on sick leave since the Chat House attack.

He pushed back his chair and stretched out, arms in the air, looking at the ceiling in his untucked blue check shirt, faded black jeans, and trainers with soles worn almost smooth. He was wearing yellow socks with Snoopy on a skateboard.

He turned to Jess. 'How's it going, Jessica? You've had a hectic couple of days.'

She looked up from her screen. She was feeling crap. 'I'm sorry – but Ben Tremblay and his girlfriend and that poor chauffeur,' she said. 'We were with them all only yesterday. It's so horrible. That woman, Sue, she was horrified. She was sure something would happen, but Tremblay just brushed her off. And I keep seeing that driver's lovely smile, Dan, and now he's dead.'

Dan looked at Jess, cocking an eyebrow and tilting his head with his mouth slightly pursed. Jess thought it must be his hardened newsman's 'shit happens' expression.

She forced a smile. 'I've got to ask. Why those silly Snoopy socks?'

'Careful,' he said. 'I got them for Christmas from Harriet, my daughter. I'll be in a black suit tomorrow for Howard Wyler's funeral, but I'll still be wearing these. I love them.'

'Oh,' Jess said, turning to look at her computer screen, pretending to study its contents. She could still see Dan's smile; he was enjoying her discomfort.

It was better to talk business. 'I've got a date tomorrow with a hotel security guy,' she said. 'He was there when the bomb went off.'

Dan swung his chair to face her. 'Jess, are you sure about that? You've had bylines on this story. Someone there might know by now you're a journalist. If anyone in that hotel helped them, they'll know you've been lying to them.'

'Don't worry, I'm certain he's not part of some wicked plot. He's a nice guy. He's already spent hours being interviewed by the police. He'd be inside if they had any suspicions. When the law works out what happened in that hotel, he could be a great contact.'

Dan didn't look convinced.

'I'll be fine,' she said. 'Anyway, you know I checked out of that place. London got cheap and moved me to another hotel.'

'Where are you now?'

'A dingy place in Yorkville. Apparently, even your hotel was too expensive for a mere cub reporter like me.'

Dan didn't answer. He was staring at his phone, surprised at what he saw.

'*The New York Times* says Ben Tremblay is going to sell his papers or close them if he can't find a buyer.'

'Yes, that's what he said he would do.'

'You knew?'

Dan stared across the desk they were sharing, waiting for her answer. She could see for a moment why he scared people.

'He told Siobhan in the apartment,' she said. 'He said newspapers were doomed anyway and he wasn't going to get himself killed for them. His editor was there. He looked very upset.'

'Jesus, Jessica – that wasn't in your story. Why the hell didn't you file it?'

'Because Siobhan agreed to take me to the apartment on the condition I didn't use anything Tremblay said.'

'For goodness' sake. It's a vital part of the story.'

He stood, pacing the little room, then turned to her, shaking his head so slightly it hardly moved, a mixture of anger and disbelief.

'Don't you see? This means the terror tactics of these crazies is working. It's exactly what they want. What were you thinking? That no one was going to find out if you didn't write anything?' He folded his arms and looked back at his computer. 'How fucking stupid can you be?' he muttered. Jess guessed Dan thought he was talking to himself, but she heard him.

She jumped up and put on her angriest face.

'What did you say? Don't you dare talk to me like that. What I was thinking was I had given someone my word and I was bound to keep it. She was a new contact for me. I wanted her to trust me. She'd have cut me off forever. When did that become a crime? No one else heard what he was saying except for Siobhan and the editor.'

Dan sat down and put up his hands. To her surprise, his anger was evaporating. 'Jess, please, let's calm down,' he said. It looked like a surrender.

But Jess gave an angry laugh. 'Calm down? *The Daily Courant*'s number one tantrum merchant is actually telling someone to calm down?'

'But Jess, don't you see what happened? Journalists are crap at keeping secrets. The editor of *The Herald* leaked it to someone he knows at *The New York Times*. You should've spoken to me. There are ways to tell these stories without getting people in trouble.'

Jess could see he had a point, but no one was going to speak to her that way. She remembered Jory's advice . . . 'He's like a golden retriever with a personality disorder. Every now and then he thinks he's a pit bull.'

'Well, thanks for your tutorial on the fucked-up rules of this game,' she said. 'I must have missed the class on lying and cheating.'

'The number one rule of this game is telling people what they need to know.'

Jess pulled the jacket from the back of her chair to tug it on, grabbed her bag, and headed out of the room.

'Hang on, Jess, please come back,' said Dan, a golden retriever again, following her to the elevator. 'I'm sorry. I was over the top. You've done some great stuff. It's just . . . I can't tell you how much difficulty I'm having.'

'Oh, you poor boy,' she said. 'No one's feeling any pressure but for you.' She punched hard at an elevator button. 'I'll prove to you how fucking good I am.'

Jess maintained her angry glare until the elevator doors closed.

Chapter Twenty-Six

News had broken that Cressida Chatstone was dead, and New York's high and mighty seemed to be forgetting their manners. Mourners were gathering at a synagogue on Fifth Avenue for the funeral of Howard Wyler, the poisoned boss of the New York World Company; but the terrible death preoccupying them was not the terrible death they were here to grieve.

'Awful, awful business . . . dreadful,' the New York governor, his hand wound freshly bandaged, was telling the city's mayor . . . 'It's just heartbreaking, she was so young and talented,' a US senator's wife said to her husband as they passed by . . . 'She spent the week with us at Sagaponack last summer. Terrific lady . . . a load of fun,' said Manhattan's richest property developer.

Dan and Perry were on the sidewalk, out of the rain beneath a grey canopy at the synagogue's entrance, while Dan finished his cigarette. They were there on orders from London, representing ChatCorp.

'These press moguls, Daniel,' Perry said in a low voice. 'They're dropping like flies.'

Dan wasn't shocked at the news, just dazed. He wondered what becoming numb to grief meant and imagined how handy it would be to develop some emotional scar tissue to protect yourself against its destruction. He knew he would never manage it.

'It's fucking terrible,' he said, dropping his cigarette end onto the wet sidewalk. He ground it out with his foot, then put it in a trash can on the corner.

'We must drink a toast later to a great lady,' Perry said. 'She never expected the burden, but she carried it well. It probably cost her life. She could have turned her back and lived in idle luxury with the family billions like the rest of those Chatstone ne'er-do-wells.'

They headed into the synagogue. 'What time's your flight?' Perry asked. Dan had agreed to return to London to help with the coverage of Cressida's death, and the growing fear Leila could face more serious charges. 'I'll let Jess know why you've vanished. She has a date tonight with one of the hotel security people.'

Dan came to a sharp halt and turned towards Perry. 'She still intends on seeing that guy? Please talk her out of it. That hotel will know about her by now from her stories. She shouldn't risk it. Be gentle – I went over the top with her yesterday about a mistake she made.'

'Okay, okay,' Perry said, at the same time looking Dan up and down. 'I've got to ask, wherever did you get that outfit? Haven't seen you in a suit for years.'

'Men's Wearhouse, one hundred and ninety-nine bucks,' Dan replied, with an unsmiling wink. 'Got to look my best when a titan of the press is laid to rest.'

In its impressive history of security threats, the Temple Emanu-El could surely never have been subjected to tighter security than it was today. Uniformed police were everywhere. Plainclothes men and women with tiny lapel pins, dark glasses, and unreadable faces escorted VIPs into the synagogue. Four blocks of Fifth were closed to unauthorised vehicles. Two police motorbikes cleared the way for an unmarked white van cruising the blocked-off streets. 'That's an NYPD X-ray van,' said Dan. 'It sees through walls. The military had them in Afghanistan.'

Howard Wyler's corpse arrived in a simple wooden coffin borne on the shoulders of six men in black, followed by his mourning family. His widow, Cornelia, held a white hand-kerchief fringed with lace in one tiny black-gloved hand. The other grasped the arm of her only child, Francis, now head of the company founded by his great-great-grandfather in the mid-nineteenth century.

'He'll be shitting himself more than he's grieving,' whispered Perry. 'I spent three weeks on the road with him covering the Obama–Romney campaign. Total dunce. Before you know it, *The World* will be going downhill faster than ever, along with the rest of the family empire. You wait and see.'

A gigantic bunch of white lilies had arrived from Wyler's friend the president, and the first gentleman. Media people were heavily represented: newspaper editors and publish-ers, owners of news websites with their chief content officers, a couple of TV network CEOs. There was someone familiar from Facebook and people Dan recognised from Google and Amazon. But none of the tech age founding fathers was pres-ent – no Zuckerberg or Brin or Bezos. Their creations had swallowed much of the globe's advertising revenue and they owed no homage to the fading empires of print. Jeff Bezos, the world's richest man, or thereabouts, had bought *The Washington Post* with his own money ... *The Washington Post*, once a tower of profit and prestige, had become a rich man's amusement. To him, it was dropping pennies – like other billionaires dropped pennies for a sports team, a Tuscan vineyard, or a yacht big enough for its own ballroom and landing pad.

Dan was at the back of the synagogue with Perry, ready to make a quick escape. The service was just about to begin when a man squeezed into the pew next to him. 'Make a little room, please,' he whispered.

'Sure,' Dan replied, pressing against Perry as he slid along the pew. When he looked up at the man, their eyes met. 'George Frobisher,' Dan said.

'Well, if it's not Dan Brasher,' the man answered, reaching out to shake his hand. 'How's your old dad getting along?'

'He's doing very well, thank you. Working hard as ever. Away in Asia at the moment.'

'Why are you in New York?' Frobisher asked.

'I'm working on these Wrath of God attacks.'

'Terrible business. Poor Howard and Jim Slight, and now this awful news about Cressida.'

'You've had your own close scrape with them.'

'Yes, poor Jorge – took the poison meant for me. He worked with me for years.'

'I tried calling you the next day,' Dan said. 'You must have had a lot going on.'

Frobisher nodded. 'Let's chat later.'

As the service ended, the congregation stood to watch the Wyler family following Howard's departing coffin.

Dan whispered to Perry: 'I'm seeing Frobisher straight after this.'

Perry smiled. 'Very impressive, hobnobbing with a president's son-in-law. You always did make a speciality of high-falutin' contacts.'

At the exit, Dan and Perry joined the line of mourners offering sympathies to the Wylers. George Frobisher was ahead of them. 'I'm so sorry for your loss,' he said, holding Cornelia Wyler's

174 · LES HINTON

gloved hand. 'Your husband and I once enjoyed a great friendship and I wanted to be here today to honour that friendship.'

'I'm sorry for your loss also,' Cornelia replied.

Frobisher squeezed her hand with both of his.

Outside, he turned to Dan. 'Want to get a bite to eat?'

. . .

Bodyguards hastened Frobisher and Dan through the wet towards a big, brutish SUV waiting on Fifth. A back-up car followed as they travelled a few blocks to a diner on the corner of 73rd and Third, where they waited in their vehicle while two of Frobisher's escorts went ahead into the restaurant. Every eye followed Dan and Frobisher as they were led to a booth tucked into a far corner, away from the windows.

Dan was mystified by Frobisher's lunch invitation, but eager to find out what he knew. They'd last seen each other a few years ago at a lunch Jim Slight was hosting, when Frobisher was in London to be honoured by the Tate Modern after donating two Picassos and a Jackson Pollock to the gallery. Not long after that London visit, his father-in-law's administration was drowning in scandal and Dan had gone to Washington to cover the story. Frobisher hadn't changed much: the same lean look and flinty scowl, his short, streamlined hair still maintained in an ageless shade of brown.

A server arrived. 'Tex Mex chicken salad, Mr George, as usual?'

Frobisher nodded, and added, 'And some decaf black.' Dan ordered a sandwich, toasted cheddar and tomato on rye.

'I come here pretty well every day,' Frobisher said. 'I like it here, it's down to earth. My security guys think I'm crazy. We can't be long – they get nervous when I spend too much time in the same place when I'm out.'

'You're the only non-media person they've tried to kill.'

Their meals arrived and Frobisher looked in silence for a moment at his chicken salad. 'It's why they still give me this protection,' he said. 'The intelligence people are always picking up evidence there's a plan to get me.'

'Do you think they have a clue yet who's doing this? They seem wary about nailing it without doubt on Islamist extremists.'

Frobisher poured sweetener into his coffee. 'They're pretending to keep an open mind, but they've made it pretty clear to me they know it's coming from the Mideast. It's got to be. I've made enemies in my life, but they're the only people who for certain want me dead. And whoever they are, they went after me and Howie Wyler on the same day in the same way.'

Their meals were only half eaten when a bodyguard at the next table came over. 'It's time to get moving, sir,' he said.

'Okay, okay, gimme a second.' Frobisher put his napkin on the table. 'Sorry, they'll keep getting antsy if I don't move.' He put some cash down and stood. 'We should keep in touch, give me your number. I might be able to help. I have to be careful, but they tell me sometimes more than goes public. And no attribution – that goes without saying, right?'

'Of course.'

Frobisher smiled. 'You gave me a hard time in *The Courant* when poor Gene was in trouble, but that was long ago and no son of Trevor Brasher can be all bad.' He reached out to shake his hand. 'Tell your dad to look me up when he gets home. Things got in such a mess I lost touch with him. He's a fine man. I got a couple of projects he might be interested in?'

As Frobisher's little convoy cruised uptown, Dan figured he had solved the mystery of his lunch invitation: Frobisher was using Dan to get close again with his father. Frobisher had been through tough and tragic times and was looking to build bridges.

Dan would definitely keep in touch with him; Siobhan never told him much, and that line about the Feds being pretty sure it was Islamists was worth pursuing. But there was zero hope his father would ever again do business with Frobisher.

Chapter Twenty-Seven

Jess walked along Lafayette Street downtown with Angelo Caputo, the Plaza-Asturias chief of security. She quite liked him, and it would have been unfriendly to refuse his dinner invitation. If Dan and Perry met him, they would see she had nothing to fear, and knowing him might be handy as this story developed.

Caputo had been very formal about making it a proper date, even arriving at her new hotel to escort her to the restaurant. Over dinner, he hadn't seemed to care much about her under-cover deceit. He was even keen after they'd eaten to take her to a club he knew, which made Jess hope he wasn't expecting too much from their friendship. It was true she enjoyed his company and liked his gentle eyes, but she found it difficult to feign interest as he talked about the Yankees and the Jets and the Knicks, and the varying talents and injuries of their stars, and the mysterious rules of the games they played. Plus his beard was trimmed too fussily. Even if she lived in New York, their friendship was unlikely to blossom into anything more.

She was also in no mood for clubbing. 'Do you want to give the club a miss?' she said, hopefully. 'I'm very tired and I've got a busy day coming up with what's going on in London and here.'

Angelo looked so stricken by her suggestion that Jess felt more guilty than ever for leading him on. 'No, no. Please come – please,' he said. 'It'll be great fun. The band is fabulous.'

The club was called CrashLanding and it was in a basement on the West Side. It was rowdy and hot, with many blinking lights directed at a small stage crowded with three male guitarists and a female drummer. The drummer impressed Jess with her ability to twirl her long, sweat-wet black hair through the air to the same frantic rhythm she was maintaining with a complicated set of percussion instruments – two bass drums and five others, four cymbals, and a Chinese gong. She didn't know enough about music to put the performance into a category, but never enjoyed the kind that crashed into her like this, so loud and metallic it was impossible to make sense of.

She was amazed by the drummer's acrobatic performance, though, and took a video of the action with her phone.

'That is Sasha,' Angelo said loudly into Jess's ear. 'Star of the show.'

A big-shouldered man with long blond hair and a beard returned from the dance floor to the bar and Angelo gave him a high five. He was wearing a red baseball cap, pushed back, and his beard reached far down to the beginning of his large belly. He had his arm around a short, wiry man with a pug face, a black beard, and severely misaligned eyes. A black T-shirt hung loosely from the short man's bony shoulders. Jess had seen the men dancing together, each swigging from a can.

'That big man's name is Craig,' Angelo told Jess. 'He worked at the hotel for a while.' Jess and Craig waved at each other through the crowd and noise.

'This is my friend Fitz,' Craig shouted, ruffling the dark hair of his shorter companion.

Sasha's routine came to a climax as she swung around wildly, striking each of her drums and cymbals at increasing speed, the guitars building the crescendo with her, until she fell from her stool, crashed to the floor, and lay still among her instruments. For an instant in the silent room Jess was alarmed, but then the crowd roared with appreciation and Sasha sprang to her feet to perform elaborate curtsies.

Sasha waved towards Angelo as she left the stage. She came over smiling broadly at Angelo and gave him a long, tight embrace.

'He's a beautiful boy. I love Angelo,' she told Jess. 'You make me jealous.'

'Jess is a reporter,' said Angelo. 'She's come all the way from London to report on these Wrath of God terrorists. She was sneaky. Checked into the hotel and asked a lot of questions. We thought she was a tourist – but no! She was operating undercover.'

About eight people were in the group by now. Jess wasn't happy at being exposed like this, but some of them smiled admiringly at her trickery.

'That's very clever,' one of the men said. 'Who the hell do you think these people are?'

'They say they're Islamists, but no one knows for sure.'

'Did you discover any secrets at the hotel?'

'Ah, well, they would be my secrets, wouldn't they? I'm piecing together a few clues,' she said with a smile, exaggerating to add some mystery.

She could see Fitz looking at her with his ugly screwed-up face.

'Do you know what I think?' he asked her.

'Please do tell.'

'I think maybe these people are too smart and nobody's ever going to catch them.'

'Oh, they'll get them in the end, you can bet on it.'

Sasha was back on stage sitting among her drums. The music began again.

Jess wanted to get away from the group and grabbed Angelo's hand. 'Take me for a dance,' she said.

He looked unhappy at the idea. 'I'm lousy at it. I love the music, but I've got no rhythm for dancing.'

Another man in the group linked his arm with Jess's. 'Come on, let's go,' he said.

Angelo was left leaning against the bar with Craig and Fitz as Jess got lost in the crush of the dance floor. She was only away from the bar a few minutes, but when she got back Angelo was gone.

Craig and Fitz looked at her in an odd, unsmiling way.

'Your boyfriend had to leave,' Craig shouted above the music. 'He asked us to take good care of you.'

He put an arm around her and Jess pushed it away. 'Where's Angelo gone? Is he all right?' she said.

'Don't you worry about him, sweetheart. You're with us now.'

The bar around them was crowded. The two men were standing tightly either side of her.

'I can take care of myself, thanks,' she said. 'And I'm not your fucking sweetheart.'

'No need to be unfriendly now,' Fitz said, grabbing her wrist.

Craig moved in front of her. 'This place is so noisy,' he shouted. 'Let's get out of here.'

'I'm leaving by myself,' she said, but when she tried, Craig pushed her back hard against the bar.

He held his face so close Jess could feel his rough beard and his spit when he shouted. 'You've been snooping around where you've no fucking business, lady. There's some people want to talk with you.'

She screamed, but in the din of the crowd and the blasting music it was like she made no sound. In the packed heat of the club, no one seemed to see her struggling.

'What the fuck are you doing?' she yelled. She thrust her glass at Craig's head, aiming for his eyes. The glass splintered and there was instant blood. Craig reeled back, clutching his face. Some of the crowd were noticing now, but all they did was look, or retreat. Jess turned to Fitz, biting hard into the hand holding her wrist and aiming a knee into his groin. She ran towards the exit. The music was still playing.

On the street, a woman was getting out of a yellow taxi. Jess ran for the open cab door and slammed it behind her. 'Just drive, quickly,' she shouted. Over her shoulder, she saw her two attackers standing in the street.

It was after midnight when Perry answered his phone. He was instantly wide awake, hearing the fear in Jess's voice. She was heading uptown to the Yorkville hotel where she was staying. 'I'm sure I was set up by my date,' she said. 'I don't know what the hell they planned to do with me.'

'You've got to get out of New York right away,' he said. 'Go straight to the airport.'

'My passport's at the hotel. I'll head straight from there.'

'Call me from JFK. I'll organise the first morning flight.'

As Jess's head cleared, she remembered taking the video of the wild drummer. Sure enough, she also had video of both Fitz and Craig dancing. The images weren't very clear, there were a lot of flashing lights, but it was definitely them. She texted the video to Perry. *It was the two guys drinking from cans*, she wrote. *The big one said his name was Craig. The other was Fitz. My date from the hotel was Angelo Caputo.*

At the hotel, she gave the cabbie twenty dollars and told him to wait five minutes while she picked up her passport and bag. It was a small hotel and the main door was locked. She hammered on the glass until the lone doorman let her in.

In her room, Jess grabbed her bag and stuffed it with clothes and shoes. She packed so roughly she was struggling to close the zipper when she heard a key in the door and saw it open.

Craig's head was still bleeding and his T-shirt was stained red. 'Hi there, Jess,' he said, as Fitz appeared from behind him with a puggish, cockeyed smile.

After thirty minutes, when Jess still hadn't reappeared, the taxi drove away.

. . .

Perry waited for her call, pacing his suite at the Ritz-Carlton, too fraught even to drink, cursing himself for letting her walk straight into a trap. When he still hadn't heard from her, he took a cab to her hotel. There were police cars and an ambulance in the street. Two medics were wheeling out a gurney carrying a body. They were in no hurry and the body was covered.

He ran from his cab towards the blue barricade blocking the street. Two cops turned towards him with their on-duty, workaday faces.

'What's happened?' Perry panted. 'Who's on that stretcher?'

'Calm down, sir.'

'Please, you've got to tell me. I'm a journalist.'

'Oh yeah?' the cop said. The two officers looked at each other, smiling, and Perry realised what they were seeing was an old man with wild white hair, a flapping blue shirt undone to the waist over his white vest, and a sweaty, panic-stricken face.

'Please believe me.' He pointed over their shoulders at the gurney. 'I might know that person. Is she dead?'

The officers turned to look as the medics loaded the gurney's covered occupant into the ambulance. Then they looked at each other and one said to Perry, 'It's a good guess, sir, that whoever's on that gurney is – yes – deceased, on account of the fact the body's completely covered.'

Perry took hold of the blue barrier, abandoned by his practised professional cool, unsure he could keep standing. 'Oh, my God,' he said. 'I can't believe it. I think I know who it is. That poor young woman.'

'We don't know who it is and no one's likely to tell us,' the cop said. 'We're only here to keep folks out of the way while Homicide do their job.'

'But I need to find out,' Perry said, ducking quickly under the barrier to head for the little hotel.

Both the cops took hold of him. 'Take it easy, guy,' one said. 'You don't want to get yourself arrested for messing up a murder scene.'

Perry knew it was pointless struggling. The other cop said, 'Look, if you're a journalist, head over there. There's a whole mob of you. They'll all be asking the same questions. They'll get told at the right time, but it could be a while.'

Perry stood helpless, looking at the departing ambulance and the two unruffled cops. It was just one more Manhattan homicide statistic to them; one more corpse off to the city morgue.

Chapter Twenty-Eight

London

Dan switched on his phone the instant he touched down at Heathrow. Moments later he was listening to Perry's frantic message. 'Something's happened to Jess. I think she might be dead,' he said. 'She went on a date with someone from the hotel. I told her, Dan, I told her not to go. They took away a body from her hotel, but no one would tell me who it was. I knew it was risky, but how could I have imagined this?'

Dan phoned back, but Perry didn't answer. He sent a message: *I'm on the ground. Call me.*

The plane crept across the tarmac for so long Dan felt imprisoned. He looked out at the half-lit London morning and at the mist drifting across the damp flatness. He remembered Jess's determined face the last time they were together; her anger as the lift doors had cut them off, and her last words to him: 'I'll prove to you how fucking good I am.' What brave, eager, dumb thing had she done?

He imagined Leila Chatstone, sitting alone with her secrets at the family estate, bail tag on her ankle, mute even in the face of a trial and prison; a prime suspect – the *only* suspect. Whatever she knew, Leila was no longer entitled to her silence. If she wouldn't talk now, the only explanation was the thing Dan most hoped against: she was working with these people; she was an accomplice, along with her vanished father.

He texted Roy Jory: *I'm not coming to the office. I'm heading straight for Chatstone House. I don't care who she is, or what Fiona Chester or anyone else thinks, Leila has got to tell us what she knows.*

By the time Dan arrived at Chatstone House, Chester and a company lawyer were in a car outside the gatehouse. Chester left the car and stood with her walking cane on the pathway to the gatehouse door.

'Don't even try to stop me, Fiona,' Dan said. 'I'm going to find out what she knows.'

'She's not answering the door,' Chester said.

'I'll break a window if I have to. Get me kicked off the paper if you like, but I'm going to make her talk, and if *The Courant* doesn't want the story I'm giving it to *The Times*.'

'Dan, you surely don't think she's involved with this.' Chester shifted her body to stand in his way.

'I don't know what's going on, but she knows something she's not telling us. She has lied to everyone. Her Pakistani father is an activist and critic of the West, and he's vanished. She smashed up her own iPhone to prevent the police getting into it. No one has any idea where she was during the five days before the Chat House bomb. For Christ's sake, Fiona, who are we kidding? If she were a citizen of Afghanistan or Iraq, by now she'd have been vanished somewhere on a rendition flight to be waterboarded and God knows what else.'

'Dan, please – her mother's just died,' Chester said.

'A lot of people have died, and they keep on dying,' Dan said, and he headed past Chester towards the gatehouse.

At the door, he took a few deep breaths. *Slow down now. Interrogation experts at the Yard have tried for days to intimidate her, with zero success. Shouting and screaming might not be the best first option.*

He knocked on the door. 'Hey, Leila, it's Dan – Dan Brasher. It's terrible news about your mum. I'm really, really sorry, but it's very important we talk. You have to tell us what you know. So many people have been killed or injured.'

'Please go away, Dan. Honestly, I don't know who's doing these things. I swear to you it's got nothing to do with me. Please leave me alone.'

Dan raised his voice a little. 'Leila, love, people are dying. If what you're saying is true, you've nothing to be afraid of, but you've got to tell us what you know.'

'I swore to my mother never to tell anyone what happened to me. She made me promise.'

Chester and Dan looked at each other. Chester whispered, 'That's bloody weird. What does she mean?'

Dan kept talking to Leila. 'But your mother's gone. Haven't you kept your promise to her? You don't need to protect her anymore. Nothing you say can harm her now.'

They could hear Leila sobbing on the other side of the door.

'Leila, listen to me, please. We think one of our reporters has been murdered. She was a young woman – your age. She had her whole life ahead of her, like you do. She was just doing her job. And one of my oldest friends is being held by them. He might be killed as well unless we stop these people. Would your mum want people to keep dying if she knew?'

There was a long silence before they heard the door unlocking. When it swung open, Leila was walking away into a room crowded with big game trophies.

She was barefoot in a sleeveless cotton dress. An ugly grey GPS bail tag was attached to her tiny left ankle, and an

Irish setter sat nearby on a tiger-skin rug, so placid it looked medicated.

Chester walked into the tiny kitchen. 'I'll put the kettle on,' she said.

Leila pulled her legs up under her in a large armchair next to the unlit fireplace. The lawyer, who had followed Dan and Chester in, placed himself in a corner chair beneath a big buffalo head, pulled an iPad from his briefcase and began tapping the screen.

Dan knew he had broken through and that Leila was ready to talk. It wasn't the time to pile on pressure. He crouched to stroke the setter.

'Is this dog going to be okay?'

'The vet says yes, eventually. She's lucky. Bertie was killed on the spot.'

Dan gave a small smile, looking around at the game trophies. 'Don't you hate these things? I thought your mother got rid of them long ago.'

'Mum banished them from the house when she took over after Grandad died and Uncle Neal killed himself. She couldn't bear to throw them away. I definitely will.'

Dan sat on the other side of the fireplace and took out a recorder to place it on the low table close to Leila. She looked startled at the sight of it.

'Leila, nothing is more important right now than telling the truth,' he said. 'Whatever happened ... whatever you did ... whatever you know ... just tell me. People are making up all sorts of terrible things because you have kept silent. They're saying you're a terrorist, that you're responsible for blowing up your own home.'

Chester came into the room with a tray and delivered mugs of tea to everyone. Leila's mug shook in her hands.

'I don't know what to do,' she said. 'I think I'm going to be in terrible trouble. Mum told me never to tell anyone. She kept saying "promise me, promise me", and I did what she asked. I kept asking her why anyone would do such a thing. She wouldn't say, but she must have known. It's been wrong to keep quiet, I know that. I knew everything had to be connected in some way. But she was very frightened and so was I. Every time, she said the same thing. "Promise me. Say you were on holiday in Venice, no matter what."'

Dan put his hand on Leila's arm. 'Leila, just tell me what happened to you.'

'They grabbed me. They dragged me out of my car. They covered my head and drove me somewhere.'

'Who did?'

'I don't know who they were. There were two smelly bodies pressed against me in a car. I didn't see any of them, ever. I was driving home from seeing friends in Gloucester. I was going to Venice the next day. I was almost home when a red car forced me off the road. Next thing I was in the back seat. They gagged me and put something over my head. We drove for a couple of hours I think and no one spoke to me the entire time.'

She was speaking quickly now – desperate to tell her story.

'Then I was locked in a room. It must have been a basement. There were no lights and no furniture. I slept on the floor on a hard carpet. All I heard from outside was music and singing. I think it was Arabic music and it was all I heard for days. They gave me food and bottles of water but not much to eat – the same wrapped Marks and Spencer roast chicken and salad sandwiches on white bread. The first time they brought me pork, which I told them I wasn't allowed to eat. I thought that was weird.'

'Very weird,' Dan said.

'I had no real idea of time, but later I knew it must have been five days. They took me away in a car. When they put me out, I was in Gloucester on a back street right next to my own car. They must have driven it there. It had a ticket. They didn't steal anything. They gave me back my bag and my cash and cards, and my phone and watch. It was a bit before twelve o'clock. They'd even charged my mobile and there was a note stuck to it. The first thing the note said was if I told anyone what had happened they would find me and punish me. I didn't know what they meant at first. The note also said to check my voice-mail and then to throw away my phone. It said to listen to my mother's message first. I kept the phone for a while but I knew the police would want it after *The Courant* ran the story about me lying about Venice. I hit it hard a few times with a rock and threw it in the rubbish. The police were very upset when I refused to tell them my password. I guess they've been trying to get into my backed-up data, but they can't have succeeded yet.'

Leila stopped to drink a mouthful of tea. The lawyer typed intently on his iPad. Chester gripped her mug with both hands, slack-jawed in blank disbelief.

She asked for an iPhone and the lawyer offered his. Leila punched in a number, entered her passcode, and put the phone on speaker to play her mother's last message. There were voices in the background – voices from the party, Dan thought – and Cressida was speaking in a frantic, whispering voice:

'Sweetheart, by the time you hear this something terrible will have happened. You must listen carefully to what I'm saying and please, please do exactly what I ask. Everyone thinks you went on that trip to see Kirsty in Venice. Please tell that to everyone who asks – it's very, very important. You mustn't tell them what really happened to you. I love you very much. I would do anything in the world for you. Anything. You must delete this message after you hear it – that's very important. I love you.'

Leila shut off the speaker and the lawyer reached out for his phone back.

'That's it. I'm so glad I didn't delete the message. They were her last words to me before the bomb went off. I had lots of other voicemails that night. There was one from the police telling me to call urgently, and there were loads from friends saying how upset they were, and sad, and how awful it all was. They didn't say exactly what happened, but I knew it must be something very bad. Then I checked the news on my phone and it said there had been an explosion at the house. I called the police and made up a story about being on a plane from Venice and they told me about the explosion and people being dead and that Jim Slight and Mum were seriously hurt.

'The police came to visit Mum in hospital before she lost consciousness altogether, and she went completely crazy. She was screaming and waving her arms. The stand with her drip bags went flying. The doctors made the police leave. They asked me about people Mum had seen recently and visitors to the house and whether I knew if anyone had ever threatened her. All I told them was the family had been getting threats for years, but nothing that seemed to worry them. That was the truth, but I didn't dare tell them what had happened to me.

'If I told anyone, I was afraid she would be in terrible trouble. She begged me to keep it a secret, but you're right. She's gone now and nothing can harm her. But I'm still going to be in serious trouble, aren't I? I'm not even sure why. I don't know what happened. Why would anyone do that to me?'

She stared at Dan with her wide, wet eyes, waiting for an answer. She looked different. Her shoulders, hunched and tight as she told her story, were looser now, and her face of pure terror had become one of relief more than fear. She was finally free of her secrets.

'I don't know why anyone would do what they did to you, Leila,' Dan told her. 'But we're going to London now to tell the police everything.' He reached out to touch her hand. 'There's no choice. Maybe you are guilty of withholding information, but you have an incredibly powerful explanation. I know they'll show a lot of sympathy.'

As Leila stood, Chester pointed to her ankle tag. 'That thing will send the police crazy the moment she leaves here. I'll call to tell them what's happening.'

Chapter Twenty-Nine

When Perry called, Dan was waiting in a visitors' room at New Scotland Yard while the police questioned Leila. He didn't give Perry time to speak. 'Why the fuck did you let Jess spend more time with those hotel people when you knew her cover was blown? How stupid was that?'

'I tried, Dan, I told her not go, but she wouldn't listen. What was I supposed to do?'

'She's a kid, Ainsworth. It was your job to talk sense into her. I'd have tied her up and locked her in a room.'

Perry went quiet. Dan thought he might be in tears. It was useless being angry. 'Okay, mate, I'm sorry. It's my fault for getting her into this mess in the first place. I tried talking to her myself. She was young and pig-headed. I guess we were the same once . . . Perry, are you still there?'

'Dan – I've got news,' Perry said. 'Maybe it's good news, I don't know, but the body's a man. It was the hotel doorman. He'd been stabbed and dumped behind the reception desk. That's all I know. It's not Jess, but she's vanished, Dan. These bloody animals have taken her. She managed to send me a short video of the two who attacked her. I couldn't make out much. It's grainy and there's lots of flashing lights, but I gave it to the police.'

Within minutes of Perry's call, news of Jess's disappearance began flashing on the visitors' room TV. Until then, it had been mostly about Cressida Chatstone's death, with historic footage of the Chatstone family. The first Viscount Chatstone appeared in a helmet and goggles, waving in black and white from the open cockpit of his doomed biplane. After that, he was walking jerkily along between Lloyd George and a young Churchill, all three with long black coats, top hats and swinging umbrellas. More recent video showed Cressida Chatstone as a young woman departing unsteadily from a Mayfair nightclub, and later sitting responsibly at her desk for a company portrait as the new executive chair. There were photos and video of Leila Chatstone, the twenty-five-year-old heiress, with talking heads arguing whether she was heading for the boardroom or for prison.

Dan had just filed from his laptop the story of Leila's confession. It would be online soon and her tale of terror and kidnap would be filling hours of TV and acres of newsprint. Friends would be interviewed, and friends of friends, and old teachers and university tutors, and former boyfriends. Every detail of her life would be hung out for all to see, and she would become one of the most talked-about people on the planet.

A *BREAKING NEWS* head ran across the TV screen: *MISSING JOURNALIST CAUGHT HER ABDUCTORS ON VIDEO.* The video was only about ten seconds. Two men were dancing to heavy rock in blinking lights. One was bearded and big but Dan couldn't see much more. The shorter guy was dark-haired, possibly Arabic. He knew the FBI would be trying to enhance the images. These men had murdered someone in order to take Jess alive. If that meant they attached value to her life, then Jess had become a commodity in these killers' plans.

He was exhausted.

· · ·

'Mr Brasher? . . . Sir?'

Dan stirred stiffly on the hard-backed chair where he had crashed into his first sleep for more than twenty-four hours.

'The commissioner would like to see you,' said a young police officer. Her solicitous expression made Dan uneasy.

'Really? What's happened?'

'Let me take you to her office.'

Commissioner Daneen Hassan came from behind her desk, which was empty but for a computer monitor and keyboard, and a red Costa coffee cup alongside two opened Sweet'n Low packets.

'Dan, I heard you were in New York. What a completely ghastly time this must be,' she said, directing him to sit at one end of a long grey sofa as she sat herself alongside him. 'It's awful news about the young woman you were working with. I'm so sorry.' Then she looked at him with wide, attentive eyes. 'How are you?'

'I'm okay, thank you. Where is Miss Chatstone?'

Hassan placed her hands in her lap and looked down at them. 'We've decided we should keep her detained.'

'Not again. Why? Didn't she explain everything?'

'This story she's told us, Dan. It's pretty incredible. She's refused to talk for days, destroyed her phone to hinder us, and now she's come up with this wild story about being kidnapped and held by mysterious masked men. Why on earth would she have kept this from us until now?'

'Because her dying mother made her promise—'

The commissioner put two fingers to her mouth to silence Dan.

'Just listen, please, and consider this lady's background. As an undergraduate at Cambridge, she attended classes in Islamic studies at the Faculty of Divinity. Then she changed her religion and kept it secret.'

'What's wrong with following the religion of the father she never knew?'

The commissioner went on. 'She's made headlines for her criticism of the government's Middle East policies. She's been accused of having sympathies for Hamas. She made secret trips to Pakistan, and she hates her family's own newspapers – among other things because she thinks they're too pro-Israel.'

'There's nothing much new in that. Her politics don't mean anything. They're all over the place. A few years ago, she thought it might be a good idea to exterminate the world's cows to save the ozone layer. And it's definitely no crime to search for your own father.'

'But what's happened to her father, Dan? Where's he vanished to? How can we be sure she's telling the whole truth?'

'Have you heard her mother's voicemail message?'

'Yes, we have, Dan, and all it might mean is that her mother *believed* her daughter was kidnapped. We don't know it wasn't a trick intended to blackmail Cressida Chatstone into cooperating with them.'

'So you're still ready to believe she was an accomplice in the murder of her mother and numerous others?'

The commissioner held up her palms to Dan and raised her shoulders. 'Who knows?'

'For what it's worth,' Dan said. 'Leila was bloody convincing when we were talking. I had to drag it out of her and she was completely terrified. Did she tell you about the pork sandwich? Why on earth would she make up something like that?'

The commissioner looked quizzical.

'She told me her captors gave her a pork sandwich,' Dan said. 'What Muslim gives another Muslim pork to eat?'

Hassan made a note. 'Thank you, but you'll forgive me for not allowing the Metropolitan Police's inquiries into multiple murders to hang on a prime suspect's claims about the contents of a single sandwich . . . a sandwich she claims was given to her by people she alleges kidnapped her.'

The commissioner stood. She was getting impatient.

'Thank you, Dan. We do this kind of a thing for a living, you know. We're keeping an open mind about the culprits – we've always kept an open mind.'

'Really? From what I can tell the only people you've hauled in for questioning have been Muslim.'

Hassan headed back behind her desk.

'All we can do is follow the evidence, and you know as well as I do which direction it's been heading. We still don't know Leila isn't lying to us. We don't know why she's played games all this time. And the father, Dan . . . why on earth is he hiding?'

. . .

Dan hurried along the Thames Embankment from New Scotland Yard to the Westminster Underground. He was shouting into his phone at Roy Jory.

'Listen to me, Roy. You can tell the human resources director, whatever his bloody name is, he can fuck off. I'm going to see Jess Hunter's father now and I refuse to be accompanied by some woke note-taking minder from HR, there to make sure I don't say the wrong thing. I don't give a shit about corporate liability, or whatever the fuck he's saying, and here's why . . . I AM LIABLE, okay? I'm liable for getting her into this mess. I'm liable for not taking proper care of her. I'm liable if they've killed her. And I'll thoroughly fucking deserve it if her father beats me to death on his doorstep. Goodbye.'

Dan kept walking. His pulse was racing. His head was thumping, his entire body ached … poor helpless Jess … crazy rich Leila … these maniacs who were stalking him. All his neural pathways were caving, his entire nervous system was blowing fuses. If he stopped, if he lost the momentum from rushing along this pavement, he was sure he would collapse in a useless heap.

He checked his phone on the way to catch the Tube to Jess's Brixton home. The Leila news had leaked:

CHATSTONE HEIRESS HELD AGAIN: TERROR CHARGES IMMINENT

Christ, she's going to be crucified.

Chapter Thirty

William Hunter sat in his fireplace armchair. His living room was dark, but for the flicker of a muted TV and the yellow beam of a reading lamp. The curtains were drawn to conceal him from the clutch of people with notebooks, microphones and cameras pacing the pavement outside.

Next to him, a wall of untidy bookshelves contained mostly beaten paperbacks. The only motion on his face was the reflected animation of the TV screen in his metal-framed spectacles.

His hands rested limply in his lap. On a small table was a mug with the *Daily Courant* masthead, and on the wall were two framed photos: in one, a gleeful girl, maybe four years old, was held high in the air by a laughing young man; in the other was exuberant Jess, in a graduation gown, her mortar board teetering as she pressed her head against her father's chest. On the mantel, a small black-and-white shot showed a happy young couple – the groom in a broad-lapelled double-breasted suit with a thin bow tie and a carnation, the bride in a lace bonnet and billowing white gown. Jess's parents had married in London soon after arriving from Kingston, Jamaica.

Dan didn't even try to imagine how William Hunter must be feeling about his lost daughter, or the visitor who had arrived at his door drowning in guilt.

The people camped on the pavement outside had said the police had told them not to knock. 'I've got an appointment,' Dan had said, and pressed the bell.

'He's from *The Courant*,' one said to the other. 'We're fucked.'

A uniformed police officer opened the front door and stepped aside for him to enter the hallway. He was a police liaison officer – assigned, along with a plainclothes detective, to be with William on the outside chance his daughter's kidnappers made contact to demand a ransom. No one was expecting that call.

The officer left William and Dan alone in the living room, where a black retriever eyed Dan without moving from its owner's feet.

William looked away from the TV as Dan sat in an armchair crowded with loud-coloured cushions.

'I've heard a lot about you over the past few weeks. You're quite a hero to my Jessie.'

'I'm so sorry, sir,' Dan began. There were other things Dan imagined saying, words of comfort, but when the moment came it seemed pointless.

The TV was showing Sky News. Jess's disappearance was a running story in Britain, the States, and much of the world. It had all the right ingredients: 'a tasty tale', they'd be telling each other in tabloid newsrooms – a pretty woman investigating a string of terrorist attacks had vanished without trace in Manhattan after fleeing two men who tried abducting her at a nightclub named CrashLanding.

All the channels and websites had picked up her painfully happy social-media pics and videos – in a pink bridesmaid's dress dancing a jig with the bride, throwing sticks for the family dog, posing mock-sultry in a flowery bikini.

Images from the cameras in Jess's hotel showed her running through the lobby towards the lift soon after midnight. Forty-five minutes later, three people were seen leaving the hotel, each wearing a hooded top. They were impossible to identify, but they were walking tightly together, and the New York police were confident the images showed two abductors leading Jess away.

When Dan had called Siobhan, she'd surrendered a little inside information. 'I've got to have something to tell the father,' he told her. 'Not for me to use, I promise.'

'Don't get his hopes up too much,' Siobhan said. 'The only good news, if you want to call it that, is we've had no claim of responsibility. After every other attack these people wasted no time claiming the credit. Maybe — just maybe — they're keeping her alive for some reason. But, between us and being realistic, I can't see why. Whoever they are, there's no doubt they're ready to kill anyone who gets in their way. Chances are they took her from the hotel to kill her and dump the body.'

'I'm not telling him that.'

The police had arrested Jess's date, Angelo Caputo, she said. 'He won't tell them a damn thing. He's terrified.'

Now, Dan told Jess's father what he knew as they sat together in the darkened living room. He tried hard to offer at least some reassurance and optimism, hoping it was enough to conceal his own deep fears. William listened without a word, glancing towards the TV as he drank from the *Daily Courant* mug. He held up the mug. 'It was a gift from Jessie a few days after she started work,' he said. 'You're sitting in her favourite chair. Those cushions she brought back from Benidorm when she was nineteen. It was her first trip abroad. She loved bright colours when she was young.'

'They're pretty lively,' Dan said. 'She dresses mostly in greys and blacks now.'

William nodded, with the shadow of a smile. He picked up a scrap of paper next to the landline phone beside him. 'I've had lawyers on the phone. They left a voice message. They said if Jessie comes to any harm I could make millions in the courts and it wouldn't cost me a penny – they'd only take a share of the damages. They said your newspaper exposed her to dangers she didn't know enough to handle.'

Dan didn't care. 'Do what you think is right, Mr Hunter. I wouldn't blame you or try to talk you out of it. This would never have happened but for me.'

They kept watching the TV. There was coverage of Ben Tremblay's search for a buyer among the private equity operators swooping on ailing newspapers all over Britain and the US. Someone was telling the TV reporter they would drive the newspapers to ruin while harvesting extravagant profits. Tremblay had already done a good job of that himself.

'Jess said she made a bad mistake when she was working on that Ben Tremblay attack,' William said.

'It was a small thing.'

'She said you were furious with her,' William said, without taking his eyes off the screen.

A new headline appeared, with a photo of Jess. *MISSING JOURNALIST FEARED DEAD*. William's head gave an involuntary jerk.

'Please don't pay too much attention to the headlines,' Dan said. 'They can be meaningless – it's how newspapers and television keep people's interest. You'll find out very quickly if there's any real news.'

'I know. It's hard to stop watching. I'll check in again later.' William switched the TV off. 'And don't worry about any lawyers. I already told them I'm not interested. I don't blame you or anyone. I know the woman Jessie has become. There's no stopping her and she's doing the work she wants to do.'

Dan was glad William was still talking about his daughter in the present tense.

'Jessie loves working with you,' he went on. 'She was crazy with excitement getting to go to New York. She said a lot of the reporters were afraid of you.' William's faint smile reappeared. 'My Jess doesn't scare so easy. The only trouble she ever had at school was when two white boys were giving her a hard time – two of them, mind you. They'd been at her for weeks before she let fly. One of the poor lads needed stitches. I think the coppers who came to see us were secretly impressed.'

'I've seen that in her myself,' Dan said.

William went on talking about his daughter, about her childhood and the bedtime books she had wanted read to her over and over – *Where the Wild Things Are*, Dr Seuss's *The Sneetches* – and the first poetry she liked hearing – *Nobody else but the rose bush knows / how nice mud feels / between the toes* – and about her spirit and mischief as a girl, her wild ambitions growing up, her charm and popularity, her fearlessness, her teenage heartbreaks, and the mother she hardly knew.

'I promised Jean we would both be proud of her,' he said. 'She'd be very proud, I know she would.'

His eyes brightened as he talked; he began looking almost happy, as if by reliving his daughter's life and imagining wonderful things to come, he was keeping her alive – that his stories were holding back the terrible possibility of what had happened.

'Her big dreams used to frighten me,' he said. 'I worried that the disappointment would crush her. She would talk crazy stuff, like becoming editor of *The Times* or writing a bestselling book. I would tell her, "Don't get ahead of yourself, it's a hard world out there." She would give me such a look of pity when I did. I wish I'd had her dreams at that age.'

Dan only listened. This man had invested all his lost ambition in his only child, made her the object of all his hope and love and purpose, and now she was gone – dead or alive, no one knew. There were no hopeful words of comfort he could offer. He felt like he needed to confess, but confess to what? How reckless he had been with the enthusiasm and trust of an eager and inexperienced girl? Pouring out his guilt might make Dan feel better, but it would be no help to William Hunter.

Dan had taken his own risks again and again, been too careless sometimes with his own life, but he had never put anyone else at risk. He had felt bad enough years ago, when he was doing a news desk stint and told a keen young casual there were no more shifts for him at *The Courant*. The casual immediately took off to Syria to freelance, covering the civil war. Within a few days, he'd disappeared and was never seen again. Dan had tried telling him Syria was too dangerous, that he didn't have the experience, but he wouldn't listen. Even so, Dan knew the man might never have died if only for a few extra shifts on *The Courant*. Who knew asking Jess Hunter to hang around a hotel for a few days could be a lethal assignment?

'I didn't dream I was putting her in any danger,' Dan said. 'I would do anything – anything – to bring her back safely, but we don't even know exactly why this happened. No one has a clue.'

William nodded. 'You've done lots of dangerous things, right? Wars and the rest?' he said.

'Yes.'

'That's one of the things Jessie wants to do. She reads all about female war correspondents. It's a terrifying life. I can't understand why she would want to see things like that. Why do you do it?'

'People need to know what's going on in these places. It's frightening, but it's exciting too, I've got to admit.'

William gave Dan a long, determined look.

'Jessie's going to be fine, I know it,' he said. 'She's a lucky girl; she's always been lucky.'

'Yes, sir,' Dan said.

PART
THREE

T*he man watched the video at his desk. The camera panned
along a bright palm-lined street, stopping at a corner by
an ivy-covered house with a blue front door. He saw the
camera come closer to look over a fence covered with purple and
white bougainvillea. As it did, a little girl came into view playing
on a scooter by a kidney-shaped swimming pool. She was wearing
pink shorts and a white sunhat and speeding towards a laughing woman, who was tall with long brown hair and balancing a
younger girl on her hip.*

He closed the laptop and reached for a phone to type.

Email it to him now and then we must talk about the
Hunter girl.

*The man had been looking at the latest news. He'd read with
the most interest the website of* The Daily Courant *of London.
An article by Daniel Brasher told Leila Chatstone's story of being
kidnapped by masked men. The story was already being picked
up by websites around the world. There were additional stories
on other websites saying the Metropolitan Police did not believe
Leila Chatstone and she was back in their custody. Dramatic headlines accompanied these stories:* KILLER IN A GUCCI GOWN
. . . HATRED OF THE GOLDEN GIRL WHO HAD IT
ALL . . . HIGH SOCIETY HEIRESS WHO PLOTTED
MANSION MASSACRE.

TV news had shown footage of the beautiful suspect meeting the King at Buckingham Palace and arriving with her late mother for a reception at 10 Downing Street, wearing a sweeping crimson dress.

The man made some notes on a yellow legal pad, sent another text, then walked towards the large four-poster bed to kneel and pray. He had prayed every day since his marriage twenty years before; but now his prayers had changed.

Chapter Thirty-One

'Oh, Danny, Danny – what have you got yourself into?' Laura could barely speak through her tears. Dan had called his wife the moment he saw the video. It was evening in London, early afternoon in Santa Monica, and his daughters were crying in the background.

'I can't explain now, but you must trust me,' Dan said. 'You and the girls are not safe staying at the house. People know where you are – dangerous people. They have been very close to you.'

Dan heard her new man Charlie Dugdale's angry voice: 'Gimme the phone, I want to talk to him.'

'Do not put that man on the phone. Just listen to me.'

'Where are you?' Laura said. 'What's going to happen?'

'I don't know what's going to happen, but you've got to get out of there straight away. And wherever you go, don't tell your folks. Don't call the police. Don't tell anyone. Don't tell me. Don't talk about it over the phone or text anyone. Don't use your mobile at all, or your bank cards. Buy a burner.'

He could feel his hot face and his racing heart and his tears. 'Laura ... I'm so sorry, but please do what I'm asking. I miss you. I can't even say how much. I've been crap to everyone, but most of all to you. I don't know what's wrong with me. I waste things and I wasted you and everything we had. My life had so many crazy moving parts, I just lost control. I stopped noticing how much you matter, how much we mattered to each other, but I love you. I'll always love you and want you forever. Please, please get out of that house.'

'What are you going to do, Dan? Where are you? Why don't you just get out, run away?'

'It's too late for that. These people are insane, and for some reason they're interested in me. There's no use stopping now. They'll find me if they want to. They killed Jim and Cressie Chatstone and Larry. They're holding Jake. Leila says she was kidnapped. This young reporter who's vanished – it's my fault. If you stay there, they'll take you and the girls too.'

Laura was crying again. 'Take care, take care,' she said. 'We'll leave straight away.'

Dan hadn't told Laura about the video, or the words that came with it: *You will be hearing from us again within hours, Mr Brasher. Tell no one. Remember your loved ones.*

The video had arrived moments after Dan reached his home in London after seeing Jess's father. He'd played it over and over, listening to Harriet giggling on her scooter, coloured ribbons streaming from its handlebars, aiming it straight at her mother. And Laura, a loose orange shirt over her swimsuit, making sounds of mock horror as she ran away. Amy in her arms, shrieking with delight. Laura's mother sitting on a sun lounger, laughing and clapping. That had been the moment the exact address of the house in Santa Monica appeared on the screen.

They must have parked their car in the street right outside and walked to within feet of his family. They wanted him to know they had his loved ones at their mercy. There was nothing these people weren't willing to do. But what did they want from him?

If Laura and the girls made it out of Santa Monica, he didn't know where they would go. He didn't want to know.

If he didn't know, no one could force him to tell. They might go to Queensland, where Laura's brother owned a property, or Alaska, which Laura had grown to love at school attending summer camps.

In his kitchen, Dan opened the fridge and took a beer from among the out-of-date food and cartons of sour milk. Ever since they'd left, he'd hated being in this house. The cold loneliness terrified him.

He pulled back the living-room curtains and looked through the fading light at the back garden. It was untouched since they'd left. The black trampoline by the apple tree was speckled grey, blitzed by birds. The play pool was mostly deflated, its happy colours dulled by dirt, the rainwater it had collected green and pungent. Dandelions and other weeds had reoccupied the flower beds Laura had loved and tended. Upstairs in the girls' room he looked for some of the clothes they'd left behind, just to smell them.

He collapsed on a sofa. It was unbearable to look at the mantelpiece and the line of family photos, with all their freeze-framed happiness. He put on loud music. He loved the body-throbbing sound of the cello and sat with his eyes closed, feeling his bones keep the rhythm. For a while, half asleep, the vibration of the mobile in his pocket got mixed up with the music.

When he looked, the screen showed *JESS HUNTER*.

'Is that Mr Daniel Brasher? '

The voice was muffled. Dan couldn't even tell the caller's gender.

Chapter Thirty-Two

New York

Dan prowled the Terminal 8 concourse at JFK, trying to avoid the bars, as he waited for the next call. It was mid-afternoon, and it had been three hours since he'd arrived on the first morning flight out of London. The call in London had been specific: 'Wait at JFK for our instructions. There will be a surprise for you.'

The next message was quick when it came: he should take a taxi ten miles to a one-way street in Brooklyn off Bushwick Avenue, and find a church. Outside, he would see a blue Honda Accord with a black towel draped over the front passenger seat. 'Your surprise will be in the trunk,' said the same muffled voice. 'Make sure no one is following you.'

As his taxi crawled through streets choked with traffic, Dan dreaded what waited for him. He thought of Jess's father, in his living room fixed to his TV, holding himself together with the unreasonable belief his daughter would be safe.

He arrived in a modest street lined untidily with brick and clapboard houses and a stunted tree now and then. Glorious graffiti covered an abandoned building. An old man, mumbling angrily, was bent so far into the hood of a battered SUV his feet had left the ground; an Amazon lady carried a box back and forth, puzzling over house numbers. He envied their everyday priorities. A young woman pushed a stroller, whispering comfort to a tearful toddler as he reached up for his mother to hold him, and Dan remembered the cry of an outstretched child and the joy of knowing your touch was the only thing in the world it wanted.

He took for granted that they knew where he was. They would be tracking his phone, or watching him from one of these buildings, or a nearby car. He didn't care if he was walking into an ambush to be snatched himself; it would be a relief almost.

The church was modern, with a blank façade of orange brick. The blue Honda was parked at the entrance; he saw the black towel, but he kept walking, unable at first to face what he had to do. He wished he hadn't come, had just called the police and left everything to them, but he knew that was impossible. These people were toying with him, this was some kind of sick game, and he knew he had to follow their rules. They wanted him to be here – for him to open the trunk and look.

The old man was now hammering at something under his hood, but he was fifty yards away and otherwise there was no one in sight. Following his caller's instructions, Dan opened the unlocked driver's door and pulled the lever to pop the trunk.

The body was on its back, naked, bound with black rope at the hands and feet. A plastic bag over its head was tied at the neck and clung so tightly to the face Dan could see the wide eyes and open mouth. He tore open the bag with both hands to expose the face. Its skin was a pale shade of blue and the open eyes red with blood. Dan slammed the trunk and leaned against the car.

It was Jake Abrams.

Jake had been so sure they would get him in the end. He had begged the family for sanctuary – the family he had risked his life for again and again, the family he had made proud with Pulitzers, who'd enjoyed power and celebrity thanks to his newspaper. Now, here he was, after thirty years of loyalty, suffocated by a plastic bag and dumped in the trunk of a car in the back streets of Brooklyn, denied even the swift dispatch of a bullet to the head. The news would reach the Wylers soon in their Park Avenue bunker. What good had it done them, leaving him out there to die? What was cold-hearted Howard Wyler's reward?

Dan should have guessed it might be Abrams; his guilt over Jess had blinded him. Perhaps she would be next, perhaps they were keeping her alive for a purpose. Dan hid the caller ID on his phone and dialled 911. He gave the dispatcher the details and the address, asked her to repeat the information, and hung up. He had gone a few hundred yards when he heard the first sirens and the next text arrived:

You have been looking for this man and now you have found him. He has suffered the punishment he deserved. The girl is still with us, Mr Brasher – for now.

Chapter Thirty-Three

Dan had finished four large drinks at the Second Avenue bar by the time Perry Ainsworth heaved onto the stool next to him. The bartender had been leaning next to the register, looking at Dan. She could tell something was wrong.

'What are you having?' Perry said to Dan, catching the eye of the bartender as he spoke. She was shaking her head. 'For me, a gin martini with plenty of olives,' Perry told her.

'And the same again for me,' said Dan, pushing his glass in the bartender's direction. The glass was empty but for ice that hadn't had much time to melt.

'You sure, sweetheart?' the bartender said. 'It'll be your fifth in the last half hour.'

Dan looked at the bartender as he pointed into his empty glass. 'Same again, please,' he repeated.

Perry put his arm around Dan's shoulders. 'Dear, dear boy,' he said. 'You do look bloody rough. You don't have the experience to drink like this.'

'I'm learning fast,' Dan said.

Perry raised his arms in surrender, and then reached to pick an olive from the cocktail stick in his glass.

'They're saying Abrams had been dead only a few hours,' he said. 'They didn't even waste a bullet on the poor chap. The office couldn't get hold of you so I filed a quick story. They'll get more detail from the news agencies – I needed to get here to see you. Do they even know you flew back to New York? You didn't tell me.'

Dan hunched over the bar, swirling his drink and staring into the glass like a tea-leaf reader looking for a message.

'The Wylers sacrificed him to save themselves,' he said. 'Like barbarians appeasing the gods. They thought abandoning him would keep them safe. He was an offering.'

'Yes, well, that hasn't worked out so well for them, has it?' Perry said.

'They left poor Jake out there to burn. And now Jess . . .'

'We can't blame anyone but ourselves for Jess.'

'Yeah, us – a couple of buccaneering hacks ever eager to please . . . cogs in the machine. That poor kid. Her dad's heart-broken. I don't know why he didn't kill me. Such a decent man. He's sitting at home trying to persuade himself she'll be fine. He's so proud of her; she's his whole life. God, I wish I'd sent her back to London. She was so pissed off with me over that stupid Tremblay story. It was nothing, and I treated her like shit.'

The bartender tried pouring extra tonic into his glass, but Dan pushed her hand away.

'It looks like the Met will be keeping Leila inside,' Perry said. 'They still haven't decided what else to charge her with beyond obstruction. They seem set on the theory she conspired with her father and others to blow up the place, and it's one part of a much bigger conspiracy.'

'Do you believe that?' Dan asked.

'Goodness only knows. It's odd the Pakistanis still can't locate her father. He's bound by now to know they're looking for him.'

'She wasn't fond of her mother, that's for sure,' Dan said. 'She hated working at ChatCorp, but couldn't bring herself to leave. There's something tragic about her. She's always been so helpless, like she's trapped in a fire she can't escape unless someone gives her permission.'

Dan threw back his drink and rattled the ice to attract the bartender. She was pretending not to hear.

'Who cares about this job?' he said. 'We lease our lives out to these fucking people.'

'The Chatstones? You sound like you hate them.'

'They don't care about us and I honestly don't care about them – well, maybe the girl. It'll be fine for all the media moguls. The Wylers, the Chatstones – they'll be fine.'

'Those two moguls are stone dead, Dan,' Perry said.

'It's the dynasties I'm talking about, mate. They'll live on. Thousands of people are losing their jobs, but it'll make no difference to them.' Dan rattled his ice again. 'Miss, can you please come to the rescue of a thirsty man,' he called. He held up his empty glass, but Perry took it from him.

'Calm down, old man, that's enough for today.'

'Ha! Peregrine Ainsworth pleads for restraint at the bar. That's a headline.'

Perry pushed Dan's glass out of reach and the bartender took it away.

'What are you going to do?' Perry said. 'We can't stop now.'

'People keeping dying, Perry, and it isn't going to stop.'

'It's our job to tell the story, isn't it?'

'Come on, man – Jim, Larry, Jake, Wyler, the Honourable Cressie – they've all been murdered, and for all we know so has Jess. We *are* the fucking story, and we're helpless.'

Perry took hold of Dan's hand. 'Do you remember those wonderful lines from *Waiting for Godot*?' he said.

'Oh, please, spare me any smart-arse literary quotes.'

'Listen now, it's about us. One desperate character says, "I can't go on like this," and the other replies, "That's what you think."'

Dan looked at Perry. His cherry-coloured face was a road map of broken veins, the vivid evidence of his life's high mileage; but his pale blue eyes were bright and humorous – you could see that even now. It was a sturdy, honest face, full of stories – stories of sunshine and of storms, like the rings on the trunk of an old tree.

'I fucking know I've got to go on, Perry,' he said. 'Because they've got me by the throat.'

'What on earth do you mean?'

It was in that moment Dan decided to trust his old friend with everything.

Chapter Thirty-Four

The bird was pecking hard again on the barred window. It had arrived every dawn for three days, as regular as an alarm, a beautiful thing with a white and reddish chest and dark wings. Jess thought it might be insane, every day at war with itself, never working out it was mistaking its own reflection for an unwelcome intruder. That, and the rat – and the black-haired arm, if it counted – were the only living things she had seen since they'd locked her in the basement.

The only light was coming through the bottom of the locked door and the small window. The rat was awake, tugging with its teeth at the old mattress she was lying on. If she kept still, it would stay with her. It had scared her at first, but now, after three nights trapped here, she almost appreciated the company. The basement was cold and the air had a sweet and putrid smell. The smell had been more bearable before she'd traced it to the decomposing remains of two mice in traps. Her lavatory was a small metal wastepaper bin she had positioned as far away as she could in the empty room; it had yet to be replaced in spite of her numerous appeals shouted through the locked door.

Jess had heard voices, but never clearly enough to be certain of the words or even the language – not until five minutes ago, when she'd heard a man on the phone outside the door.

'She's okay. She's eating and drinking.' It was an American voice with no trace of an accent. An unintelligible voice was coming through the phone.

'When will he be here?' the man outside asked. He listened again. 'Okay. What will we do with her if he doesn't cooperate? . . . Yes, understood. There'll be no choice. What about the others? . . . We'll be ready, let us know.'

The door opened and the black-haired arm reached into the room with her latest meal. The same arm always delivered food, usually a sandwich containing pastrami or processed turkey with a bottle of water.

This time it came with a voice, the same voice that had been on the phone. 'You'll be seeing your boss later today,' he said, and the door closed.

Jess called out, 'What boss? When will my boss be here?' There was no reply, only the sound of disappearing footsteps. The rat was gone too.

She could feel another panic attack coming. They were always waiting to pounce – the pounding heart, crushing chest pain, the sweating, shakes and sobbing. It felt like she would die before they had the chance to kill her.

Whenever they happened, she would try conjuring up an ideal memory. Sometimes it worked . . . she was in the living room with her dad, her stockinged feet tucked under the sleeping dog, watching TV – something stupid, like *Love Island.* Her dad was ignoring the screen, his head in a book, but he'd keep annoying her by interrupting to read something out. He always did that and it had always got on her nerves. Now it was her happy place.

But these tricks never worked for long and, when Jess thought she couldn't possibly survive, she would see her father in his living-room chair hearing the news of her death, and cry again imagining that. She didn't know who was keeping her or why, but she did know what they were capable of and that she was helpless against them.

She tried exercise to stay calm: jumping jacks and push-ups. She managed one hundred push-ups non-stop and could have kept going.

Jess had expected to be killed when they came through her hotel door. They were too strong for her to put up a useful struggle, and her neck had bled, they'd pressed so hard with the knife. When they took her out of the hotel, the body of the old man who'd unlocked the hotel entrance was on the floor at the reception desk. They told her he was dead.

She hadn't thought they would find her hotel – but, of course, that had been why Angelo, her fake fucking friend, had wanted to pick her up.

Other than voices, the only sound she'd heard here was the Islamic call to prayer coming from speakers on the other side of the door. At first it was a beautiful sound, but after hearing it five times a day, it was like a death threat.

What had the voice meant about her boss? It had to be Dan. What had happened to him?

Chapter Thirty-Five

Dan had never in his life felt this afraid. This was not a risk based on cool calculations. His life was in their hands and nothing he did could have an impact on his chances of survival.

It had been a sunny day and at lunchtime the streets were crowded, and he felt safe. When someone in a hooded coat, whose face he couldn't see, approached him outside a shoe repair shop on East 66th Street, he thought they must be looking for directions.

'Excuse me,' a voice said. It was a man with an East End accent. 'See that SUV double-parked fifty yards along the way?' When Dan said yes, the man told him, 'They said you'd come with us without making a fuss, and you knew why.'

They walked towards the black-windowed SUV and its yellow rear lights flashed as the back door began to rise. A hood came over Dan's head and the man's hands pressed him into the vehicle's seatless rear.

The door closed and Dan was handed a bulky plastic bag. 'Take everything off. Everything,' the man said. 'And put this on.'

Dan could tell it was a tracksuit in his hands. He put it on and the tailgate opened again. Two men whispered for a few seconds, then the SUV took off with the tailgate whirring shut.

'Is anyone there?' Dan said into the silence.

'I'm here,' said the English voice. 'Me and the driver.'

'What's happened to my belongings? My clothes, my phone, my wallet?'

'They'll be safe,' was all the man said.

The SUV moved at a tame pace, the driver no doubt keen to avoid the inconvenience of a police stop. Dan knew at first they were travelling west, but soon lost any sense of direction.

He didn't know who these people were, or where they were taking him, but Jess was out there somewhere and, whatever was going to happen, Dan was doing this for her and his family.

His one shred of hope was the knowledge that if they wanted simply to kill him, he would be dead by now.

After about fifteen minutes of stops and turns and traffic slowdowns, they were moving more smoothly and faster on a winding road. He could hear traffic but no heavy trucks. Dan guessed they were on a parkway. He heard humming. His companion must have been browsing music on his phone; it sounded like 'Satisfaction'. A piece of bread was pushed into Dan's hand, but he wasn't hungry.

After a couple of hours the English voice said, 'This is the exit,' and he heard the driver's acknowledging grunt. They turned onto a slower road. When they turned again, it was a rough and unfinished road. When the SUV pulled to a sharp halt, Dan was pretty sure he heard the steady grind of an electric gate opening.

It was windy outside. The rush of leaves and the creak of trees, and birds, plenty of birds, were the only sounds. He was taken down some stairs and placed on a hard stool. He heard footsteps leaving, and a man say, 'Take off the hood.'

The only furniture in the room was a square table with a green Formica top and a stool. On the table was a black Lenovo laptop between two small speakers and a phone plugged into a charger. There were high shallow windows along one wall and the mechanical drone nearby of what sounded like a boiler.

The laptop came to life and the screen showed it was a little after three in the afternoon. Through the speakers, a muffled voice began: 'Good afternoon, Mr Brasher. We hope your trip was not too uncomfortable. We are sorry to have taken your possessions, but it was a necessary precaution to be sure you were not being tracked. If you speak, we can hear you.'

Dan replied, 'Why am I here? Why have you been pursuing me?'

'You are here to be our messenger, and this message will be the most important of your life. Many lives will depend on your obedience. You must deliver this message exactly as we say.'

'Are you the people responsible for these bombs and deaths?'

'We are serving a righteous cause, and God is our guide. We are delivering his wrath. But our work is not yet complete and you are going to help us.'

'I don't know how I can help you. You have killed innocent people and no one understands why. How have the murders and misery you've caused served God? How did Leila Chatstone help you in your attack in England?'

'Our work has depended on many helpers and no one has died except for our great cause. Unless you cooperate with us, there will be more attacks and many more deaths. We are not giving you a choice, Mr Brasher. We have little time. You must follow our instructions.'

'But who are you? Who do you represent?'

'We have never met, Mr Brasher, but we have a shared experience,' the voice said. 'Do you remember Afghanistan, when the British and American occupation was at its height? Do you remember the wedding massacre you saw with your own eyes?'

'I remember it very well,' Dan said.

'Your report in *The Daily Courant* seethed with anger at the barbarism you had witnessed, about the women and children who were slaughtered by the American drone.'

'It was the most horrifying thing I'd ever seen,' Dan said. The voice he was hearing was muffled but its English was excellent.

'For me, it was the greatest tragedy of my life. The unbearable suffering has stayed with me all these years. The grief and sadness have never faded. The anger lives inside me still, growing and growing. I want to tell you all about it.'

Dan was then told what he must do.

'We want you to use the phone in front of you to dictate to your London office every word of what will now appear on the computer screen. It must appear in *The Daily Courant* under your own name.'

Dan was horrified by what he read. 'This can never appear in *The Courant* under my name. I don't know who you are, I only have your word. You want me to help you hold the free press to ransom, but I've no way of knowing if this story is telling the truth.'

'The demands we make are real and must be carried out. We demand no ransom. We do not want money from anyone. It is justice we seek.'

The laptop screen went black, then flickered grey, before an image appeared. The camera was handheld and moving shakily as it came close to a face. 'Speak to him,' a voice said.

'Dan?' Jess said, raising her right hand weakly. 'I can't see you. Can you hear me?'

Jess moved close to the camera and her face shocked him. It was dazed and vacant. Her feelings seemed to have gone beyond her ability to show them. Her hair reached below her shoulders over a sleeveless top that was black and sequined. She was wearing a necklace of small green stones. She was still dressed from her night out.

'Hey, Jess,' he said. 'Oh, it's so good to see you.'

'I've been locked away in this basement by myself for days,' she said. 'I'm so scared.'

'Jess, I'm talking to them. We're talking things through. I'm doing everything I can. We're going to get you out of this.'

'I don't know where I am,' she said. 'I don't know what they want. I don't know who they are.'

The screen went black again and the muffled voice resumed.

'Mr Brasher, you know what you must do to save your friend. You must deliver our message. Even if you were to take your own life, people you love will pay for your failure. We will find your family, however long it takes. If you follow our orders, your family will be safe and this young woman will be released. But, if you fail us, they will be punished. They will die if we even suspect you of talking to the authorities.'

'Why are you doing this? What do you think it will achieve? You have murdered innocent people. You have not served God – you have sinned against Him.'

'You will have that answer soon, Mr Brasher. Perform this task and it will be a matter of days until we meet again one last time. Then you will understand our grief and anger. Dictate what you read, Mr Brasher. Do not dare to change one word.'

Dan took hold of the phone. Within minutes of filing this story, millions all over the world would be reading it. Every newspaper, every news website and TV channel, in every language, would repeat it. It would look like the story of his career, yet, for all he knew, it didn't contain a single truth; one line he knew for sure was a glaring lie. But he had no choice.

'I'm in a difficult situation,' he told Roy Jory. 'But I have a huge story. It will explain itself, but I have no time to reach a laptop so I need someone who can take copy.'

'Are you okay, Dan?'

'I'm good, just under rather a lot of pressure. You'll understand from the story.'

Dan began dictating, amazed in the circumstances to find himself worried about the story's clumsy phrasing. When he had finished, Jory came back on the phone.

'Good grief, man, this is unbelievable,' he said. 'Where are you?'

Dan heard footsteps from behind him. 'I can't speak now,' he said. 'Sorry if the copy's a bit rough. I need to go.'

As he disconnected, two arms reached to place a hood over Dan's head and he glimpsed a tattoo in the light of the desk lamp. He recognised at once what it meant. It was two eights – 88, that's all – but Dan knew 88 meant Heil Hitler; H was the eighth letter in the alphabet. It was a symbol popular round the world among white supremacists. The man who had hooded him could not be a Muslim. No devout Muslim would be seen with that, or any, tattoo: tattoos were haram in Islam – forbidden by God. Who were these people?

Chapter Thirty-Six

The FBI director, Alexander L. Livermore III, was standing behind his desk. He was tall and his white hair was military-short. His deep voice and gritty features might have projected gravitas if he hadn't been licking his lips between every sentence.

Livermore had based himself in New York on the orders of the president, and Siobhan had been summoned before dawn to talk about her friend the English reporter whose story was shocking the world. The call hadn't woken her; she had been phoning and texting Dan all night without success.

Director Livermore was in a panic, she was told. The White House chief of staff had been on the phone to him, and the president was not happy. The FBI, the NYPD and the entire US intelligence network already looked like fools in the face of these attacks. The news industry was afraid and furious. Howard Wyler had been one of the president's oldest friends and *The New York World* her most reliable champion. And now this incredible story.

When Siobhan had arrived, Livermore was alone in his office. She could see him through the glass door on the phone. 'You better wait,' a man told her as she was about to knock. 'That's an important call.' But Livermore had seen Siobhan and waved for her to come into the room. The man moved reluctantly aside.

On the phone, Livermore was listening more than talking.

'I understand . . . I'm not familiar with the author, no, but we're making inquiries . . . With respect, I understand very well. We are doing all we can . . . Yes, Madam President.'

The call ended and he dropped the phone on the desk, letting out a low groan. 'Oh, boy,' he said.

He sat across from Siobhan, tongue still sliding, bony hand moving oddly back and forth above his desk like he was stroking an invisible cat.

'She called as soon as she woke up,' he said.

'I see it's being leaked she's talking to the defence secretary about using the military.'

Livermore didn't respond.

He reached over to shake Siobhan's hand. 'Hi there,' he said. Siobhan had known Livermore since she'd joined the FBI, long before he got the top job.

'This English reporter,' he said. 'You and he are old friends, am I right?'

'He's my oldest friend, sir. We met in high school.'

'I'm told these Brit newspapers sometimes get a bit loose with the truth. What kind of journalist is he?'

'*The Daily Courant* is a trusted newspaper and Brasher's their most high-profile correspondent. He began his career on *The World*.'

Livermore picked up an iPad with an image of that morning's *Daily Courant* front page. 'I see . . . well, this story of his is quite extraordinary.'

The Courant had abandoned its traditional, muted display, resorting to an all-caps headline with three decks across the entire front page:

TERRORISTS THREATEN
MORE ATTACKS UNLESS
NEWSPAPERS CLOSE

The Courant and New York World
given 72-hour deadline

Beneath the headline was a large photo of Dan – younger, and better groomed. Next to the photo were three lines of bold type:

By DANIEL BRASHER
who met Islamist terror leaders
somewhere in the United States

His story occupied the newspaper's first five pages, with photographs of Cressida Chatstone, Howard Wyler, Ben Tremblay, and Jim Slight and Jake Abrams. Slight and Abrams were together in one shot, arms around each other's shoulders. There were pictures of the devastation left by the bombs at Chatstone House and the Plaza-Asturias Hotel.

The story set out an encounter at an undisclosed location with two men who had told Dan they were father and son. The father had said his name was Joram and the son Hayyan. Dan described sitting in a windowless room with the men, who said they were Afghans. They were dressed in jeans and plain white T-shirts, with their faces covered. Joram, who did more talking, had a bulky frame; Hayyan was taller and muscular. Dan wrote that two more masked men had stood on either side of him as he asked questions and took notes.

Joram was quoted at length talking about the deaths of his wife and four of his five children at a wedding outside Kabul. 'They were killed from the air by the Americans,' he said. 'My three-year-old daughter died in my arms. Her beautiful mother was blown to pieces.'

Joram identified numerous stories in the *World* and *Courant* he said were filled with lies and hid the truth about American and British 'barbarism' in Iraq, Afghanistan and Syria.

He said these lies had been repeated around the world in other media. They had misled millions, and enabled 'the aggressors to continue their oppression and savagery'.

Both men claimed they were not acting alone. 'We are agents of the global jihadist struggle,' Hayyan said. 'The full might of their holy cause is with us.' Jihadists inside the United States and Britain were working with them, along with American and British sympathisers who shared their anger. Their aim was 'to decapitate the messengers who have deceived the world'.

'These newspapers deserve to die,' Dan reported Joram had told him. 'Let their deaths be a lesson to media everywhere of the vengeance awaiting them if they lie again about the murderous military imperialism of America and Britain.'

This group, Joram was quoted as saying, had shown it could defeat the highest security, and its members were prepared at any time to do so again. The deadline for announcing the closure of both titles was seventy-two hours from noon today New York time.

'If this deadline is not met, many deaths will quickly follow,' Dan said Joram had told him.

The last sentence of this long story said: 'The managements of *The Daily Courant* and *The New York World* would make no comment for this article.'

The appearance of Dan's story on the *Courant* website had already led to scores of law enforcement raids on addresses in Britain and the United States. Averaging out various media estimates, it appeared more than three hundred people, almost all of them Muslim, had been detained for questioning.

'We need to speak to this friend of yours so he can tell us everything he knows,' Livermore said, still looking at his iPad.

'Sir, I've not been able to make contact with Brasher. I've been calling his cell all night. For all we know, he might be a captive of these people. They might have already killed him.'

Siobhan paused, shocked how clinical and detached her words sounded, as if this were just any case.

Livermore looked indifferent. 'We'll know soon enough whether he's dead or alive,' he said. 'But if he's alive, and not their captive, Brasher should be eager to tell us what he knows. Lives are at stake, and so is his newspaper.'

Siobhan pushed on. 'I last spoke to Brasher four days ago, and I know of only one person who has spoken to him since. His newspaper's editor-in-chief told us they spoke when Brasher filed his story to London last night. They haven't heard from him since. We know his debit card was used last night at an ATM in uptown Manhattan. We linked the withdrawal with CCTV cameras and the card was used by a man in a hooded white tracksuit carrying a black bag. We don't know for sure it was Brasher and I can tell you he never dresses that way. If he's free and alive, it makes no sense that he hasn't been in touch.'

Livermore clutched the iPad to his chest and turned his furrowed face upwards, his tongue still sliding between his moist lips. He kept gazing at the flickering strip lighting, seeming to hope it would give him some solutions.

'The Lord alone knows how the newspapers will react,' he said. 'The Met can't get any sense out of the *Courant* people in London, and that sad sack Francis Wyler is apparently in a total panic. I'm hearing he's inclined to shut the paper down. The president's quite rightly keeping out of it, but she told a security briefing this morning she hopes they follow the administration's firm rule never to yield to threats like this.'

'That's easy for her to say, sir, but we're in no position to guarantee we can keep them safe,' Siobhan said.

Back in her own office, she felt a helpless tear on her cheek. She sent another text to Dan's phone – *Where ARE YOU?!?!?!* – but, as with all the others, it wasn't delivered.

Her job was hard enough. She had seen plenty of evil and anguish and forced herself to toughen up. Years ago, with the DEA in Mexico, she had visited a shack in Veracruz where a man, his wife, and five children had all been murdered in some local drug dispute. Their bodies were piled in a bloody heap with flies crawling all over them. They had been there for days in this little shack where they'd lived. But the shack was so hot, and so filled with the sweet stink of rotting flesh and the hideous droning of flies, that she ran outside and collapsed. She'd had bad dreams for weeks, and the sound of a single fly would bring it all back.

There were other shocks, and even though they didn't compare with that sweltering afternoon in Veracruz, the job at first had seemed overpowering. But she'd coped – she'd had to. She'd seen other mutilated bodies, and the heartbreak of survivors, at home and in other countries, and had learned, with time and determination, how to detach herself.

But with Dan it was different; she couldn't detach herself from him. Dan was almost all she could think about – whether his body was somewhere riddled with bullets, or in a car trunk suffocated with a plastic bag.

Chapter Thirty-Seven

'Amazing, old boy, what an extraordinary story. I can't remember anything like it, not ever,' Perry said. He was at Dan's hotel door in his pinstripe suit and fedora, shillelagh in one hand and a bottle of Johnnie Walker Blue in the other.

'It's the biggest story of your career. So big I gather the techies in London are afraid all the traffic might bring down our website. I'd say congratulations if it wasn't likely to put us both out of work. Have you any idea at all where you met them? Were you able to record their voices?' Perry paused and peered around at Dan's room. 'What are you doing hiding out in a dump like this?' He frowned at the sight of two glasses he had taken from a shelf above the sink and began washing them.

It was a tiny room, with a single bed against the wall, a corner sink, and a sunken red armchair next to a wicker side table in front of a small flat-screen TV. It was a third-floor walk-up hotel west of Broadway, ninety-nine dollars a night. Dan felt like a fugitive in a 1950s gangster movie; there actually was a neon sign on the wall outside his window. He had crashed for a couple of hours on the bed, and already he could see a red row of bed-bug welts on his right forearm. He would have preferred a wilderness hideout like Jake Abrams's, but had no time to work out where to go.

His abductors had driven him back to Manhattan, freed him in Harlem – still wearing the same white tracksuit – and given him forty dollars, a receipt from a luggage storage address, and a blue flip phone with instructions to keep it turned on at all times. With the receipt, he'd retrieved a bag containing his clothes, credit cards, passports, and his phone. Then he'd taken out cash at an ATM to pay for the hotel and a cheap laptop from Best Buy.

It was too risky seeing anyone; Dan was afraid he wouldn't stand up to hours of questions from the FBI if they were to get their hands on him. He'd turned off his phone and found a hotel that was content to deal in cash only. Dan had invited Perry because he needed someone who could tell the real story in case it all went wrong for him.

Before Perry arrived, Dan was deep in the red chair with the weight of the world pinning him down. It was his life's worst hangover without a drop to blame for it. He had been watching wall-to-wall morning coverage on the news channels and finding it hard to look each time *The Courant* front page appeared.

Perry handed Dan a generous shot of whisky. Dan set it aside on the wicker table and drank from his soda can. He had already told Perry everything about how these people were tracking him, and about their messages and threats and how they had led him to Jake Abrams's body. Now he had to tell him the truth about his 'greatest exclusive'.

'It's all bullshit, mate,' he said.

Perry's glass came to a halt halfway to his mouth. 'You what?' he said.

'It's bullshit. It isn't true. They told me exactly what to write. They showed me Jess trapped somewhere and said they'd kill her. I didn't even see anyone. One muffled voice spoke to me over a laptop and made me file it. They set it out on the screen and gave me a phone, to dictate to London.'

Perry's drink was gone before he spoke again.

'Good lord, old boy. Why would they do that?'

'I think I know why. I don't believe they're Islamists at all.'

'How do you work that out?'

'I saw a white supremacist tattoo on someone's arm in the basement. Two eights, that's —'

'I know. It means Heil Hitler. The German neo-fascists came up with it as a secret sign after the swastika was banned. That's evidence, but it's not conclusive. They said they had Americans helping. They could have recruited all sorts of nutters. Maybe he's a neo-fascist reborn as an Islamist terrorist. Some of these people are crazy enough.'

'But that's not all,' Dan said. 'The man I spoke to through the laptop told me he was the father of the family wiped out years ago in a drone blunder at a wedding near Kabul. He knew I covered that story and was there at the scene.'

'Why doesn't that support his story?'

'Because I know that father is dead. He blew himself up in a suicide attack six months later. I filed it at the time, but it never made the newspaper. Even the bombing only made the bottom of a left-hand page. Whoever these people are, I think they saw my piece and they've spun a bullshit story around it.'

'It's a big *if*, Dan – the world's got a long history of crackpot alliances . . . your enemy's enemy is your friend and all that. If you're right, these people have pulled off one of the greatest bluffs in the entire history of murder and mayhem. A gang of homicidal neo-fascists have tricked the world into hunting down Muslims while they go about their evil work. But why, Dan? What would they do it for?'

'Fuck knows,' Dan said.

They sat in silence for a moment, Perry sipping more whisky and Dan with his soda. A garbage truck clattered in the street below; a couple were shouting at each other in the next room.

Dan couldn't regret what he had done. Wouldn't Perry – wouldn't anyone – have done what he had? If the act of writing that story had saved the lives of Jess, Laura and the girls, he didn't care what anyone thought. No story he could ever write would make him happier. And yet he felt wrecked all the same. Hundreds of people had been detained, governments were in crisis talks, two of the world's most distinguished newspapers might close; and at the office, they had no doubt, absolutely none, that he was telling the truth. Jim Slight had trusted his stories without question, and the top people at *The Courant* still did.

There was no more reliable reporter on *The Courant* than Daniel Brasher. Sometimes, in his columns, Perry blended separate characters into one and refined their quotes to fit the smooth flow of his prose. Perry never regarded this as dishonest. 'I'm subtle sometimes with the truth, that's all,' he once told Dan. But Dan never toyed with the facts. 'Unimpeachable,' he once heard Slight tell a sub-editor with questions about his copy.

Perry reached for the whisky bottle. 'And you couldn't put anything about the tattoo and the fake dad in your piece for fear they'd kill Jess and go after your family.'

'They'd kill Jess for sure. They've killed everyone else, and Laura can't stay hidden forever.'

'Whether it's Islamists or not, the threat isn't a lie,' Perry said. 'A lot of people are dead already. The newspapers will need to be bloody quick making up their minds what to do. The office says the prime minister has asked to see Roy Jory.'

The *Courant* front page was filling the TV screen again, and Dan turned it off.

Perry stood. 'I need to go. I've a couple of hours to file a column and they'll think it very odd if I don't. If they decide to close, I daresay they'll order my immediate return to London. They'll definitely stop footing my Ritz-Carlton bill.'

He checked the angle of his fedora in the cracked mirror above the sink.

'One last word, old pal. I've got to get this off my chest. You know I can be relied upon to say nothing, but if you want my advice, it's too dangerous taking these people at their word. Don't you at least have to let the law know this whole business might have nothing to do with Islamists?'

'But if I tell them and it gets out, they'll know for sure it came from me. They'll kill Jess.'

Perry grabbed his shillelagh. 'But you can't trust these damned people. Look at what they've done – they could kill Jess no matter what you do. Can you get the information to Siobhan somehow without anyone knowing? At least if she knows, she could do something without telling anyone the details.' He paused at the open door. 'I'll keep quiet, I promise, but think about it, please.'

The door closed and Dan crushed the empty soda can in his hand and dropped it on the stained carpet. It was true he couldn't be sure Jess's captors would keep their word, but what choice had they given him? He wasn't sure he would come out of this alive himself: they wanted to see him again, and he knew he couldn't refuse.

The flip phone Dan's abductors had given him was on the wicker table waiting for their call.

If anything happened to him or Jess, at least Perry could help tell the truth about what he had tried to do. Dan was writing the whole story, the whole truth, on his new Best Buy laptop.

But Perry could be right. Maybe these people would go on killing no matter what.

Chapter Thirty-Eight

Siobhan looked at the video and the row of people, side by side in black high-back chairs. Most were wearing headphones and staring at large flat screens, their fingers flying over keyboards. A few leaned back, swinging in their chairs, drinking from paper cups, eating sandwiches and burgers, and chatting. One hunched forward in a hooded white top, bowed over the keyboard – the lone person in that internet café who was obviously no gamer.

When he finished typing, Dan swung his chair round, pushed back the white hood, looked up towards the security camera, and gave a wave and a smile. Siobhan knew that smile was meant for her – that Dan was still alive.

He knew his message would be traced to its source. That wave was his way of making sure she knew he'd sent it. Fuck knows how he could find a smile in his situation, she thought, but there it was. She turned her back to the glass walls of her office. No one must see her crying.

Dan's email had arrived in Siobhan's personal account, telling the truth about how he'd been forced to file his story and the details he had omitted about the 88 tattoo and the man who'd claimed to be father of the family killed in Afghanistan.

I don't know whether they're white supremacists or Islamists, or if it's some coalition of killers with a common grievance, he wrote – and at the end of his message: *Please, please take care how you use what I'm telling you. We know how leaky the FBI can get with things like this. It would be one hell of a story for someone. I know it might be nuts to trust them, but doing what they tell me is the only hope of saving Jess. I know they might kill her anyway, but I'm certain if any of this message reaches these people, she'll have no chance, and they'll find Laura and the girls.*

FBI technicians had traced Dan's message to an internet café off Broadway. Siobhan had told no one yet of its contents, only the IP address and other information needed to trace it. But she had to tell Livermore, the director, and work out what to do next. And there was one other person she was certain she could trust.

Siobhan waved from her office at Bridget Kenny, who was at her desk on the phone with AirPods. Kenny touched her watch and held up five fingers with a questioning look. Siobhan nodded – a few minutes would be fine.

Siobhan's desk phone rang. 'Miss Mac Stiofain, the director needs to see you straight away. He said to tell you it's very urgent.'

She walked quickly from the elevator two floors up, and found Alexander Livermore leaning, arms folded, against the glass wall of the office, more distressed than ever. As she entered the room, Livermore closed the door, telling the young man on the desk outside, 'No interruptions, Ben. None.'

'I'm going to get straight to the point, Siobhan,' he said. 'I've just seen this.' He lifted a piece of paper from his desk and offered it to her. 'It's an email you received three hours ago from Dan Brasher.' For a moment, she was too surprised to speak. The director of the FBI was snooping through her personal email?

'When were you going to tell me about it?' he asked.

'Sir, I don't understand,' she said. 'Why are people accessing my private emails?'

'I'll answer that when I'm ready. Meanwhile, this is vitally important information.'

'I know that, sir, and you can see from its contents keeping it secret could be a matter of life and death. I didn't know for sure it was genuine until a few moments ago. We traced the message to its source and a security camera shows it was Dan Brasher who sent it. If this information leaks to the media, that young journalist will certainly be killed.'

Livermore ran a hand over his bristly white hair, his anxious tongue sliding again between his lips. 'And no one else in this office knows of its existence?' he asked.

'I've told no one.'

'Thank God for that.'

'But since my private email's been accessed,' Siobhan said, 'I've got no clue who else knows.'

'Don't worry about that,' he said. 'Your email was caught in DC by the internal corruption unit.'

'Why would the corruption unit be looking at my private emails?'

'Don't take it personally, Siobhan. Something very serious has developed . . .' He seemed to hesitate over what to say next. 'We think there's a mole in the Manhattan office. We don't know who it is yet, but someone in this office has been spying, and right now everyone is a suspect.'

'Well, it's not me, sir. You can't believe it's me—'

Livermore waved his arms to stop her. 'We're looking at everyone's personal comms,' he said. 'But it's sure to be a waste of time. No one trained by us would be dumb enough to use comms registered in their own name.'

'How have we even discovered there's a mole?' Siobhan asked.

'That's what makes this email of yours so critical,' he said. 'We've heard from an agent working inside the outfit calling itself Hard Core.'

Siobhan nodded. She knew plenty about Hard Core. Its members were white supremacists believed to have established training camps for a violent insurgency against the federal government. Some of its members had been charged with plotting the assassinations of members of the Antifa anti-fascist movement.

'Our man says he heard someone bragging about high-level information being leaked from inside the Manhattan field office,' Livermore said. 'The undercover agent doesn't know the leaker's identity.'

'What information do we believe this mole has gained from us?' Siobhan asked.

'We don't know. It wasn't until today we made a connection to these Wrath of God attacks.'

'So we think Dan Brasher is right?'

'Not only that,' he said. 'But after enhancing the video that woman Hunter sent of her kidnappers, DC has identified the man who called himself Craig, the big one with the beard. He's Wilbur Johnson. He's thirty-four years old, from Georgia, and it seems he has links to Hard Core. They've already found video of Johnson at a number of right-wing rallies.'

'Sir, how safe is Dan's email? If it's shared with the wrong people . . .'

'I know, I know,' Livermore said. 'Only a small group in DC knows of it. There's no need right now to tell anyone else.'

. . .

Kenny came into Siobhan's office as soon as she returned from her meeting with Livermore.

'You vanished in a hell of a hurry,' she said.

'Livermore needed me,' Siobhan said. 'It was nothing much. He's in a panic, a lot of pressure coming down from the very top.'

'You were looking for me,' Kenny said.

'Oh, it was nothing – just whether you were up for dinner tonight.'

'It's a date,' Kenny said, standing behind Siobhan to massage her shoulders.

'Quit it,' Siobhan said. 'These walls are made of glass.'

Chapter Thirty-Nine

ChatCorp HQ, London

Roy Jory looked up as the directors took their seats. He was making notes for his presentation to the ChatCorp board's late-night emergency meeting, still seething from his encounter with the prime minister and dreading the decision the board would have to reach. He wasn't hopeful about the outcome. Print veterans had once dominated this boardroom, but they'd yielded long ago to computer scientists and high-tech entrepreneurs. *The Daily Courant* had been reduced to a tiny player, the runt of the multicontinental giant ChatCorp had become.

Earlier, at Number Ten, the prime minister had greeted Jory with an unfriendly grin, his big, crooked smile reserved strictly for public display. He seated his guest on a low sofa and himself on an elevated chair next to an unlit fireplace. He wore a blue open-neck shirt and his sleeves were rolled up above his elbows. It was already evening, and he held a glass of white wine; Jory had declined the offer of one.

Jory detested the prime minister, and the feeling was mutual. No matter how serious things were, a perpetual expression of amused indifference seemed to play on his face, like everything was rather a lark. Jory considered him lazy and disloyal; he knew the PM had been the 'senior cabinet source' in many efforts to undermine previous prime ministers and his cabinet rivals. *The Daily Courant* had never been his supporter.

'Thank you, Mr Jory, for taking the time to come,' the PM said. 'First, it's important you understand this conversation must be off the record. To be clear, that rather means it's not happening.'

'Thank you. I'm well aware what *off the record* means.'

'Good, well, for a start you can stop writing things down and put away that notebook.'

Jory kept looking down at his notebook.

'Prime Minister, what are you afraid of?' he asked, pointedly still writing. 'You know I understand the rules. There's a difference between wanting to remember what is said and putting it in the newspaper.'

The PM shrugged in surrender. 'Well, you should understand if anyone were to claim I have said what I'm about to say, I will issue an immediate and indignant denial.'

Jory glanced up from his notebook. 'I've no doubt at all you would.'

The PM turned his gaze away from Jory and towards the blank, beige wall of his office. 'So, this is the situation,' he said. 'In my view, you must close *The Courant* immediately. You have no choice. Our police and security people have no idea who's doing this. The Americans now have this theory there might be some new axis of evil involving jihadists and fascists, though our people remain unconvinced. And no one appears to have any leads on what's happened to that poor woman who works for you, or Dan Brasher. But whoever is responsible, we know they mean business and we can't ignore their ultimatum.' Then the PM went quiet, studying his bitten fingernails.

'What about Leila Chatstone,' Jory said. 'Is she being charged?'

'The police are very suspicious about what she's been up to.

She seems to have ties with some bad people – I mean, where the hell has her father got to?'

'Do you think she plotted to kill her own mother? A lot of people do.'

'She may have been a pawn in their plans, God only knows, but what matters right now is if you defy these killers, whoever they are, you can be sure others are going to die. It could be you, or another Chatstone, or members of your board. I wish we could offer you protection, I really do, but we cannot guarantee the lives of all your employees.'

He paused, looking for Jory's response.

'What if we decide to keep publishing? You'll have to keep protecting us, otherwise we'll be at their mercy and it'll look like the government's abandoned us.'

'Come off it, Roy – you know very well there are limits to what we can do. We can protect your headquarters to some extent, but that's not going to help if they decide to go after individuals. And you have offices and printing plants all over the country. We can't guard everything.'

Jory and the prime minister looked at each other. Jory was sure he could see signs the PM was enjoying himself; that he would delight in the death of his least favourite newspaper.

'But *The Courant* has been around more than a hundred and fifty years,' Jory said. 'Are you going to stand back and see it killed off by a gang of murdering thugs? The government's refused forever to yield to terrorists, even when they were murdering innocent British captives.'

The PM said, 'I can tell you *The New York World* is very likely to announce its closure in the next few hours. From what I'm hearing, the late chairman's son is entirely in favour of an immediate shutdown.'

Jory stood to leave, determined to limit the pleasure his host seemed to be getting from the meeting.

'I will be telling board members about this meeting later tonight. It will be their decision.'

'Good, let's hope they act sensibly.'

Jory turned towards the door, but the PM hadn't finished.

'Wait, there's something else. As you've said, this government is unequivocal on the issue of never bowing to threats. We can't ever be seen to give in. Therefore, you need to know, should you make the decision to close your newspaper, we will be bound in public to disagree with that decision.'

Jory strode back. 'Are you serious? You're ready to give us a kicking for the very decision you're leaning on us to take?'

The PM kept his eyes on Jory. 'I promise you our statement will be mild, but you must understand as the government we cannot be seen to approve of any surrender.'

Jory glared at the prime minister, searching in vain for some sign of sympathy or concern. 'Bullshit,' he said, enjoying the jolt of shock on the PM's face, and he turned to leave.

'Remember, all this is off the record,' the PM called after his departing guest.

Jory laughed. 'Of course it is,' he said.

. . .

'I can't believe I'm having to do this,' Fiona Chester whispered to Jory. She was at the head of the board table, brass-handled walking cane leaning against her chair. Chester, the late Cressida's oldest friend, could never have imagined being elected interim chair for the most momentous board meeting in *The Courant*'s history. But the hierarchy at Chatstone was in chaos with the death of Cressida, the arrest of Leila, and the novice status of the acting CEO, Ambrose Cracknell.

Chester began the meeting.

'There's no agenda,' she said, 'because there's only one thing to discuss. We're here to make an historic decision and we must make it today. You all know *The Courant* was the foundation of this company, and remains at its heart.'

She laid out the practical matters facing the board: it was now ten thirty in the evening on Tuesday, and five thirty in New York. She had spoken to Francis Wyler and they had agreed that, if both newspapers were to close, the decisions should be announced immediately online and in Wednesday's print editions.

'Before our discussion,' Chester said, 'our acting editor, Roy, has just come from a private meeting with the prime minister.'

Jory outlined what had happened in the meeting: that the prime minister was urging them to close *The Courant*, and that, if the newspaper did close, he would be obliged to criticise ChatCorp for surrendering to the blackmail of murderers. 'He won't publicly tell us to shut the paper because he knows it'll make him look weak,' Jory said. 'At the same time, he's terrified of being landed with the responsibility of keeping the entire staff of a newspaper alive. Every death would be blood on the hands of the police and security services, and therefore on his hands as well. I should add, for what it's worth, he said any criticism of us would be mild.'

The moment Jory finished and went to a chair near Chester, the rich Welsh tones of Lord Alun Rees-Jones rumbled through the room from the far end of the table. He was sitting erect in his chair, in a well-worn grey pinstripe suit, waving his fist.

'We're being cast off, disowned, washed from the hands of His Majesty's Government,' he said. 'It's unbelievable, a bloody disgrace. That man is a disgusting fellow – a frightful weakling, always was.'

Far into his eighties, and the company's longest-serving employee, Rees-Jones had been at Cambridge with Cressida's father and risen to become Jim Slight's predecessor as editor of *The Courant*. Later, he became chairman of Chatstone's newspaper division, in the days it was making millions.

'Thank you, Alun, thank you very much,' Chester said, curtailing the old man's rant. 'Someone needs to propose a motion. It might as well be me. I propose we reject the ultimatum of these ... these heartless killers, and announce we will never yield to their threats.'

One or two of the remaining print directors muttered approvingly, but most of the room stayed silent. Jory wasn't sure Chester believed her own words; more likely she couldn't bear being remembered as the person who'd championed a great newspaper's execution.

But Rees-Jones's face lit up. 'I second the motion – and with the utmost enthusiasm,' he said.

Ambrose Cracknell stood to remove the Levi's jacket he had on over his black T-shirt. He planted the palms of his hands on the table, spreading them wide, invading the space of his neighbours.

'Well, I know this is super difficult for some of you,' he said. 'But I must say to the chair – with all due respect, Fiona – the motion she proposes is totally nuts. I believe firmly closing this newspaper is the only right thing to do. I know for sure how important this newspaper is to the family, and to the country as well, but we're in a very dangerous place right now, and from a business point of view … well, let's face it – this newspaper makes no damned money. Our stock price has gone down the drain because of the trouble it's caused, and this great corporation will go down the drain as well, unless—'

'Excuse me, if I may,' Rees-Jones interrupted. His face quivered and a droplet at the tip of his old nose caught the light. 'Please, I beg you, let's not reduce this debate to the crude terms of profit and loss …' Then he stopped, pointing towards Cracknell, who had turned to studying his phone. 'I'm so sorry, Mr Cracknell. Am I keeping you from something more important?'

Cracknell dropped his phone on the table with a grunt.

'Thank you, sir,' Rees-Jones said. 'Let's show some respect, shall we? I'm sure you think of me as some crumbling antiquity, just as you look upon the entire newspaper industry, but this is a very important moment.'

In the ensuing silence, Rees-Jones reached for his glass of water and took a couple of sips, taking pleasure in this young upstart having to wait for him to resume.

'Now, as I was saying, in the wild and unreliable world of modern media, *The Daily Courant* remains among the world's most trusted newspapers at a time when trust in journalism has never been lower. *The Courant* has earned that trust over more than one hundred and fifty years. Its importance might no longer be evident in the company's balance sheet, but surely we cannot squander what it represents in the face of these nihilistic brutes.'

Cracknell was massaging both temples with the knuckles of his index fingers.

'Sure, Al, I get it, honest I do,' he said. 'So, let's look at it another way. This newspaper employs more than a thousand people. They've got husbands and wives and lovers and children and hopes and dreams. And you know what? Right now, they're all still alive. Poor Jim and Larry are gone, but everyone else still lives and breathes. Right? And what about Jess Hunter and Dan Brasher? What will happen to them?'

Rees-Jones raised his hand for attention while pulling a red chequered handkerchief from the breast pocket of his jacket; he used it to dry his nose.

'No, Mr Cracknell. You *don't* get it. Honest you don't,' he said, attempting with some success to replicate his adversary's American tones. 'You, sir, need to understand we're not involved here in some kind of orderly corporate negotiation. We are not considering a give-and-take deal with some commercial rival. We are not dealing with rational people. They are mindless killers. You really think they will lay down their arms if we simply surrender to their demands? Are you that naive? Capitulation will only empower them. They will never stop until they are crushed. For all we know, and God forbid it, Dan Brasher and Jessica Hunter might already be dead, but if they're not it would be madness to think we can keep them alive by yielding to these animals.'

Cracknell slapped the table so hard Rees-Jones flinched and spilled a little of the water he was on the point of drinking.

'That's one hell of a risk you're asking this board to take, my lord,' he said. 'If we ignore them, what will they blow up next? Very soon we could be counting the bodies of people who work for us, people who are depending on us to do the right thing.' Cracknell scanned the long table and all the anxious faces. 'Well, I'm not willing to live with that, and I have a powerful hunch I'm not alone here.' He kept looking around the table, but there wasn't a flicker of dissent. 'You should all know if this vote goes the wrong way, you can count on my immediate resignation.'

Cracknell leaned away from the table and picked up his phone again, talking quietly, as if the words were for his own information. 'To hell with that "beacon of freedom" stuff. This world's got more free speech flying around than any time in history.'

A murmur swept the room along with a few mutterings of 'Hear, hear' and 'Quite right'. The directors on each side of Cracknell reached over to pat his back. Others sent approving smiles in his direction. Roy Jory could tell Cracknell had won and so could Rees-Jones, who was looking dolefully at a large portrait in oils of his departed friend, viscount number three. It was gazing down on them all with a proud, unknowing smile.

The room was silent except for the sound of Alun Rees-Jones's angry breathing.

'Well, let's vote,' said Chester. She checked the company secretary was making the proper notes for the minutes, and continued. 'This is an historic moment and one of the most important in the company's history. For all the financial success of Chatstone Corporation, no asset has brought more pride and been more treasured than *The Daily Courant*. The only modern British newspaper to close its doors under duress was the *News of the World* in 2011 during the phone hacking episode.'

Lord Rees-Jones growled. 'In my own opinion, it was an appalling newspaper, but still it was wrong to close it down. I wish the people in this room were not about to make the same frightful, weak-kneed mistake.'

He looked around the table, but no one met his eye.

Roy Jory had to look out the window. He couldn't bear the sight of Alun Rees-Jones, sat there with everyone hiding their eyes from him – that lion from a forgotten country called Fleet Street, where they did things differently, with that look on his battered old face of disbelieving defeat, like he had stumbled into some hostile future world where they spoke another language, and he was stranded in a place he no longer mattered.

Chapter Forty

It was late when Fiona Chester called. Francis Wyler had been at the window of his eighth-floor office looking down on the New York World Circle. It was raining and the streets and the fountain glowed with the lights of the whirling traffic. A circle of one hundred flights of water poured in high arcs of homage towards the statue at the fountain's heart. Carved into the plinth were these words:

TO THE MEMORY OF OTIS JEREMIAH WYLER

1820–1904

HIS VISION AND INDOMITABLE

COURAGE

SHAPED OUR GREAT CITY

It was one of Francis's first memories: standing with his father, looking up at that statue of his great-great-grandfather. It was the image of a man in full stride, head high in a searching gaze, long jacket swirling behind to demonstrate the subject's dynamic haste. He wore a goatee beard and flowing hair, and clutched in his right hand was a stone replica of his greatest creation – *The New York World*.

Beyond the statue, an electronic headline streamed across a building. Such an out-of-date gimmick in a world of handheld information; Francis would have torn it down years ago but for his late father's resistance.

The World's presses had been primed to run with that night's edition, as everyone waited for its new chairman to reveal his decision. Two front pages were prepared:

THANK YOU
AND
GOODBYE

or

NEW YORK WORLD DEFIES
WRATH OF GOD THREATS

But Francis had made up his mind within moments of reading Dan Brasher's sensational story. There was no need for board-room debate about the future of *The New York World*. Chatstone Corporation was in turmoil with the death of Cressida Chatstone, but Francis was alive and well and the company share structure gave absolute authority to the family trust, and therefore to the thirty-nine-year-old new boss.

He had no hesitation about what he would do, or any interest in hearing the dissenting voices of his journalists and executives. Francis had inherited none of the sentimental feel-ings of his father, or his demented grandfather, or that ancestor out the window with his granite glare. He would not fret for the existence of *The World* and nor would his far-flung family.

Francis had conveyed his decision the moment Chester called with news of the Chatstone board's vote – sixteen to two in favour of closure. As agreed, their decisions were already up online; and Thursday, the day after tomorrow, would see the final editions of their famous newspapers.

In London, the prime minister had issued an angry statement. 'This is an extremely disappointing decision and a huge stain on the history of a fine newspaper. We can never yield to the demands of terrorists. We stood ready to provide every protection to *The Courant* and its staff. Our brave military and police forces, our embassies overseas, our public servants, and every citizen – they all face danger. This is an astonishing action – the complete surrender of a newspaper once so brave with its words.'

A rival newspaper website quoted a source describing the prime minister's private fury. 'They're a bunch of spineless bastards,' the PM had apparently said. The *Times* website ran a story saying the prime minister had put pressure on the newspaper to close, but Downing Street retaliated with an outraged denial.

The White House said, 'The president feels sadness at *The New York World*'s decision and pledges we will find these murderers and they will pay for their atrocities.'

In London, Roy Jory sat in his abandoned newsroom drinking wine with a handful of colleagues, glad he had leaked the story of the prime minister's treachery to *The Times*. Their phones buzzed with messages, but they had stopped checking them. They knew what they were saying. The news had spread across the world to the abandoned employees of both newspapers. It had reached press halls waiting silently for the news in London, Ireland and Scotland, and in the South Bronx and all across the United States to Washington state and Alaska and Hawaii. It had reached correspondents everywhere across both countries, and in the world's great cities. And it had reached the inveigling politicians and corporations, and their armies of public relations operatives, though they cared less these days about newspapers; they had the web and social media and the granular technology to understand and influence, one by one, their millions of voters and customers.

News media outlets everywhere waited for what might happen next, hanging some hope on these lines in Dan Brasher's report: 'These newspapers deserve to die. Let their deaths be a lesson to media everywhere of the vengeance awaiting them if they lie again about the murderous military imperialism of America and Britain.'

Much agonised debate was guaranteed about how a free press should behave with this death threat hanging over it. Ben Tremblay at least was in no doubt as he searched for buyers: he had imposed a total ban on all mention of the Wrath of God attacks, or criticism of Islamist violence.

Afraid though they might be tonight, executives at *The Times* and *Daily Telegraph* in London and *The New York Times* and the *New York Post* had given away their theatre tickets and cancelled their dinners and postponed their trysts, to work all night plotting marketing campaigns and alluring promotions to bait the abandoned online subscribers and newspaper buyers.

When newspapers die, the battle commences without delay over their warm corpses. The pickings might be fewer these days, but old habits die hard.

PART FOUR

H e looked from the window, waiting for his final dawn. In the south, a stormy black fringe lined the horizon. In better times, when it was very early, the man would make his first phone calls. He always called his people first thing: he needed the voices. He could not bear to be alone, sure that as a castaway he would quickly become insane. The subordinates who had survived in his employment accepted their boss's pre-dawn calls. There were many other rules to follow, and questions never to ask, in order to enjoy the financial success and status that came from existing within the inner circle of one of the country's wealthiest men.

But on this, his last morning, the man had no more business calls to make and no corporate subordinates waiting to receive them. His life had changed: all the power and prestige had gone; all the rich and important friends had disappeared; and the life he had worked so long and hard to build had fallen apart. Fame and prosperity had once made him admired and hated in equal measure; but in those days, he never cared. There were always bitter victims buried in the foundations of other people's triumphs. There was always enough celebrity and happiness, and wealth, to outweigh the darker side. It had been a golden, weightless time compared with the wreckage of his motherless childhood and the life he fled at sixteen, afraid he would be taken into care when his father went to prison for twenty-five years.

Alone in the world, he had scrabbled and charmed his way. He'd washed dishes, served tables at dingy diners and later at better restaurants and, finally, at an upscale steak house. When he was twenty, a regular diner liked how the young waiter connected with customers and offered him a job as a sales assistant in his downtown clothing store. As the rich man's business grew, he gave his promising recruit a store to manage, and then two stores. The rich man helped him pay for a degree in business management and, at twenty-seven, when he was managing all six of the group's stores, the owner took ill and his young protégé bought him out.

On he went from there, from retail into insurance, and investments in aviation manufacturing and New York City property. His great wealth came from oil and natural gas, when he made friends among the Russian oligarchs who were pillaging their broken nation's wealth. And that was how the boy with nothing, with every reason to have no hope at all, became a storybook American success.

He sat now at his desk in the bedroom corner. He liked working there while his wife slept. The corner walls were covered with photographs, his face prominent in each of them: in the Oval Office in a line with others, looking solemn as the president signed a trade agreement with Russia; in the Caribbean off St Bart's, on the deck of his yacht with some of the celebrities and media personalities who had once sought his hospitality; at the Kremlin with the Russian president before their relationship went sour; with Oprah Winfrey when his memoir, The Secret Art of Beating the Odds, *was her book-club pick of the month, and one of that year's bestsellers. His was an irresistible, almost impossible, story.*

Now, amid the ruins of his life, he raged against the people he blamed for his destruction. His vanished friends had become mortal enemies. His life was darker than ever, darker now than the years he'd looked from that high window imagining his wandering mother.

This time, the man knew he was doomed. He knew because the doom he faced was according to his own plan. He had written the script, and he had followed it in every scrupulous detail. Hardly a thing had gone wrong.

Although he had no empire left to manage, still there would be final calls to make. His last project was not quite finished and there were helpers waiting to carry out his wishes.

On the TV, with the news of two dying newspapers, the disappearance of two British journalists had faded from that morning's headlines. The man knew one of the journalists, at least, had hours to live.

He went back to the window. Feeders hanging from the tall maple were crowded with chickadees and tufted titmice. Beneath them on the grass, dark-eyed juncos competed with sparrows and a loud, cranky blue jay. He watched the smaller birds stage temporary retreats when the big ones jostled in. Nothing had changed for them. These visitors kept returning; they returned every day. They were his unquestioning guests, and he their welcoming host.

He read the letter on his bedside table once more and knelt by the bed for his last morning prayer.

'Blessed be the Lord, my rock, who trains my hands for war, and my fingers for battle. The day of their calamity is at hand, and their doom comes swiftly. Eye for eye, tooth for tooth, hand for hand, foot for foot, burn for burn, wound for wound. They will suffer the punishment of eternal destruction, away from the presence of the Lord and from the glory of His might. Those who seek to destroy us, first the wrath of God will destroy.'

The man wept.

'It won't be long now, my darling,' he said. 'Our task is almost done. Soon we will be together again and safe, and the world will know the truth of our great crusade.'

The news on the bedroom TV was still playing. There was a short item about a service of thanks to be held at St Patrick's Cathedral in New York City for the former president's daughter, who had donated millions to the Catholic church weeks before her death. She had died three months before, when the car she was driving crashed at high speed. The crash had happened on a straight, traffic-free road, and there was speculation she had committed suicide. Her death had come after a succession of scandals forced her father from office.

The man pulled the curtains to shut out the morning light, picked up the cold coffee by the bed, and left the empty room.

Chapter Forty-One

SCARED TO DEATH

The Sun

IT'S THE END OF *THE WORLD*

New York Post

New York

He had been such a fucking idiot. It was more than forty-eight hours since Dan had fed their story to the world, exactly as they'd demanded. But these people were killers; what did honouring their side of the deal matter to them?

People must think he was already dead. Siobhan at least knew he was alive, but not Laura and the girls and his parents. He didn't know what had happened to Jess, but he couldn't give up hope. The phone her captors had provided was still on the table beside him – plugged in, fully charged, and silent.

The morning news had been consumed with the pending deaths of *The Daily Courant* and *The New York World*. Dan had been desperate for them to close; he was terrified what would happen to Jess otherwise.

There was no news of Leila Chatstone facing more charges, but newspapers in America and London – most of all the free-wheeling tabloids – were enjoying themselves piecing together evidence against her. They'd published reports from Pakistan about Leila's missing father, a bitter critic of the Pakistani government who had been arrested at numerous protests. Many were happy to guess at motives that might have driven him to kill. One offered the portrait of an academic of modest means enraged at seeing his daughter raised without him in a media family worth billions, whose newspapers were forever attacking his homeland. Another imagined him incensed at the lover who ran away pregnant with his child and never got around to letting him know. A third speculated Leila had funded the attacks.

Francis Wyler was quoted everywhere saying, '*The World* belongs to our company's past. We will now reshape ourselves for the future.' An anonymous New York donor had offered to finance a new title to fill the vacuum. A Labour MP in London had been reprimanded by the Speaker for using the protection of the House of Commons to mock Leila's 'preposterous story of kidnap and terror'. He had demanded of the home secretary, 'Why have the police failed to charge this woman with the crimes that have been committed? Is she receiving special treatment due to her great wealth and privilege? Would a woman from a Birmingham council estate be so lucky as her?'

There was a knock on Dan's door. He muted the TV. 'Who's that?' he said, then jumped to his feet hearing the familiar voice. 'You're still here!' he said to Perry. 'I thought you'd be sacked by now and heading back to your bolthole in the Cotswolds, or off drinking too much by some Caribbean lagoon.'

Perry surveyed Dan's accommodation like he had forgotten how shabby it was. He looked for somewhere to hang his fedora, but gave up and put it back on.

'You think I'd leave you stranded?' he said. He was at the sink washing glasses again. 'Of course, the office demanded my prompt return to London. After deciding to murder our wonderful newspaper, they called to say I was booked on a flight back to London last night. But I thought to hell with them. Why should I be such an obedient employee? Why should I have a single care what they want?'

He perched himself tentatively on the edge of Dan's unmade bed, with two glasses in one hand and the Johnnie Walker Blue in the other.

'My company credit card was still working,' he said, 'so I used it to extract a few thousand dollars in cash from a local bank. And I prepaid extra days at the Ritz before the card was cancelled. Now I've come here to this frightful hideout of yours. I wasn't even sure you'd still be here.' Perry held up the glasses. 'Care for a heart starter?'

'It's a bit early for me, mate, it's only just seven.'

Perry poured his own. 'You should be grateful I'm here,' he said. 'I could have chosen Saint Lucia. Tonight, I would be enjoying a cocktail on my porch, admiring the Pitons, far away from this awful mess.'

Dan knew about Perry's villa. It was famous in the office that Jim Slight so valued Perry he allowed him to work there in the winter months, with the Caribbean lapping warmly at his feet as he raged about the hardships of Britain and the foolishness of its politicians.

Perry held up the Johnnie Walker. 'You sure?'

'Oh, fuck it. Yes, please.'

'That's my boy,' Perry said, pouring generously.

It's surprising, Dan thought, *after knowing someone for years and thinking you understand them, how they can turn out to be someone else entirely.* Perry was so manufactured, such a self-invented fraud. He had betrayed his accent and his roots – even his bloody name. He was a forgery, a chameleon, and every other metaphor you could throw at that out-and-out phoney, Ernest Scruggs from Wigan. But you had to think again about a man who appeared in a dump like this, with nothing to gain, pouring more of his expensive Scotch, to be with someone who was in the deepest shit of his entire life.

Perry pulled some pages from his pocket. 'I've been brushing up a little on domestic terrorism in this great nation,' he said. 'Interesting stuff. Listen to this from the Justice Department a few years ago: *The violent extremist threat is rapidly evolving. People may be drawn to social media sites and then to encrypted communications channels. There they may interact with like-minded people across the country, and indeed the world, who want to commit violent attacks. And they then may connect with others who are formulating attack plans as well as mustering the resources – including firearms and explosives – to execute them.'*

Perry turned to another page. 'And this from the FBI: *The problem of domestic terrorism has been metastasizing across the country for a long time now, and it's not going away anytime soon.'*

He folded the paper with a sigh. 'I found other stuff specifically warning that small self-organised cells are the mostly likely to mount attacks. We've been hearing things like this for years. We can't say we weren't warned. But if it is these home-grown lunatics, what on earth are they up to? What are they killing newspeople for?'

'There's nothing novel about killing troublesome journalists,' Dan said. 'It just doesn't happen much in America and the UK. People in high places have been dropping shit on us for a long time. Charismatic liars can send people crazy – there's centuries of evidence for that.'

The couple next door were shouting at each other again. Something shattered as it hit the adjoining wall. Perry smiled. 'It's a wonderful neighbourhood you selected. My mother and father used to fight like that. How much longer do you plan to stay in this shithole?'

Dan nodded towards the silent blue flip phone. 'I don't really know. If they don't get in touch in the next couple of days, I think I'll break cover. I can't hang around here forever. Why did I even think I could trust these people?'

'You've had little choice,' Perry said. 'But everyone's desperate about what's happened to you and Jess. I didn't say a word, of course, but they're thinking the worst. It's not been easy keeping my mouth shut. I'm not sure it's been wise of me. I keep getting calls from your friend Siobhan.'

'I took your advice and got a message to Siobhan about the tattoo and the fake father.'

'Well done. She didn't mention that, but she's desperately anxious about you. Phoned my hotel last night and I thought she was going to burst into tears. She was in the hotel lobby at first light this morning just before I headed here. I'd told the front desk to tell everyone I was out.'

Perry went quiet, looking at Dan as if he wanted to say something but wasn't sure how.

'What, mate . . . what is it?'

'Look, old man, if you're going to meet these people again, might it be the right thing to let her know?'

'Don't you say a fucking word, Perry,' he said. 'My family . . . Jess – their lives are at stake.'

'Okay, okay, only . . . what I think you should consider . . .' Perry said, but Dan didn't want to hear it.

'Have you got any inside info on Leila? Are they going to charge her with actual involvement in the attacks?' Dan asked.

'I don't know. Roy Jory says she told the police a story about discovering a letter her father wrote to Cressie. She found it in a drawer with a photo of the two of them arm in arm. She tracked him down to a college in Rawalpindi. Apparently the poor girl wanted to live with her father, but he wouldn't allow it without her mother's consent. Leila knew Cressida would never agree. Perhaps she was afraid Cressie would cut her off from the family money.'

Dan gave a slight smile. 'Wow! I knew she wanted nothing to do with running the company, but running off to live in Pakistan? Abandoning that life of luxury? She must have been desperate.'

On the TV, a CNN reporter was yet again performing a live stand-up at the ChatCorp entrance. Gun-draped police were wandering in the background.

'What's going on back at the newspaper?' Dan said.

'What newspaper? Everyone's about to leave the offices and they'll lock the bloody doors. Last I heard, there was even talk of not publishing a final edition tomorrow. Meanwhile, the corporate folk are busy going through the formalities of shutting things down. The rest of the building will be busy as ever. We don't matter much anymore.'

Dan laughed drily. 'That whole crowd will be happy to stop pretending they care about us. The board hasn't given a toss for years. I can picture the top floor back there, with all those lawyers and dickhead MBAs. They'll be studying this whole thing like it's nothing more than a health-and-safety headache, calculating the company liabilities, fretting over damage claims and our insurance premiums. None of those people gives a fuck. When this is over, they'll be researching titles for some dumb animated movie, or they'll disappear to companies making concrete, or aircraft engines, or to online stores selling groceries and cheap TVs. It's all the fucking same to them.'

Dan helped himself to more Scotch. 'You know what one of those MBA pricks said to me in the pub once? "Oh," he said, "I've heard of you. You work for *The Daily Relic*." Cunt. I tipped my drink on him.'

Dan paced the small room, a few steps each way, like an animal in a cage. 'People have no time anymore for what we do. They spend their hours on social media lying and abusing each other.'

'People have been lying and abusing each other for thousands of years,' Perry said.

'Sure, but now billions of people can tell the world whatever crazy shit they want. They've all been armed and set free by TikTok and X, or whatever the hell it's called. This is a world that's never been so honest with itself and never so disgusted with what it sees. Meanwhile, the tycoons are off already looking for the next thing to keep them rich and powerful.'

Dan came to a halt. 'What are you smiling at, Perry? It's not fucking funny.'

Perry laughed. 'You've got a bit of a cheek, pissing on the rich and powerful. Be honest, your family's worth a bloody fortune. I'm the working-class kid who's tried all his life to hide the fact. And you? You're ashamed to be rich, going around railing against the bosses and dressed like a scruffy oik from a council estate.'

'I don't need to be ashamed because I'm not responsible. My father's success was nothing to do with me and I sure as hell would never work for him. I love him, but I never wanted to be like him. He hasn't given me a cent since college. Even then, he only paid my tuition. I did night shifts at the *New York Post* to pay my food and board.'

'All right, settle down, old chap,' Perry said. 'You've got far bigger worries right now. 'The sooner you get out of here, the better. I think it's sending you mad.'

The blue flip phone buzzed and Dan grabbed it to read the text.

'They want to meet tonight,' he said. 'You need to rent me another car.'

'Really, Danny, are you sure about this? They're madmen. I really think you might be doing the wrong thing here . . . I mean . . .' Dan wasn't listening and Perry grabbed him by both shoulders. His twinkly eyes looked terrified. 'For God's sake, man, please . . .'

Dan just looked at him. 'They'll find my family. They've still got their hands on Jess. They will kill her at the slightest hint I'm not doing what they want. It's my fault they took her – I'm to blame. I'm not going to abandon her.'

'But why won't they kill you too? Please, Danny – you're totally out of your depth. The FBI do this kind of thing for a living.'

'You're wasting your breath, mate,' Dan said. 'And I need one more favour from you.' He held up his Best Buy laptop. 'I've got to work on this now, but I need you to come back here later to get it, in case something happens to me. My whole fucking story will be on it.'

Chapter Forty-Two

Siobhan's death-ray style of interrogation had been a helpful aid to her rise through the ranks of the FBI, but it wasn't working so well right now. Her angry gaze was fixed on Perry, and although he looked uneasy in her sights, he showed no signs of wavering.

Siobhan and Bridget Kenny had been waiting for him out of sight in the lobby when he arrived that morning at the hotel, back from visiting Dan. Offered the option of a trip downtown to Federal Plaza, he took them instead to his suite. It was early, but Siobhan could tell in the elevator he'd already been drinking.

In the suite, he leaned back on a grey sofa with brown checked cushions, sipping now and then from a can of Diet Coke. At one side of him a window showed the green canopy of Central Park; behind him on the wall was a large black-and-white photo of a woman's face – her eyes appeared to have been turned into flowers.

Perry wasn't so relaxed as he tried to appear. His smile was too still, but, after an hour of questions, Siobhan saw no signs of him breaking.

'I can see you must be very good at scaring people,' he told her. 'But you should know I'm a seasoned victim of hostile interrogation. In Cambodia, the Khmer Rouge came close to shooting me. They thought I was working for the State

Department, can you imagine?' He shuffled on the sofa, pulling at his French cuffs to make sure they appeared beneath the sleeves of his jacket. 'In the Congo once, a bad-tempered rebel leader might have chopped off my hand if the UN hadn't turned up. And I've also had to deal with the police in countries where extreme brutality is a basic requirement of the job.'

'Don't get cute with me, sir,' she said, and Perry's smile slipped a little at the sudden high volume of her voice. 'We need to know where the hell he is, and why he's hiding, and I have a very strong feeling you're holding something back.' Siobhan was bluffing; she had no such feeling, but figured if Dan had spoken to anyone, Ainsworth was the likeliest candidate.

Perry gave a heavy sigh. 'You can detain me for as long as you wish, or cast me into a dark, damp cell, or waterboard me to the point of death. It won't make any difference. No matter what you may think, there's absolutely nothing I can tell you. If he's alive, God willing, isn't he most likely to be someone's prisoner? And if he's not a captive, what reason would he have to hide away? He's not a fugitive from the law.'

'Well, you think about this,' Siobhan said. 'If you're keeping something from us that could have saved lives, you're going to have to live with it for the rest of your days.'

Perry faltered when she said that, but not for long. 'Oh, please, miss,' he said. 'Mine has not been a blameless existence, but nothing about this meeting will add to the already heavy burden of my sorrows and sins. Trust me, there's absolutely no way I can be of help to you.'

Siobhan's phone buzzed and she handed it to Kenny while continuing her fruitless grilling. As she did, Perry left the sofa to walk across the room. He reached into a wardrobe and held up a carry-on-sized Louis Vuitton suitcase. 'This is all very interesting,' he said. 'But, if you will forgive me, I must pack in order to liberate this suite for its next guest – unless the Federal Bureau of Investigation is inclined to foot the bill.'

Smart ass, she said to herself. *He's going nowhere. I'm going to drill into this guy until he caves.*

Kenny interrupted, speaking quietly to Siobhan. 'You need to take this call. There's some weird news about the Wyler butler's family.' She pointed towards Perry's adjoining bedroom. 'Better go in there to speak.'

Within sixty seconds of the call, and without saying a word, Siobhan and Kenny hurried from the hotel room, leaving Perry alone. He went immediately to rent that car for Dan.

He was puzzled by their sudden departure, but pleased with his performance during the interrogation. He had kept Dan's secrets, but felt even less sure he was doing the right thing. Dan had been in a state of shock and grief; he wasn't thinking straight.

Chapter Forty-Three

Siobhan and Kenny headed north on the Major Deegan Expressway, travelling fast through the Bronx. Siobhan was catching up on her phone as Kenny drove. The sister of Walter Kravits, Howard Wyler's Ukrainian butler, had told an extraordinary story to FBI agents based at the US embassy in Warsaw. Three weeks ago, masked men had broken into her flat as she was having breakfast with her three children. All four had been driven away in the back of a van with their heads covered, and held captive. The only sound they ever heard was Middle Eastern music.

'It appears the sister and her kids only got home about ten hours ago,' Siobhan told Kenny. 'They were put out of a van about a mile from where they live. At home, there was a voice message from her brother. It had arrived a few days after she was kidnapped. Kravits was in tears, talking of how much he loved his sister and her children and how sorry he was about what had happened and that he would never see them again. When the sister called her brother's number in New York, whoever answered told her he was dead.'

Siobhan put down the phone and looked out the window. They were passing the ugly concrete hulk of Yankee Stadium. 'Go Mets,' she said to herself.

'What you thinking?' Kenny said.

'I'm thinking what it doesn't take an Einstein or Stephen Hawking to figure out. I'm thinking Walter Kravits poisoned his boss and then killed himself from guilt. I'm thinking Leila Chatstone really was kidnapped, just like the Kravits family, and these killers held them hostage to force others into helping them.'

Siobhan and Kenny were on their way to the home of retired NYPD captain Chuck Healy. Kenny said, 'What do you think Healy's going to tell us?'

'I'm thinking maybe his show of mad grief had nothing to do with fucked-up security at the hotel.'

They turned into a dead-end street of clapboard colonials and ranch houses. Leaves whirled everywhere in the rising wind. 'This weather's going to get mean pretty soon,' Siobhan said as they left the car.

Kenny finished sending a text message and knocked hard several times on the Healy front door. No one answered. 'Captain Healy, it's the FBI,' she shouted. 'We need to talk to you about the attack.' She waited for a minute, but no one came to the door. She knocked again. 'We know it's been hard for you, Captain Healy, but it's very important we talk. It shouldn't take long. There have been developments and we're visiting everyone.'

'What's wrong with this guy?' Siobhan said, banging hard on the door herself. 'Come on, Captain Healy. You know how this works. We can be back here in no time with a warrant.'

They heard voices on the other side of the door. 'Are they laughing or crying?' Kenny whispered.

When the door opened, Chuck and Maria Healy looked wrecked; Chuck's breathing was raspy and uneven, like he was having an asthma attack. Maria was pressing her tiny frame against her husband and holding one of his big hands in both of hers. With his free hand, Chuck wiped away tears. Siobhan couldn't explain the odd trace of a smile that kept showing on Maria Healy's face.

'Come on in, please,' Maria said as she and her husband stepped back to make room in the small hallway. Siobhan and Kenny followed them into the living room.

'Sit down, honey,' Maria said to her husband, leading him quickly to a yellow chair with a studded back. On a table beside him was an overflowing ashtray. Maria brought a green-cushioned footstool and lifted his legs one at a time to rest on it, and then attempted with limited success to pat into place her husband's thick, disorderly hair.

She sat next to him on a wooden stool, and gripped his hand again. Chuck Healy said nothing. Maria was whispering to him and stroking his hand. Then she sat up straight and decisively. 'Ladies, we have something to tell you—'

But Chuck Healy interrupted her. 'I'm going to . . . I want to tell them. It was me. I did it. I killed them, it was me. There was nothing else I could do.'

Healy choked like he was holding back tears. He tried lighting a cigarette, but his hands shook too much.

'He did it for Ashley,' Maria said. 'He did it for him, but he's okay now.'

She began crying, but with the same odd mix of pain and happiness she had shown at the front door.

'It's our son,' she said. 'Ashley is free. He's safe.'

Kenny leaned towards Siobhan. 'We need to read them their rights.'

Chuck looked up. 'Then read them, quickly. We won't need an attorney.'

His wife nodded. 'It's time to talk.'

Kenny rapidly recited the words of the Miranda warning, but Chuck began his story before she had finished.

'He'd just graduated college and taken a summer job upstate – him and his girlfriend, Meghan,' he said. 'They were sweethearts all through college. They were waiting tables in Woodstock, saving for a trip to Europe. It was a week after he left that the first phone call came. The voice was muffled but it was a man speaking. He told me I had to do something if we wanted to see Ashley alive again. It sounded weird to me. Over the years, with cases I've worked on, I've had all kinds of threats and nothing came of any of them. And there had been a rash of these virtual kidnaps where people get suckered into paying ransoms even though no one has been taken.

'So, I said prove it to me – that's all I said – and he hung up. I tried straight away to find Ashley. I called a dozen times and sent texts but he never answered. Twenty-four hours later I got a text that just said *Meghan* – one word, *Meghan*, nothing else.'

Maria lit a cigarette for her husband and placed it in his hand. He took two deep drags as she began to speak.

'An hour or so after that, Meghan's dad called,' she said. 'I picked up and he was frantic. He said his daughter had been hit by a car outside a bar near Woodstock, and that the driver didn't stop. She was in the hospital with all kinds of injuries.'

Chuck said, 'I felt sick. When I got the next call, I knew it was legit. They said if I didn't do what they said – even if I thought of killing myself instead – then Ashley would die, too. Honest, I didn't even hesitate. There was nothing else I could do. I had no clue who these people were or why they wanted me to do it, not until they claimed credit after the explosion.

'They told me I had to pick up a package. They left it in a luggage storage place on Lexington and the claim check arrived in an envelope for me at the head office. They called one last time to tell me how to prime the bomb and set the timer and what to do with it. They knew I understood explosives from when the bomb squad was part of my patch.

'It was easy for me, getting around the hotel, obviously. I was the last person anyone would suspect. I went there early in the day, had a meeting with all the key people, walked around checking things, the usual routine. It was no problem placing the bomb. I was in a daze really. I just knew I didn't have a choice. But when it happened, when I saw what the bomb had done, it was just. . .' He began sobbing.

Maria said, 'But we never heard from Ashley. We didn't know what had happened to him, whether he was dead, or still their prisoner. We were afraid to say anything in case they still had him. But he just called. Less than an hour ago. We couldn't believe it. He had no idea why he was kidnapped.'

'Where is he?' Siobhan asked.

'He's in Massapequa on Long Island. They set him free from a van near town and he called from a gas station. He didn't know anything about the explosion.'

The doorbell rang. Siobhan had called for the NYPD to take the Healys into custody and for officers to wait for their son's return.

Two uniformed officers came into the living room. Chuck pointed at the handcuffs they were holding. 'You won't be needing them, boys,' he said.

'Better let them, captain Healy,' Siobhan said. She took one of the officers aside. 'They're in a bad way, especially him. They need to be on safety watch.'

The Healys were handcuffed, and as they were leaving the room, Chuck stopped and turned back towards Siobhan and Kenny.

'What else could I do?' he said. 'What choice did I have? Both of you, ask yourselves – what would you have done? He's my son, our only child. He has his whole life in front of him. What would you do for your own flesh and blood?'

Siobhan and Kenny watched from their own car until the patrol cars had turned out of the road. Heavy rain clattered on the roof. Kenny looked at her phone. 'Doesn't look like this storm is going to weaken much,' she said. 'They get more intense every year.'

'I think it's sent him crazy,' Siobhan said. 'That guy's at war inside his own head. But that was a good question he asked.'

'It was?'

'Think about it. It's between your family and three total strangers. What's your choice? At what point does love outweigh everything else? Is there a point when the cost of another life – a stranger's – means nothing against the love you feel for a child or a spouse, when nothing you do is too wrong if it will save them?'

'I guess,' Kenny said. 'People with passions do amazing things. They'll kill and they'll lie if they believe enough in something. Look what our Irish kin have done. A lot of people died in their cause.'

'That's different. Right or wrong, the Provisionals saw themselves as classic revolutionaries. What Healy did was a transaction – he traded three lives for the life of his son. He acted purely out of love. It would take a bunch of heartless psychos to put anyone in a situation like that.'

'It's not so different,' Kenny said. 'Good people through history have been willing to fight and to kill for the country they love, and for the safety and happiness of people they love.'

There was an accident on the Henry Hudson Parkway and the traffic ground to a halt by the George Washington Bridge.

Kenny turned on the lights and siren, cursing at cars for failing to move aside.

'Turn it off, Bridge,' Siobhan said, putting a hand on hers. 'It's jammed, it's okay. There's no way we can get through this. We're in no crazy rush.'

Kenny turned off the siren, still muttering angrily. The strain was getting to her.

'Calm down, lady,' Siobhan said with a smile. 'It's a rough day for both of us.'

They were at a standstill and Kenny took her hands off the wheel, stretched her arms, then put down the windows. A cool breeze from the river drifted through the car.

'What's motivating your pal Dan?' Kenny said. 'He met those Muslim murderers when he knew they could kill him. Is he in love with that Hunter girl? Is he trying to save her? Is he even still alive?'

Siobhan couldn't tell Kenny the answers to her questions. She wasn't sure herself how to answer the last one – was Dan alive? Wherever he was, he was still in danger. The trauma of losing Laura had triggered something in him. His guilt over Jess Hunter was killing him. What chances was he taking if he didn't care enough about staying alive?

Siobhan's phone buzzed. It was Perry Ainsworth calling.

Chapter Forty-Four

Perry's eyes darted around as if he kept discovering things in the utterly featureless room. He was holding tight to the damp fedora in his lap, his face so red it looked luminous.

'What?' Siobhan said in her angry voice, peering at him a while before going on. 'What is it you've got this sudden urge to tell us all about?'

They were downtown at the FBI's Manhattan HQ in a tiny room with walls of frosted glass. Siobhan and Kenny sat across an empty table waiting for his reply. He gave them a feeble smile, but they didn't smile back.

'Look, I know you're going to be angry with me,' he began. 'I've been going over and over everything since our meeting this morning and I know you're going to tell me I should have told you this before.' He looked at Siobhan. 'You see, my dear, I've been rather torn, to say the least. By the time I knew, he was so deep into this I felt keeping quiet was all I could do. But now I think, whether I keep quiet or talk, they're in exactly the same amount of danger.'

Siobhan's hands were behind her head, her fingers locked so hard together she could feel them going numb.

'Keep talking,' she said. Kenny sat beside her, making notes.

Perry started telling them about the kidnappers summoning Dan, how Dan had seen Jess in tears, how they had sent him the video of his family, and about the fake story they'd forced him to file. Siobhan knew most of that. She looked into Perry's penitent eyes and at his stupid, guilty smile, and felt like throwing a punch into his fat face.

'Where's Dan? What's happened to him?' she said.

'That's what I want to tell you. I saw him early today before you came to the hotel. He was fine – at least, he's not hurt in any way, but he's got himself into a dreadful spot.'

'You're telling me you were with him this morning and you said nothing to us? What lunatic games have you been playing? Where is he now?'

'I don't know where he is now. They wanted to meet him again. He had to go. I couldn't stop him and he didn't have a choice. I've tried to do the right thing . . .' Perry's voice faltered.

'The right thing would have been to tell us what you knew from the start,' Siobhan said. 'People's lives are at stake here, and this is *our* business, not yours. You write high and mighty columns for your millions of readers, and some of them might even care what you think. But it's not your job to go chasing mad killers. And Dan Brasher is a total and complete moron for ever falling into this trap. He's been forced into telling the world a complete fiction. They played him completely, and for what? They haven't released Jess, and now they've used her to lure him back again. There's no guessing what they'll make him do next.'

She banged her fists on the table. Perry jumped.

'I need to . . .' he began.

'I think you need to shut right up. You know what my Bogside granny used to say? "Don't keep putting your foot in your mouth when you've not got a feckin' leg to stand on."'

'Please, my dear—'

'Stop saying that! I am not your fucking *dear*. Do you want me to throw you out that window?' she shouted. She felt Kenny's hand grip her arm.

Perry's head fell into his hands.

'Please will you stop yelling at me,' he said. 'Have me hanged tomorrow if you want' – he looked up at her – 'but there's something else I need to tell you.'

Kenny leaned towards Siobhan, still holding her arm, and whispered, 'Let me do this for a while, take a break.'

Siobhan nodded and pushed her chair back from the table.

'What is it, Mr Ainsworth? Tell me,' Kenny said.

'After you left the hotel, I went to hire a car for Dan. He thought it less likely he'd be found if the car wasn't in his name. They called him with directions to meet. He didn't tell me where, but I put my mobile phone beneath the spare wheel in the boot. That was about three hours ago. The battery was run down a little, but I didn't have time to charge it.'

Siobhan raised her hand. 'Wait,' she said. 'Do you have the hire car receipt?'

Perry pulled the receipt from his pocket and handed it to her, and Siobhan left the room.

Kenny sat quietly, texting on her phone.

'Where's she gone?' Perry said.

Kenny was still texting as she answered. 'Most hire cars have a built-in GPS locator,' she said. 'She'll be trying to get the company to turn it on in the car you hired. If your phone doesn't work, that should.'

'Ah ... I didn't know that about them,' Perry said. 'What will you do if you find out where he's gone?'

'Try to save Dan and Jess Hunter, naturally,' she said. 'Those plans get made way above my pay grade.'

'Dan's been sick at the thought of his family worrying what's happened to him,' Perry told her. 'He's writing the whole story on a cheap laptop he bought in case he doesn't make it, the entire story, and all the lies they made him tell, the lot. He left the laptop in his hotel. I was stunned when he told me ... the thought he was preparing to die. That's what made my mind up to come here. He's convinced himself Muslims have nothing to do with these killings.'

Kenny stopped texting, but kept looking down. 'What makes him so sure it's not Muslims?' she said. 'That's only wild media speculation.'

'Most of all it's the Hitler tattoo on that man's arm and the lies the so-called father told him in the story they made him write.'

She looked up. 'Does Siobhan know about this?'

'Don't you all? Dan put it in the email he sent to Siobhan.'

'I don't always get told everything,' Kenny said.

'Well, if he's right, you'll soon be hunting for a gang of neo-fascists.'

Kenny went back to texting. Perry looked at his watch and put his hand in the air like a schoolboy seeking permission.

'When do you suppose I'll get released from here? I need to go and rescue that laptop as soon as I get out of here. It's a dodgy hotel ... don't want it getting pilfered.'

'Where was he hiding from us all this time?' Kenny asked.

'A dump called the Lilliput on the West Side,' Perry said. 'Is it okay if I leave now?'

Kenny paused. 'Let's give it ten, fifteen minutes, in case Siobhan wants to talk more. After that, make sure you keep in touch, okay?'

Chapter Forty-Five

Perry instantly reproached himself for being so stupid. He should never have told Kenny about Dan's hotel. The FBI were sure to want the laptop for themselves. Perry had wanted to take the computer with him when he left, but Dan had needed it to finish his story in the few hours before his rendezvous.

Dan had written what might be his last testament, his life's final exclusive. He was on his way by now to wherever he had been summoned, putting his life at the mercy of these killers. If they were jihadists, they could condemn him as an evil messenger who had lied to the world about their glorious jihad. If they were neo-fascists, they could kill him for being a fake-news merchant.

Whatever happened, Perry was guilty of conspiring with Dan. His friend's mad passions had overpowered him. From the outset, he should have told Siobhan everything.

Perry had been in plenty of scrapes of his own, but Dan was different. His risks sometimes seemed wanton. When he'd disappeared in Mexico years ago, Jim Slight had dispatched Perry to find him. Slight had warned Dan it was too dangerous trying to get close to the drug cartels. The local police hadn't much cared what happened to him; to them, Dan was just another foolhardy journalist. They said he must have been shot, and his body dumped somewhere. At the time, people were being shot dead by the dozen every day in Juárez, where he'd last been seen. If he was lucky, they said, he wouldn't have been buried alive; the drug lords of Mexico considered that an efficient and inexpensive form of execution. But Dan turned up two weeks later and produced a three-part series on the activities of the Juárez drug cartel and their bloody war with the competing Sinaloa cartel.

In Perry's hard-headed view, as well as being reckless, Dan cared too much. He had been known to weep in Slight's office when a story he cared about did not receive the play he believed it warranted — stories most often involving dying refugees or starving children in faraway places. It did not detract from these protests that Dan might be drunk at the time of them. But it was unhealthy in this job to have feelings so close to the surface. In himself, Perry recognised a sociopathic streak, and he was glad of it. In this line of work, concern over other people's hardship was something best kept in check. He certainly cared little about the offence his columns caused. He enjoyed the reputation; it was his personal brand.

The weather was getting worse and Perry hadn't been able to catch a cab. After taking a subway train to Midtown, he walked west towards Broadway, leaning into the whipping wind, hand pressed down on his fedora. It was hard to see through the mist of drenching rain.

He rang the bell at the abandoned front desk and, as agreed, paid Dan's bill and checked out of the room. Then he went upstairs to collect Dan's laptop and other belongings. At the top of the creaking stairs, he turned towards the hotel room door. It was open, and from inside he heard a noise.

Perry charged towards the door. Bloody FBI, that damned Kenny woman had kept him waiting while she sent people here.

Perry stormed into the room shouting, 'What's the meaning of this? You have no right being here.'

A lone man was on his knees by the bed, rummaging through Dan's backpack. The room had been ransacked. The mattress had been thrown from the bed; drawers were pulled from the dresser and scattered on the carpet.

In a second, Perry was looming over the man, who was small and thin. On the back of his grey T-shirt was an American flag beneath the words *I Don't Kneel*. A wet red anorak was on the floor behind him.

'This is outrageous,' Perry bellowed. 'Show me immediately what papers you have to justify what's going on here.'

The man looked up with his ugly, cross-eyed face. At the same time, his right hand reached for a gun on the green carpet next to the bag. On the man's arm, Perry saw the tattoo – double eights.

The woman at the front desk heard two shots.

Chapter Forty-Six

There was no way out now. He had walked into their trap, and here he was. Helpless. Dan kept seeing the people he was doing it for, imagining their grief if that was what it came to, and knowing he had no choice.

He had waited as instructed in the car park of a small-town pharmacy. A white Escalade had flashed its lights and stopped behind him, the driver waving in what Dan decided was a follow-me way. They had driven fifteen minutes, with the Escalade driver acting like a helpful host guiding him to a hard-to-find home – waiting when he missed a green light, slowing when another vehicle intervened between them.

It wasn't the way terrorists, or criminal masterminds, invited you to secret meetings; not if they intended to let you live. No rough-handling abductors, no windowless van, no hood to blind him for the journey. He knew exactly where he was.

He had driven for almost two hours from Manhattan through raging weather. Traffic was light as he travelled north of the city, slow in the blinding rain, into Connecticut. Wild white horses ripped across Long Island Sound. The wind was stripping trees and rocking his car.

There was shocking news on the radio. The whole bloody mess was starting to make sense. Leila had been telling the truth all along. Chuck Healy had confessed he'd planted the

Plaza-Asturias bomb to save his teenage son's life. In Warsaw, the sister of Howard Wyler's butler had claimed she and her children had been kidnapped. In other, more routine news for Manhattan, a man had been gravely injured after shots were fired in a West Side hotel.

Not long before sunset, he followed the Escalade crunching along the long, snaking drive to their final destination. They had passed through high metal gates leading to the big house. The Escalade's driver, in a hooded yellow parka, stopped to remove a heavy, fallen branch blocking their way.

The enormous stone house imitated the neat classical lines of an English Georgian mansion. It was raised above the trees on a wide skirt of lawn.

The Escalade stopped at a portico and a tall front door. When the Escalade door opened, a black-and-white collie leapt out. There was a roll of thunder and the dog shrank back in shock. Long-legged horses reared and started behind white fences in the distance.

Dan climbed out of his hire car as the Escalade moved away and turned into a red barn. He could see a cluster of trees draped with bird feeders swinging in the gale.

The man in the yellow parka trotted towards Dan through the rain and raised his hand in an unsmiling wave. In the shelter of the portico, he pulled back his hood and Dan stared in shock.

It was George Frobisher.

'Good evening, Dan. Thank you so much for coming,' he said, with an everyday briskness that made Dan feel like he'd done nothing more than turn up on time for a business meeting. The rainbow-striped woollen hat Frobisher was wearing, with a yellow pom-pom, would have made it impossible for him to seem sinister, if not for the fact he was carrying a Glock pistol and pointing it at Dan's chest.

He beckoned Dan ahead of him up the steps towards the tall black door; it opened into a large lobby as they reached the top. Inside, two masked men took hold of Dan, one arm each. They didn't handle him roughly, but their grips were firm. Without a word, they marched him past a grand, winding staircase with heavy, carved wooden banisters. Paintings lined the staircase wall and the stormy evening light was showing through a huge stained-glass window with a blue-robed Madonna and a pink and naked baby Jesus, each with a yellow halo.

They took him into a room that was dark but for thin strips of light at the edges of tall, closed curtains. The room smelled as stale and unused as his Sheffield grandmother's cold front parlour had when he was a small boy, though there was enough light to know it was far bigger.

As they entered, Dan heard what sounded like a stifled scream.

'Jess?' he said, and heard the same noise again. Over his shoulder, there was movement in the darkness.

'Take me over there,' Dan said. He swung himself around against his escorts' grip and felt the four hands holding him tighten.

'I want to go over there,' he shouted, pulling himself towards the struggling form. He was lifted off his feet and Dan flailed a little in the air before the door opened enough for the silhouette of Frobisher's head to appear.

Frobisher spoke calmly: 'It's okay, take it easy. Let them sit together. Not too close. And let her speak.'

They lowered Dan's feet to the floor and released their grip. He was pressed into a large chair and heard the rattle of metal and then the cold touch of it, on one wrist then the other, as they handcuffed him to each arm. He heard zip ties as they secured his feet tightly to the chair legs.

His eyes became accustomed to the light and he saw her silhouette about twenty feet away. The slow ripping sound was Jess's duct-tape gag being removed.

'Dan,' she said. 'What's happening? What are you doing here?'

'I came to get you out. How long have you been here?'

'Only a couple of hours. Those two walked me here. It wasn't far. What's going on?'

'I haven't got a clue,' Dan said.

'Do you know whose house this is? You should see this room in the light. It's like a palace.'

The wheels of a vehicle faded away, down the long drive.

'I'm pretty sure the owner is George Frobisher,' Dan said.

'What? That's crazy.'

'I know. It was him at the door.'

'Is he responsible for all this?'

'He's definitely part of it. He pointed a gun at me out there.'

'I don't get it. I've been listening to Muslim chants for days. That window in the lobby belongs in a church and the ceiling in here looks like a Sistine Chapel knockoff. It makes no sense.'

It wasn't necessary to make complete sense of it to be pretty sure everything, all this bloodshed and terror, involved the wishes of one of the world's most infamous men – one who, not long ago, was also one of its richest.

He could see Jess's shadow in the darkness and hear her breathing.

'Why would Frobisher be involved with Islamist terrorists?' she asked.

'It's a good bet right now Islamists have nothing to do with what's been happening.'

There were footsteps along the corridor outside. Frobisher opened the door and lights came on.

Jess was sitting on a long, ornate sofa covered with a tapestry of women in white gowns and high wigs reclining languorously in a garden of roses. She wore the same sequined black top, and looked at Dan through long strands of her black hair. Grey duct tape wrapped her ankles to a sofa leg and her wrists were bound on her lap. Dan was secured to a heavy chair of red velvet; its carved golden arms were already marked by the handcuffs. He was zip-tied so tight at the ankles he couldn't feel his feet.

The room was a blinding vision of frescoed walls, marble pillars and gilded furniture. On the high ceiling, a riot of rococo carving surrounded a mural where grey-bearded men in vivid robes held their hands together in prayer, and chubby, winged children floated on a background of clouds and heavenly blue. Hanging on a wall was a large painting of what looked to Dan like the Last Judgement, with a Christ figure surrounded by angels and saints hovering above terrified images of the damned. A huge vase with golden scrolling handles stood on a table between two tall windows. It was painted with bright images of flowers and fruit, but the bouquet of roses filling it was withered and dry petals littered the tabletop. On another wall, a portrait of the man of the house smiled across the room – proud, pleased, correct, hands tucked into his jacket pockets.

Frobisher held a silver tray carrying his gun, a small audio recorder, two phones and a bottle of water. Tucked under his left arm was a manila folder. He had changed into the exact clothes that appeared in his portrait – a blue double-breasted blazer with brass buttons and sharp-creased grey trousers. His black shoes were shining and, as in his image on the wall, a yellow rose was pinned to his left lapel. He wore a tie with diagonal black and red stripes. The collie ran ahead of him, jumping up at Jess and Dan, wagging its tail and barking.

Frobisher placed the tray and the folder on a circular walnut table by the wall, put the gun in his jacket pocket, and walked to the fireplace, which was piled with logs on top of balls of newspaper.

'I'm sorry it's so cold in here,' he said, striking a long match to light the newspaper. It looked like a copy of *The New York World*.

With surprising care, Frobisher removed the grey tape binding Jess's hands and gave her the bottle of water.

'Miss Hunter is fine,' he said. 'This is the first time we have met, but she has been fed and she has been able to sleep in some comfort, I hope?' Jess drank deeply from the water bottle, saying nothing.

Frobisher opened a tall, bay-fronted cabinet. Glasses rattled against the doors where they were hanging. He poured from a bottle of Macallan 64 into a carved crystal glass and picked ice with his fingers from a silver bowl. He took a large mouthful of the whisky and straight away topped up the glass.

At the window, he pulled wide the curtains and dead petals drifted to the floor from the tabletop. The hard rain on the window panes was louder than ever. Wind rushed through the trees and a rose bush rattling against the window seemed to be pleading for shelter. A lightning flash lit Frobisher's face. Sullen thunder rumbled in the distance. From a corner, alongside George Frobisher's triumphant portrait, came the heavy ticking of a tall mahogany clock.

'Isn't it magnificent?' Frobisher said. 'Mother nature is pitiless. Nothing can stand in her way. She does whatever she wants and all we mortals can do is to run . . . imagine that.'

He turned back into the room and lifted the manila folder from the table. 'I have a story to share with you,' he told Dan, holding the brown folder above his head. 'And when this is over, the world will want to know what happened here. They'll want to hear our conversation.' He took the audio recorder from the tray. 'We'll make a record. They will hear our voices when we are both gone.'

Dan looked across the room to Jess and their eyes met. She had the same look of exhausted terror he remembered seeing on the laptop the night he sent the fake story.

'But what about your promise to us?' Dan said. 'I have done everything you asked. You told me no one would be harmed if I followed your orders.'

Frobisher turned away again, looking out the window at the storm-blackened sky.

'Ah, but you have betrayed us, Mr Brasher. I found out only moments ago. In spite of our warnings, in spite of the consequences we promised, you have betrayed us. The FBI knows you have come here. They know about the story you sent to London at my request.'

Jess looked at Dan, mystified. Frobisher walked back to the tray and held up one of the phones.

'Also, I found this in the trunk of your car,' he said. 'Someone must have mislaid it. Possibly it was left by a previous customer, but I don't think so.'

Fucking Ainsworth!

'I can promise you, sir, it's not mine, and I have no idea how it got there.'

'It doesn't matter anymore,' Frobisher said. 'It was always planned to end tonight. I expect them to arrive in about one hour. They'll be ready for a fight, I'm sure, but they will be disappointed. We are alone now.'

'I told no one I was coming here, Mr Frobisher,' Dan said.

'You are lying to me now, but we will deal later with your treachery,' he replied.

They were trapped and Dan didn't know what to do. He was bound too tightly to the heavy chair. Even if he could stand, his feet were so numb he doubted they would bear his weight. All he could do was keep Frobisher talking, going through every detail of what he had done, and pray for a miracle.

Frobisher added whisky to his empty glass, drank some more, and sat across from Dan in front of the tall fireplace. He placed the recorder on a table between them and took out the gun to rest it in his lap on top of the manila folder.

'My story is about cruelty and injustice,' he said. 'It's about suffering, and it's about revenge.'

Frobisher removed a single page of paper from the folder and held it in both hands. It was a handwritten note.

'First, I want to read this to you. I've read it every morning since the day it happened:

'*My darling George, I write this with a broken heart. I loved you from the moment we first met and I will love you for eternity. No one in my life was truer and more generous than you have been to me. Please forgive me for abandoning you, but I think I am mad now and that nothing can be the same. Instead of giving you the strength you need, I fear I am draining it away. May God bless and keep you, my love, and give you the fortitude I no longer can. I will wait for you until we are together again. Please tell no one about this letter or what I have done. There will be pain enough for everyone without adding disgrace to their grief. Betty.'*

Frobisher kept looking at the note even though he had finished reading it.

'I have read this every day since Betty left us. Every day it has given me strength. It has reminded me of her love. And it has kept awake my anger.'

Frobisher showed the letter to Dan. 'Look how beautiful her writing is.'

'Yes, it is,' Dan agreed. It was true, considering what had been on his wife's mind at the time of writing it.

'She left the house after midnight when I was asleep and put that letter next to the bed. The police told me before I had time to read it. I never showed the letter to them. Betsy would hate it if I did.' He walked to the fire with the letter and held it above the flames. 'I will never read it again. There'll be no need. I'll be seeing her soon.'

Frobisher opened his hand and his wife's suicide note floated into the flames.

'Do you know how she died, Mr Brasher?' He pulled a photograph from the folder. 'Do you know what they drove her to do?'

He held the photograph in front of Dan. It was the shattered remains of Betty Applegate Frobisher's red Corvette. Dan had seen the photo before. The car had virtually evaporated on impact, its body compacted against a huge tree in a cloud of heat and smoke. Two rear wheels were the only remaining evidence it had once been a car. It was said to have hit the tree at a speed far in excess of one hundred miles an hour.

'It was me they asked to identify the body,' Frobisher said, still holding the photo in front of Dan. 'But there was no body.

There was no body left to be found in this. A state trooper tried to catch her, but didn't have a chance. He was half a mile behind when Betty hit that tree.'

He took more paper from the manila folder.

'I will read to you from this accident report: *It wasn't practical for the officer to search inside the car for documents to identify the driver, but he could see it had been a woman with long blonde hair who had been wearing light blue jeans, a white T-shirt with a Prada label, and light blue sneakers.*'

He pointed at the police report, looking at Dan. 'Blue jeans, a T-shirt, sneakers, and her long blonde hair. That was all that was left of my wife. She was torn apart. Scattered across the road and into that tree. It was like a bomb had blown her to pieces.'

Frobisher sat staring at the photo, his eyes shining with tears.

'She is watching over me now as I work to avenge her death.'

'Are you going to kill us too?' Dan asked. Jess groaned again.

Frobisher turned his head suddenly to stare across the room. It was like he had seen something – another presence that was demanding his attention.

'Mr Frobisher,' Dan said loudly. 'Surely your wife didn't want you to do any of this?'

Frobisher flinched at the question. 'We've done it together, she and I. She's my guide. We talk all the time. I know how she feels.'

Dan dismissed in his mind a range of sane responses to this statement. 'But she was a deeply religious woman,' he said instead.

Frobisher sprang to his feet. He pointed across the room to a wedding photo on the wall beside the fireplace. 'You don't understand,' he said. 'She teaches me everything about the Bible and God's justice.'

Right then, handcuffed to a chair, looking at the gun in his hand, it was obvious to Dan that, with the Bible's contradictions about forgiveness and punishment, Frobisher had become insanely partial to the passages on wrath and retribution.

Chapter Forty-Seven

Siobhan gazed at Bridget Kenny in silence, but there was nothing left in her face she knew. All the softness and sweet mischief was gone; her face was still as rock, her big eyes dull and loveless. It was like looking at a stranger across the aisle of a subway train.

'What were you thinking, Bridge? You were doing it right in front of me, sending them texts as we stood there outside the Healy house.'

Kenny didn't falter. She gazed away across the darkened interview room, looking at nothing.

'All those innocent people? How could you have helped them do these things? Why? Did they threaten you? Were they going to kill someone you loved?'

Kenny's face flickered to life and the handcuffs rattled as she tried raising her arms. 'Not them, Miss Mac Stiofain. It was me. It was us. My people. We did this together.'

'But why?'

'Innocent people get killed for great causes. The fight for freedom is long and hard. Our Irish kin, Miss Mac Stiofain. Remember? They saw themselves as classic revolutionaries – you said it yourself.'

'What are you talking about?'

'Open your eyes, Siobhan. Millions of true Americans have been dispossessed. Angry patriots have been forgotten by their own country, robbed of their heritage, seen their culture overrun. Armed struggle is the last option. Chaos and fear will be our friend. We will eliminate political leaders who would destroy our country and the corrupt media that enables them.'

She's insane. The woman I thought I loved is a lunatic.

'Was it you who told them where Jake Abrams was hiding? Do you know where Jessica Hunter is? Do you know what's going to happen to Dan Brasher? Why is he at George Frobisher's mansion?'

'George Frobisher is our saviour. He is our deliverance.'

'What the hell are you talking about?'

Siobhan's phone buzzed. It was the director's office. She left the interrogation room to take Alexander Livermore's call.

'What on earth has George Frobisher got to do with this?' Livermore asked.

'We can only speculate, sir, but we've tracked Dan Brasher to Frobisher's country house and we'll be on site in an hour or so. There doesn't seem any doubt they're expecting us. We can be sure Kenny has warned them.'

'We're certain Kenny was the mole?'

'Oh yes, sir, we received solid information. She's being questioned now, and calm like she's sitting in church. She's parroting a lot of white supremacist gibberish – thinks she's a revolutionary. And she's telling us Frobisher is her saviour. It makes no sense yet, but that's what she's saying.'

'It's unbelievable how someone like this got through our vetting process,' Livermore said. 'We'll need a hard look at the people who cleared her. It's unlikely she's been working alone.'

Siobhan joined the FBI Hostage Rescue Team being briefed on what to do in the coming raid. They were wearing khaki combat uniforms with flak jackets and helmets fitted with night-vision scopes. Patches on their sleeves showed an eagle with spread wings above the words *Servare Vitas* – To Save Lives. A big screen displayed a satellite view of the Frobisher mansion.

The roads were empty as they headed through the gale. Siobhan was crowded into an SUV, speed-reading a report that had just dropped about George Frobisher. She knew most of it already ... Married twenty years to the daughter of the last president, Eugene Applegate of Texas ... a rich man, Applegate wasn't happy having an armed robber's son join the family ... he grew fond of his son-in-law over the years ... told pals how 'tough and relentless' he was ... came to admire his aggressive style of business ... began adopting some of Frobisher's 'unconventional' tactics ... seized upon tempting, less orthodox, opportunities offered in such places as Russia ... things started going off the rails when Applegate was toying with running for president and gave Frobisher control of his companies ... Frobisher had learned from his oligarch pals about hiding his wealth in foreign banks and dubious property investments ... by the time Applegate got to the White House, Frobisher's tricks were embedded deep into the new president's operations and it was downhill from there. Applegate's enemies had already started burrowing into his personal and financial life ... banks called in loans, numerous countries froze their assets, all their overseas properties were confiscated, and Frobisher faced years in prison ... on the edge of destruction, fearing his son-in-law would turn against him, Applegate granted Frobisher a presidential pardon ... facing impeachment, Applegate left office. The new president had promised him a pardon, but the heat was so great she never delivered ...

What a holy fucking mess, but nothing in there to explain what might have turned Frobisher into a maniac who'd hired a gang of fascists to go round killing people.

Siobhan had no idea what would greet them at George Frobisher's mansion. Drone surveillance showed there were people in the building, but it was unclear how many. There also could be guards on the approach roads who would send an alert. A hostage negotiator would make first contact, but the team had to be ready for well-armed resistance. Dan could be there now at this madman's mercy, but she couldn't keep thinking about that; she couldn't keep thinking about Bridget Kenny. Not now.

Chapter Forty-Eight

'Look at her,' Frobisher said. He had taken the wedding photo from the wall and held it up for Dan. 'Take a look at this beautiful, God-loving woman. In all her life, she never did harm to a single person.' The bride wore a white gown with a long train sweeping behind her and a tiara of white flowers in her big hair. She was looking, in a delighted, oddly needy way, at the proud, unsmiling man beside her. He wore morning tails and a red waistcoat and held a grey top hat in the crook of his left arm.

'She looks very lovely,' Dan said.

Frobisher sat again in the chair across from Dan, fingertips pressed together in the shape of a steeple as he stared into the fire. 'These people took her life. She was harmless and they destroyed her.

'They hated me, they hated my success. Even when things went well, there were always the cheap shots about my slum-boy roots and about my father. Out there in the real world, people loved me because I escaped from it all and did well. They were going to make a movie about me. But on the Upper East Side, in the Hamptons and the Vineyard – I was never going to fit in with those people. I was the dishwasher who did too well. Something had to be wrong. When Gene got to the White House, they went crazy. They took their chance and they pounced. They hated me so much they would have done anything to bring me down.'

Frobisher took the gun from the table beside him and for a moment smoothed his palms against its black polymer casing, in the way a CEO might fidget with an executive comfort toy.

'I didn't care what any of those people thought. They were nothing to me. I got up earlier than they did. I worked harder. I took more chances, made braver decisions. And I broke a few of their rules, and they hated me for that.' He raised his glass towards Dan. 'I wasn't like them, or like you, Dan Brasher. I didn't go to some fancy college. My father was no high-powered investor like yours. Trevor Brasher – another friend who betrayed me, who made millions picking up cheap the remains of properties I spent my life building. Did you really believe I wanted to get back working with him?'

'That was never going to happen,' Dan said. 'But why did you invite me to lunch?'

'It was you. I wanted to get closer to you. To find out what you knew and feed you that line that the government was convinced Arab terrorists were the killers.' He smiled. 'Also, I wanted my people to get a good look at you.'

'Your people?'

'They weren't secret service people who took us to lunch. They abandoned me long ago. They were mine. It was two of them who tied you to that chair.'

Frobisher paused for a moment. He stared at the large rug. It was patterned around its edges with spears and swords and quivers filled with arrows. Maybe he needed time to reassess all the bad feelings built up inside him.

'The treachery of those people – the Wylers and the Chatstones. That old viscount Chatstone – he was always chasing me to put money into his businesses. And Howard Wyler and Gene Applegate – they'd been friends since college and just like that Wyler betrayed him, threw us into the flames.'

Frobisher looked hard at Dan, as if he were waiting to see something in his face. Was he looking for the sign of some understanding, some sympathy for the terrible suffering he had endured?

Dan said: 'Why on earth did you turn up at Howard Wyler's funeral? You were responsible for his murder.'

Frobisher frowned like the victim of a stupid question. He dropped another log on the fire. 'To enjoy their grief, of course,' he said. 'To see them going through the pain I had suffered.'

'What about the kitchen hand in your own home? Did you poison him?'

'Poor Jorge. He was insurance. How could I become a suspect if these terrorists had attempted to murder me in my own apartment?'

He walked to a table piled with books and picked one up. It was *Cheating the Odds: George Frobisher's Fatal Formula* by Jacob Abrams and James Slight. A couple of months ago, it had been the country's number one bestseller.

'And then these two – Abrams and Slight. They were the puppets. Their bosses set them loose on us. They won their fancy awards by destroying a president and ruining me. And then they made money dancing on my grave with this book.' He walked to the fireplace, dropped the book on the burning logs, and used both hands to pick up a heavy poker to stoke the fire.

'Jim Slight came to my birthday party in Mexico. He'd spend weekends on my yacht, drinking my wine, being charming to Betty. And Abrams – twice we took Abrams to Davos on my plane. Betty enjoyed his company, with his jokes and his newspaper stories. She sent him champagne every birthday.'

He watched as the book's red dust jacket curled in the flames. 'How could they do what they did to me? And to her – to Betty? I tried calling them, but neither of them would even pick up the phone. They didn't have the guts. Abrams nearly escaped, but we caught up with him in the end. Everyone believes we punished him for that editorial – "The Sword and the Pen" – but it was going to happen anyway. We planned that hotel attack for weeks.'

'Why did you keep him alive after taking him from that shack?'

'To begin with, his was the life we intended to trade for your cooperation.' He pointed over his shoulder at Jess. 'But your assistant here was a much more appealing hostage. Plus, she was getting too close to the truth, hounding that police chief who planted the bomb to kill Jake Abrams and digging around in that hotel. Once we captured her, Abrams was surplus to our needs. He was going to die eventually no matter what.'

Frobisher retrieved his drink from the table by Dan and stood beside the high stone hearth. His eyelids looked heavy and Dan noticed for the first time his clean-shaven face. He had shaved since they'd met on the doorstep.

He leaned close to Dan and the smell of whisky was strong. 'Abrams and Slight twisted every piece of information they could get their hands on, and the so-called prestige of those rags led the way for all the others. Every other newspaper and website and news channel – they all piled in for the kill. They set the world on fire for us.'

He smiled a smile of angry satisfaction. 'But you and I together – the two of us – we took care of those fearless newspapers. Thank you, Mr Brasher, for your help. Thank you for being my messenger.'

Frobisher picked up the wedding photo again. 'All her life, everyone wanted to be her friend. When Gene went to the White House, she became a star – a celebrity. She was the centre of every crowd and every dinner party. She looked so beautiful and happy.

'She couldn't believe it when the invitations stopped coming. Friends she'd known since she was a child stopped answering her messages. They turned their backs when she walked into a room. They had wanted her at every head table and every charity bash. In the end, most of them wouldn't even take her money. Hospitals removed our names from the clinics we funded; galleries returned millions in artworks we'd given.'

The dog scrambled to get onto Dan's knee. Frobisher picked it up. 'Hey, Spike, settle down,' he whispered, kissing the collie's head and stroking it.

Such tenderness. Reserved for a fucking dog.

'The media hounded us everywhere we went,' Frobisher continued. 'They came after us in speedboats when we were on the yacht. They trailed us down the street and waited for hours every time we went out to eat. They shouted insults at us, trying to get me into a rage for their pictures – *Hey, Betty, how's it feel being married to a criminal mastermind? . . . You gonna find someone decent when he goes upstate?*

Dan knew the paparazzi had hounded Frobisher to breaking point; he'd paid damages after a scuffle sent a photographer flying down some stairs, breaking her collarbone. After that, the insults had only increased.

'The gossip pages used to love her,' Frobisher said. 'Betty was the fanciest hostess in town. She was crushed when everything went wrong and they started mocking her. Columnists who were guests here and on the boat – they started laughing at her fashion sense and the cost of her clothes and her jewellery, how many pairs of shoes she owned. They wrote about the homes she designed; how loud and vulgar they were . . .' His angry smile appeared again. 'And, of course, they never stopped saying what awful taste she had in men.'

Frobisher pushed the dog off his lap and turned the gun carelessly in his hands, His voice fell to a whisper and his eyes were brimming again.

'She couldn't bear it. She was alone except for me. We never had children. No one wanted to see her, not even her family, because she refused to abandon me. There was only the cardinal. He came to the apartment to pray with her. For hours they sat together. Canny old priest, the cardinal. She left the church a fortune.' He took more of his Macallan. 'They murdered her and I have made them pay.'

Frobisher walked over to Jess and sat alongside her on the sofa. He waved towards Dan. 'Look at what he's been willing to do. The sacrifice he's making to save the lives of those he loves – his family and you, Miss Hunter.' He smiled at Jess and she looked away. 'You became my bait for Dan Brasher. And you, Mr Brasher . . .' Frobisher raised his weapon in the air. 'Here you are again, for the final time, with your life in my hands.'

He drank more whisky.

'People will do anything to save those who matter most to them. I weaponised their love. I made it lethal. They were fine citizens, every one of them. A police chief who'd dedicated his life to upholding the law. A media magnate who loved her daughter more than life itself. The devoted butler who sent money home every month to his beloved sister. Each of them did things that would have been impossible for an outsider. Healy organised that hotel's security himself. Who would suspect Cressida

Chatstone could plant a bomb in her own home? Or that a devoted butler would poison the boss he loved?

'Their actions saved the lives of those they cherished. I honoured my bargain with them. Today, with our work at an end, they have all been set free. I have kept my word. Unlike you, Dan Brasher.'

'What about Ben Tremblay?' Dan asked. 'How did that fit in? You didn't kidnap anyone to kill him.'

'I used to deal with Tremblay in my retail businesses – complete crook. He was so stupid, shooting off his mouth. It's a pity about his driver.'

'And the girlfriend of Chuck Healy's son?' Dan said. 'The radio says she was run down by his kidnappers.'

'That was a shame,' Frobisher said. 'But Healy had to know we were serious.'

'How come you picked me to do your work?'

'We needed a journalist of good standing, someone whose ethics were never in doubt, someone who could help us achieve the final punishment – the destruction of the two newspapers that destroyed me. There were several candidates, then I saw your Wrath of God stories. I remembered you and your father. He had betrayed me and you had savaged me in your newspaper. It was a double betrayal and I could never forgive either of you. When I searched *The Courant*'s archive, I found your story about the wedding massacre in Kabul. You became the outstanding candidate. Don't you think my story about being the father at the wedding was ingenious?'

'Not really,' Dan said. 'That was your mistake. That's when I knew you were lying. I knew that father had killed himself in a suicide attack.'

'He did?' Frobisher shrugged. 'That's too bad. It didn't stop you sending our story though, did it? It didn't prevent the completion of our plan. Everyone believed the lies I made you tell. The Muslim story a perfect decoy. Islamists – jihadists. I knew much of the world would be too ready to think the worst of them. That English aristocrat Leila Chatstone. They've kept her in jail, but she has nothing to do with any of this – she was just the tool to force her mother to follow our orders. All over America and Britain, while we finished our work, the police wasted their time arresting Muslims. We made sure all the captives heard Islamic nasheeds or the call to prayer. If one of them escaped, the music would reinforce the story.'

'Who helped you do all this? One of the men who abducted me had a Heil Hitler tattoo on his arm.'

'I had many helpers. They've gone now. We're alone.'

'Who were they? Why would they help you do all this?'

'In this country, they are proud American patriots. They love Applegate. They think Washington is a sewer – and who can argue with that? Call them whatever you want – ultra-national-ist, anti-communist, freedom fighters. They love their country and they'll fight to save it. They know that Gene Applegate, in his heart, was one of them, and that's why he was destroyed. I gave them millions for their help, just about every penny I could keep out of the hands of the banks and the government. It's no use to me anymore. One day all this will look like a side-show – you'll see. For them, this was a dress rehearsal. They've got sympathisers inside the FBI, the NYPD, and at the Justice Department. And plenty of ex-military – former Special Forces people – lethal, dedicated fighters who would give their blood to keep this country safe. They have links all over the world. They talk together and they plan and the millions I have given will help them achieve their dream of a new America.'

Frobisher stopped abruptly, looked at the tall clock, and left the sofa to walk unsteadily towards a full-length mirror alongside his own huge portrait. He looked at the portrait, then in the mirror, unfastened his double-breasted blazer and adjusted his red-and-black tie. He took a black comb from his jacket, ran it through his short brown hair, looked at the portrait and combed his hair again. Then he played with the angle of the yellow rose in his lapel, glancing back and forth between the mirror and the portrait. All the time he was humming, but Dan couldn't catch the tune.

A little smile appeared on Frobisher's face. 'Good,' he said. 'Very good.'

Dan couldn't figure out why Frobisher would care right now how he looked. He was like a kid getting ready for a big date . . . and that's when it dawned on him. He looked across the room at Jess and it had dawned on her as well. He had done everything trying to save her. Everything he could.

Frobisher walked back from the mirror, still with his smile. 'Betty loves that portrait,' he said. 'She thinks I look perfect.' He brushed his fingertips against the rose. 'She gives me a rose like this for every big occasion. It's to bring me luck. "I'm your yellow rose from Texas," she always says.'

Frobisher staggered a little on his way to the drinks cabinet. He filled his glass again. The bottle was all but empty. He tried dropping it in a wastepaper basket, but missed and the bottle fell to the floor, leaking its last drops onto the rug of spears and arrows. He was drunk and getting clumsy, but Dan was tied too firmly to take advantage.

'And that brings us to you, Mr Brasher,' Frobisher said, his whisky breath in Dan's face again. 'It brings us to your treachery and to your punishment. I warned you to say nothing, but you defied me. You might have caused a disaster for me and my supporters. You and your father I hated already, so you will die for multiple offences. His punishment will be the grief.'

'Any treachery was mine alone, Mr Frobisher,' Dan said. 'My children, my wife, and Jess – they knew nothing of this.'

'I have considered that. You helped me free the world of two cruel newspapers. That part of the deal you did keep – and for that, your family will survive.' He pointed over his shoulder without looking. 'And so will Miss Hunter.'

. . .

Jess looked from across the room at Frobisher's back, at Dan's drooping head. Whenever Frobisher looked away she had been unwinding, inch by inch, the tape binding her ankles. Her left leg was almost free.

. . .

Frobisher put his nose to his glass with his eyes closed, then swallowed its contents. He leaned forward, arms resting on his parted knees. Dan could see only his hair – his uniformly brown, precisely parted hair – and the shoulders of his blue blazer moving as he breathed.

'But as for you and me . . .' Frobisher said to Dan, then paused. He studied the gun in his other hand and, for the first time, wrapped his finger around the trigger.

He looked up at Dan with his mad, empty face. Talking about his lost wife, Frobisher had tears in his eyes; talking about the supposed injustices against him, his face was alive with anger. But at the mention of his victims, of the human consequences of his actions, there was nothing; his face showed only empty indifference, like a drugged child soldier in Africa, or a cartel killer. Whatever cranial wiring it was that helped tell the difference between right and wrong, it had blown up inside George Frobisher's head.

'As for you and me,' he repeated, his eyes lifeless as two blue marbles. 'I cannot offer you a priest, but together we can share the comfort of the words a priest would use at a time like this.'

He went down on one knee, still looking at Dan. He touched the point of the gun to his forehead, to his chest, and to his right and left shoulders. George Frobisher blessed himself with a Glock.

'What would your wife say?' Dan said. 'Ask her what she wants you to do. Ask her what the Bible says. Enough people have died.'

Frobisher, without reply, began his prayer.

'*Through this holy anointing may the Lord in His love and mercy help you with the grace of the Holy Spirit. May the Lord who frees you from sin save you and raise you up . . .*'

After that prayer, Frobisher began reciting the Lord's Prayer, his eyes shut. '*Our Father who art in Heaven, hallowed be thy name. . .*' Dan looked at the room – at the bright religious ceiling, at the painting of the cowering damned receiving the Last Judgement, at the oblivious collie, head on its paws, staring with its big eyes at Frobisher, at the upstanding man in the portrait, a portrait that was such a preposterous lie . . . '*forgive those who trespass against us . . .*' He heard the clapping thunder and the threshing wind and the hammering rain, and the imperturbable beat of the tall mahogany clock.

Frobisher began another prayer: '*This is the Lamb of God who takest away the sins of the world . . .*' Dan closed his eyes and saw, in glowing clarity, Harriet on her scooter; Laura running in pretend fright; Siobhan in high school plugged into her Walkman; smiling Alina at the Lion's Head cutting his slice of lime; the pride in his father's face. And he felt a wave of helpless finality . . . *'Lamb of God who takest away the sins of the world, grant us peace . . .'*

There was a bolt of thunder, close and very loud. An instant streak of lightning turned the room blinding white.

• • •

Jess's legs were free. The heavy poker rested by the fire, steps away. One shot; she had one shot. She grabbed it with both hands and heard herself screaming as she swung at his head. The poker struck Frobisher's temple and sent him crashing into the fire. The gun went off as he fell, shattering the big vase by the window. He shouted and struggled to get up as the flames caught his jacket. Jess struck him across the face and, as he went down, again and again until he fell back into the hearth against the pile of logs.

The gun lay on the rug a few feet from Frobisher. Jess gripped it in one hand, with the barrel pointing away, and walked with it across the room. Then she went to Dan, who was slumped forward, chained to the chair, sobbing.

'Dan, it's okay, we'll be okay,' she said. 'He's out cold. He's not moving.'

There were splashes of Frobisher's blood on Jess's face and arms. She was still holding the poker in one hand, with the other against Dan's cheek. She kept glancing back at Frobisher. 'I don't think he's even breathing,' she said.

A loud voice came over a megaphone.

'This is the FBI. We are coming into the house.'

Within seconds, there was banging and shouting and a sharp crash as they broke through the front door. Agents streamed into the room looking everywhere along the sights of their guns.

Jess was next to Dan, hands in the air. She gestured towards Frobisher and his unrecognisable face.

'That's him,' she said. 'We think we're the only people left in the house. There's a gun on the floor over there.'

The dog bristled and snapped at an approaching agent as it lay across Frobisher's legs.

'Take it easy, puppy,' she said, pulling it gently off the body, with one hand holding its mouth closed.

'They're in here, miss,' an agent shouted from the door and Siobhan rushed in.

She looked at Jess. 'Are you hurt?'

'It's not my blood,' Jess said, pointing at Frobisher.

A paramedic was already at the fireplace, examining Frobisher. He looked at Siobhan. 'One deceased,' he said.

'I did it,' said Jess. 'He was going to kill Dan. I'd be dead if Dan hadn't come for me.'

Siobhan looked at Frobisher's shattered face. 'Wow,' she murmured, and told the paramedic, 'This lady needs to go to the hospital for a thorough check-up. She's been held captive for days.'

Through his tears, Dan saw Siobhan kneel on the carpet next to him. She kissed him on the cheek and held her storm-wet face against his.

'Hey, boy,' she whispered. 'How you been?'

Chapter Forty-Nine

New York, two weeks later

Dan was at a little bridge at the south end of Central Park. The early sun sent sharp shadows and streaks of gold slicing through the trees. A young man, entrusted with the morning walk of six dogs, sat on a bench nearby, staring into the water, clutching leashes in one hand and dragging deeply on a thick joint in the other. The dogs sat serenely around him, dope cloud hanging over them, unmoved by the yapping young border collie straining at the leash in Dan's hand.

When he was young and starting out, Gapstow Bridge had been a sanctuary for Dan in the hurtling city. He would get here before sunrise, when the city was most peaceful, its pulse still at resting rate. The bridge was nothing fancy, just a high stone hump, but when he shielded the leaning towers with his hands, he could be looking down at a stream in a beautiful bit of honest countryside. Only the morning birds spoiled the illusion: they seemed louder and more quarrelsome than country birds, like everything else about Manhattan.

It had been two weeks and still Dan couldn't sleep much. The images and sounds kept repeating themselves: George Frobisher slurring through the last rites, when Dan was sure he was going to pull the trigger; Jess, like a wild avenging angel, swinging and swinging at Frobisher's head; the loud crack of the gun; the heavy tumbling of Frobisher's body as he flew back-wards and lay there half upright among the scattered logs, his limbs at crazy, lifeless angles, dressed up to die with his clean shave and best blue blazer; Jess leaning over him with the poker, ready to strike again, splattered with her victim's blood.

Dan had read and heard all the breathless explorations of Frobisher's life and mind. His life, they said, had been an ever-lasting battlefield. How could any boy have survived intact with a single father who used the point of a gun to pay the rent, buy the booze and settle an argument? How could he have had any hope of being properly anchored on the right side of good and evil? He had hidden his anger and hurt inside a shell of success and generosity and fooled the world, until his life went wrong and his inner demon escaped.

In Dan's opinion, Frobisher's crimes and shattered mind didn't deserve this kind of serious analysis or understanding. There was a tipping point to insanity waiting for everyone, that was all. Frobisher was an extreme example, along with all the other lunatics and tyrants. All it had taken for him was years of piled-up injustice, real and imagined, mixed with a lethal dose of malignant narcissism. No one knew what they were capable of until the moment.

Dylan Thomas put it best – 'I hold a beast, an angel, and a madman in me'. When Dan used that quote talking to Siobhan, she had laughed. 'Very lyrical, Danny,' she said. 'You could be referring to yourself.'

He kept hearing Frobisher's words in the last moments of his life: 'I weaponised their love. I made it lethal.' Frobisher had harnessed people's love to get his revenge, and harnessed people's hate to fool the world into blaming Muslims. Dan was glad he had not been forced to find out if he was willing to kill.

His wife had called in tears when she knew the full story. 'You risked your life for us,' Laura said. Dan was a little offended by how surprised she seemed. She invited him to LA, and he was taking the kids to Disneyland for three days. The girls had squealed with glee when he told them. Their happiness made him so happy he cried a little after the call.

Dan left the park and his favourite bridge, the dog pulling at its leash as he headed into the rising beat of Manhattan's morning, walking quickly past the boastful townhouses and peak-capped apartment building sentries. He stopped at the Lexington Avenue diner where he'd eaten with Perry and took a table outside with Spike at his feet. The place deserved a last chance, and besides, he wanted its familiar comfort. He had the same unhappy server, but this time he would leave a tip. Again, he bought copies of *The Wall Street Journal*, the *New York Post* for Page Six, and *The New York Times*. And again, there was little they contained that he hadn't read the night before. In London, *The Daily Courant* was back in print and online, but the *New York World* newspaper was gone forever: Francis Wyler had restored only the website.

The George Frobisher drama and its aftermath had pretty well smothered all other news for two weeks. Jess had become a celebrity for the way she'd saved Dan's life, taking on Frobisher and his Glock armed only with a poker – 'The Brixton Brawler', according to the *Daily Mirror*. Photos appeared everywhere of Jess in her student days, looking lethal in a white taekwondo outfit.

Leila Chatstone's father, Dr Fahad Khan, had resigned his teaching post in Rawalpindi to join his daughter at Chatstone House. He'd gone into hiding after Leila's arrest, unwilling, with his reputation as a dissident, to risk falling into the hands of Pakistan's security services. Leila had been photographed with her father by the serpentine lake. She was wearing a purple hijab. The Crown Prosecution Service decided it was not in the public interest to prosecute Leila for obstruction of justice. She had been motivated by 'misplaced loyalty' to her mother, they said. The forthcoming trial of Chuck and Maria Healy was already exciting the media. The defence intended to capitalise on their clients' heartrending predicament, and what the tabloids were calling 'Chuck's Choice'.

Dan had one task before heading for California. He went into a florist on Madison and ordered a large arrangement. Perry Ainsworth, for all his bluff and calculated ways, loved flowers. Dan could smell them as he walked along Madison, cradling the bouquet in both arms. At 81st Street, he arrived at the grey-canopied entrance to the Frank E. Campbell Funeral Chapel. This corner of Madison was most famous for its corpses. Some of America's most distinguished departed had been here: Lauren Bacall, James Cagney, Joan Crawford, Rita Hayworth, Mae West, Oscar Hammerstein, Damon Runyon, Tennessee Williams. Arriving dead on this corner was the last social brag you could have on the Upper East Side. Perry was fond of telling the story of his last visit in December 1980, when an ambulance delivered the corpse of John Lennon. 'It was in a body bag on a stretcher,' he said. 'Very undignified.'

Dan kept walking, turning left at 77th Street and walking two blocks. He tethered Spike to a post outside the hospital. 'I'll only be five minutes, puppy,' he said.

Before Dan reached his room, Perry's booming laugh resounded along the hospital corridor.

'What's improved your mood?' Dan said, dropping the flowers in Perry's lap. He was sitting in red silk pyjamas by the window of his private room, laughing at the TV.

'The news just broke,' he said. 'Gene Applegate is going to be indicted. Bank fraud, false tax returns, foreign bank accounts, illegal campaign contributions. No pardon for him after all. That's one tough lady in the White House.'

'He needs to be charged with whipping up homeland terrorism,' Dan said.

Perry turned off the TV and put his face close to the flowers. 'Very kind of you – sunflowers, dahlias, chrysanthemums, zinnia, daisies. Best bunch yet, and the last I'll be wanting here. I'm to be released in the morning.'

Dan took the flowers and put them on a chair. 'Did you see the *The Courant* ran your long piece this morning?' he said.

Perry laughed. 'They loved the part when I went to rescue your computer from that dreadful hotel. Great headline.' He raised his voice. '*The Laptop That Nearly Cost My Life.*'

'It nearly bloody did,' Dan said. 'Man, you were lucky.'

A nurse came into the room to take Perry's blood pressure, so he recounted the story again. 'Two wild shots was all that thug got off,' he said. 'I felt the thud and the pain in my leg even as I was swinging at him. He didn't even get up from his knees. Three mighty blows I struck him.'

Dan looked at the surprised nurse. 'He almost killed the guy,' he said.

'It was his life or mine,' Perry told the nurse, pointing with his thumb towards Dan. 'And this gentleman thought my shillelagh was all for show.'

The nurse departed and Perry looked from his window, resting on a single crutch. 'How's Siobhan getting on? Poor girl.'

'She's being put through the wringer, getting grilled again by lawyers right now, I think. She knew there was a spy, didn't dream she was falling in love with her.'

'I knew it had to be that woman,' Perry said. 'I hadn't told anyone else about your hotel. I called Siobhan from the ambulance bringing me here.'

They stood at the window together. Then Perry said, 'I'm off to Saint Lucia on the first flight. You promise you'll visit after seeing the little ones?'

'I promise.'

Perry laughed as Dan crossed his heart. Dan wasn't fond of hot and lazy islands, but it seemed churlish to refuse. Perry had been browsing his photos in hospital and sending shots of himself holding up icy drinks, with blue sea and lush green hills behind him.

. . .

When Dan got back to her apartment, Siobhan still wasn't home. He took a half-empty bottle of cranberry juice from the fridge and sat on the window ledge, his feet on the fire escape. A pigeon landed fearlessly a couple of feet from him and sat there, puffed up and proud. There was no citizen of New York tougher, or more loyal; no immigrant more cursed, or more determined to remain. They sat together listening to the city.

The dog leapt at Siobhan when she came back to the apartment. She pushed it away. 'Are you really going to keep that animal?' she said.

'Why not?' Dan said. 'He was an orphan in a storm and I rescued him. You said you'd take care of him while I'm away.'

'I did? Well, I've changed my mind. I hate that fucking dog. There's got to be something wrong with anything that lived with that maniac. It's going to turn savage one day, just wait. Put it in a kennel.'

'Siobhan, it's a harmless puppy. Are you all right?'

'No, sir, I'm not. I've just spent another five hours being barbecued by fucking lawyers.'

She took two beers from the fridge and slammed the door so hard its contents clattered. She offered a bottle to Dan, but he waved it away.

'Do you remember,' she said, 'when I told you that woman wanted a few weeks before telling the agency about us while she put an end to a relationship back home in Georgia?'

Dan said he did.

'Well, it turns out that was a stall so she could keep an eye on what I was doing.' Siobhan drank some of her beer. The dog put its paws in her lap and Siobhan shoved it away. 'What kind of an idiot was I? It turns out she's not even gay. I should've guessed from how crap she was in bed. God knows the consequences for me – having an undeclared affair with a subordinate, plus sleeping with the fucking enemy.'

Dan could have responded with platitudes about the blindness of love, but he knew better.

'Shut up a second,' he said, arms tight around her, lifting her briefly off the floor as he hugged. 'Let's go down to the river. I want to ride the tramway to Roosevelt Island, for old time's sake. I have to head to JFK in two hours.'

They walked along with the beautiful racing East River on one side and the machine roar of the FDR Drive on the other.

'This is the perfect walk,' Dan said. 'For the bloody deaf.'

Siobhan smiled and slipped her hand into Dan's pocket, gripping his fingers. She looked up at him. He was taller, but not much. His eyes had grown creased and weary with the years, but they still came alight when he was angry or excited, or laughing at his own jokes; they still looked shy when he walked sober into a room of strangers. Rogue streaks of grey had appeared in his hair, but it was still mostly the colour of black coffee with a drop of cream.

Dan stared back. 'What?' he said.

'I keep having the same dream about you,' she said. 'We're outside the Frobisher mansion in the storm when we hear that shot fired. That part is always exactly how it really happened. Then one of the hostage rescue guys calls that they've found you and Jess. That's the same too. But when I get in the room it's you who's been shot. You're lying on the ground and there's blood all around you, but you're looking at me and smiling. Everyone keeps telling me you're dead, but I keep saying they're wrong because your eyes are open and shining and you're still looking right at me with this beautiful smile. But then your eyes close and the smile disappears and the others start pulling me off you as I'm screaming at you to wake up.'

Siobhan leaned against him, her eyes closed, and Dan could feel her shaking. He stroked her head as it rested against him.

'Shit. I knew I'd start crying if I told you that,' she said, and wiped her tears with the front of his shirt. Ahead in the distance, the two red tram cars swung through the air against the bridge's creamy girders.

'That bullet was meant for me,' he said. 'He had his finger on the trigger. If it hadn't been for Jess . . .'

The tide was ripping along the river, and a small sailboat, bright white in the clear day, dipped through the tossing waves. A little girl with a face of frightened concentration was gripping the boat's tiller with both hands. Dan raised his hands towards her in a big thumbs-up and her face broke into a proud beam. The man next to the girl smiled and waved. His hand was firm on the tiller behind the girl's back.

Dan put his arm round Siobhan and pulled her tight against him as they kept walking.

'There's nothing more electrifying than feeling really, really lucky to be alive,' he said. 'After you've felt for sure you have only seconds to live, as certain as if you were looking down at the approaching sidewalk after jumping off the Empire State. I was sure I would never see the girls again, or you, or anything. Every little thing seems like a miracle now. Nothing's worth worrying about. The job, the poor fucking newspaper business, all the stupid anxieties and insecurities. It's all melted away. Things are so vivid. Feeling the breeze, hearing the traffic and people laughing, the happiness of a little girl who thinks she's sailing her daddy's boat. I feel shocked sometimes just being here.'

Siobhan nudged Dan with her elbow. 'You're going through some kind of beautiful, post-traumatic bliss. Don't worry. The real world will come crashing back soon enough.'

Dan laughed. 'Quit it, Mac Stiofain. You're crap at acting cynical.'

As they boarded the tram, Dan looked across the river at the apartment towers crowded together on Roosevelt Island. They'd been in high school the first time they took the tramway together. Much of the island was wasteland then.

The city shrank beneath them as the tram car pulled steeply upwards. Siobhan rested her head on Dan's shoulder. 'Here we are, Danny boy . . . both singletons again.'

'Yeah, but at least we're all alone *together*, right?' he said. 'That's not so bad.' He kissed the top of her head. 'You can count on me, Siobhan Caitlin Mac Stiofain,' he whispered. 'I'll never stop loving you.'

Siobhan turned her face up to his. 'Ha! You're alright yourself,' she said. 'And I'll take care of that damn dog.'

Dan kissed her once more. 'I knew you would,' he said.

They leaned together and looked from the window of the swaying tram car at the jet-wisped sky and the crisscrossing girders of the bridge slinking past, and at the unheard tumult of the city beneath.

About the Author

Les Hinton was born in Bootle, Merseyside, and grew up in Egypt, Eritrea, Libya, Germany, Singapore, and Australia. He has spent his career as a journalist and senior executive in a multinational media company. He lives in New York and London with his wife Kath. His memoir *The Bootle Boy* was published in 2018. *Dying Days* is his first novel.